Lacey Black

Included in this paperback

A Pine Village Prequel Short Story

Pretty Remarkable
A Pine Village Series Prequel Short Story

Cover Design by Y'all. That Graphic.
Photographer Sara Eirew Photography

Editing by Kara Hildebrand
Proofreading by Sandra Shipman, Joanne Thompson, and
Karen Hrdlicka

Format by Brenda Wright, Formatting Done Wright

CHAPTER
one

Blair

"Five miles to your destination."

I squint through the thick falling snow, trying to find a landmark I'd recognize but coming up short. Hell, I'd settle for spotting the roadway. I can't see anything. My windshield wipers are moving at maximum speed, the rapid thump of the blades angrily filling my little car. I knew better than to ignore the weather report, yet here I am trying to drive through snow much deeper than my Kia can handle.

If only I had left earlier in the day, I would be safely tucked away in my hometown of Pine Village, Wisconsin, by now, probably sipping on a glass of wine, not still trying to get there on snow-covered roads that clearly haven't seen a plow in the last few hours.

This is what I get for trying to surprise my best friend. We haven't seen each other in two long years and even though she's expecting me this weekend in Pine Village, she thinks I'm coming tomorrow.

Brilliant idea, right?

Now I'm going to get stuck in the snow just outside of town. I'll probably freeze to death either trying to walk to civilization or trapped in my car in a ditch, wishing I had packed that blanket my mom always insisted I carry and grabbed a venti mocha with an extra shot of espresso on my last bathroom break before I left the interstate.

"Come on, come on," I insist, willing my car not to stall as I hit a drift.

Unfortunately, my two-year-old Kia doesn't care about my begging and comes to a complete stop on what I can only pray is the side of the road.

"Shit, shit, shit!"

I slam the gearshift into reverse and press the gas, only to feel the wheels digging a rut. I throw it into drive and carefully try to rock out of the hole I'm in but after several attempts, realization settles in.

I'm stuck.

"Son of a bitch, whore, asshole!"

My mom would be so proud.

"Think, Blair, think," I mutter, reaching for my cell phone. I only have one bar of service, and I try not to consider it a sign from the universe.

I'm usually a much more positive person, but today has not been my day. Even the Christmas music hasn't helped cheer me up. The pediatric clinic I work at decided to close at noon, in light of it being a Friday and tomorrow being Christmas Eve. Of course, throughout the morning, I slowly started to run behind with my patients, which I hate, thanks to the weather. By the time I got out of the office, all I wanted to do was grab some Chinese takeout and a bottle of wine and settle in for cheesy Hallmark movies. I wasn't scheduled to leave for Pine Village until tomorrow morning, but the thought of surprising Hallie a day early started to grow, and before long, it was too exciting to pass up.

Now, it's almost ten at night and I'm still five miles out, with not a light or a person in sight, and no one knows where I am.

Brilliant.

I find her name in my contacts and press call, praying it goes through despite the shitty signal. I start to worry about calling her at this hour, but what choice do I have? There's really only one other person left in this town I could call, and I'd rather have a bikini wax from a blind woman than call him.

No way in hell.

"Hey, Blair!" Hallie bellows into the phone. "I can't believe I'm going to finally get to hug you tomorrow!"

I cringe a little, hoping she's happy about this surprise. "So, there's been a slight change in plans."

"Do tell," she insists.

"Well, surprise! I'm in town!"

I'm greeted with silence. "Wait, what? You sort of cut out. It sounded like you said you were in town."

Well, not yet, but I hopefully will be as soon as you come pick me up.

"Yeah, uh, that's the thing. I'm sort of stuck. In the snow."

"Seriously? No, Blair! I'm not home. Curtis and I went to Saint Paul to finish our Christmas shopping, but then the snow started to get really bad. I heard they stopped running the plows, so we got a hotel," she says, near panicking.

I close my eyes, realization settling in.

I'm going to freeze to death in my car.

Of course, I ignore the fact I have half a tank of gas and enough heat to keep me warm until it runs out.

"How far out are you?"

I glance around, even though I can't really see much. "I think I was approaching Johnson's farm. I don't remember passing the barn, but I know I already went over the old bridge." At least I hope I didn't pass it.

"Okay, so you're not too far from town. Maybe four miles?"

"Yeah, four to five."

Too far to walk, but I don't vocalize the obvious.

"Oh! You're near Gabe's house!"

"Gabe?"

"My brother. You remember him, right?"

Memories of Hallie's nerdy older brother come flooding back. Gabe storming out of his room to yell at us to keep it down while he studies. Him completely ignoring us as he plays with his friends in the backyard. Gabe throwing a roll at my head the moment his mom turned around to get more ham from the kitchen. The time he returned home from his first year of college looking like a man instead of the boy I remembered.

"Yeah, uh, I recall."

"He's right up the road. He purchased the Peterman place just 'round the bend," she informs.

"No, I don't want to bother him."

I'm met with silence on the other end of the line. "Blair, I'm not sure who else could get you right now. They're not running the plows. It might be hours before emergency services can get someone out to your location," she says with a slight hesitancy in her voice.

"Shit. You're right."

"Unless you want to call...you know."

"Nope, no way," I insist, already understanding where she was going.

"That's what I thought. So, why don't you let me call Gabe? At least you'll be safe, and I won't have to worry about you."

I take a deep breath, letting it out in a loud sigh. What choice do I have? "Fine. Thanks."

"I'll call you right back, okay?"

"Yeah, all right," I mumble, making my oldest and dearest friend laugh.

"Just sit tight, Blair. Help is on the way!"

Where else am I going to go?

I slip my phone back into the cupholder, barely refraining from slamming my head on the steering wheel. Seriously, Blair? If I would have just left tomorrow morning the way I wanted, none of this would have happened. I'd be safely tucked away in my townhouse, wearing my comfy flannel pants, no bra, and half-drunk on my favorite red wine. The snow would be long cleared from the roadways, and I wouldn't be trapped in the middle of nowhere, waiting on a rescue.

My phone rings a few moments later, my best friend's face filling the screen. "Hello?"

"He's on his way."

"Is Gabe going to be able to get to me? It's really deep, Hal. If the plows aren't running, maybe it's not safe for your brother to venture out into it either," I reason, noticing the snow hasn't let up in the slightest.

"Not a problem for Gabe," she insists with a chuckle. "I can't believe you were going to surprise me a day early. I'm so bummed I'm not there."

"I can't believe I didn't pay closer attention to the weather forecast before I took off, but once I had it in my head I wanted to go, I just packed up and left. I should have been here almost two hours ago, but the farther north I went, the worse the roads got, especially after I turned off the interstate."

"I know you haven't been up here much in the last decade and a half, but you should know it's like a different world once you exit."

Before I can reply, a pair of headlights flash up ahead. "I think someone is coming."

"That's probably Gabe, but I'll stay on the line with you until we know for sure."

"No, you don't have to do that. I've already ruined your night," I insist, hating that I've interrupted an impromptu hotel night between Hallie and Curtis.

"Pssh, please! I can see him anytime, but I never get to see you. I'm just sad I'm not there. But we'll be back in town as soon as we can tomorrow morning. Then, we're hanging out for almost two whole days."

The vehicle races toward me, faster than any car or truck ever could. "Holy shit, what does your brother drive, a spaceship?"

Hallie snorts a laugh. "Uh, no. He's probably on his snowmobile."

My throat instantly goes desert-dry the moment realization sets in. "I can't ride that thing," I whisper.

"Uhh, you're going to have to, Blair. Otherwise, it's going to be a long, cold walk to his house," she teases.

The machine stops right next to where my Kia is stuck in the snow, and this big hulk of a man climbs off. The moment he slips off the helmet, a small gasp slips from my throat.

"Are you okay?"

"Yes," I reply, a little too quickly and emphatically. Gabe walks up to my door and gives me a small smile.

Holy hell, what a grin it is.

Even in the dark, that one small gesture lights up his entire face, and suddenly, a warmth spreads through my veins, much hotter and deeper than the heater inside this car could provide.

"Is that Gabe?"

"Yes," I reply, flashing the man outside my car a quick grin. "Listen, Hal, I need to go."

"Call me in the morning, okay?"

"Will do. Have a good one," I reply, signing off after a quick goodbye.

Then, I open my door and step outside, ready to face the gorgeous man who is here to rescue me.

CHAPTER Two

GABE

The moment my sister's old friend steps out of her car, I completely forget my annoyance at being interrupted.

I had finally slipped into loungewear, after the world's longest day. Thanks to Christmas just two short days away, our office was busier than normal. I had two broken bones, thanks to falls on the ice, and more sick kids than usual, courtesy of aggressive flu and strep throat strands. Then toss in the snowstorm, which doubled the time for my commute home and added the fun of shoveling the walkway to even get to my back door. I probably should have hooked up the plow on the four-wheeler and cleared the driveway, but I was beat and just looking to unwind.

Then my sister called.

Since I hadn't taken the time to plow my driveway, I only had one mode of transportation left that would get me from point A to point B. The moment my legs were shoved into my snowsuit, I had my helmet and gloves on and headed just down the road from my property.

Now, the most beautiful woman I've ever seen is standing before me in an outfit completely unsuitable for the elements. Black leggings, ankle boots that look more designer than anything else, and an oversized sweater hanging over one shoulder.

"Gabe?"

"Yeah." The word comes out all raspy and dry, like I haven't drank a drop of liquid all day.

"Thanks for coming for me," she says, giving me a small grin that seems to do more for my libido than any woman has done in a very long time.

"You're not going to be able to ride in that. Do you have a coat, gloves, scarf?" I ask, my tone a little gruffer than I meant it to.

"Oh, yeah," she replies, opening up the back door and pulling out a thick down coat with fur around the hood.

While she removes a few personal effects from her Kia Niro, I take a look around the vehicle to see if there's any way of pulling her out, which of course there isn't. She's good and truly stuck. It's going to take a shovel and a tow truck to get her out of this drift. "This an electric car?" I ask, meeting her back at the door as she retrieves a suitcase.

"Hybrid," she confirms, trying to tug the large piece of luggage through the snowdrift.

"Uhh, that's not going to work."

"What?" she asks, stopping and facing me.

"That's too big to hang onto while I drive the snowmobile. You're gonna need to just grab a few things out of it and leave it here."

Her pretty green eyes widen, and her sexy little mouth falls open. "What? No! I can't just leave it here, with all my things."

"It's not safe to try to hang onto that thing on our return ride."

She huffs, her breath coming out in little puffs of steam against the falling snow. "What do you suppose I do?"

"Take a few things, and we'll secure them in my suit," I suggest, taking her suitcase and tossing it on top of the hood.

Blair sighs and carefully steps up, her leg dropping into the drift and sinking in the cold, wet snow. She yelps, pulling her leg free and shaking her boot. I almost tell her those aren't the best boots for the weather, but something tells me it would be an unnecessary statement. She works quickly grabbing a few items of clothing and a cosmetics bag. "You're sure I can't take the whole thing? What if I just sit on it?"

"And have you bounce off at the first rut I hit? Not happening, sweetheart," I mutter, zipping up the suitcase and tossing it back into the car. "Ready?"

She lets out a deep breath and turns her attention back to the snowmobile. "I suppose."

I reach over and unzip my suit, grabbing her clothing and shoving it inside. As I do, something falls to the ground. Something tiny, pink, and lacy. My cock notices instantly and twitches with approval.

Blair snatches the panties out of the snow and huffs. "Why can't I just put my clothes under my own coat?"

My brain focuses on the strip of lace in her hand. "Because they'll fall out the bottom of your coat. In my suit, they aren't going anywhere," I state, holding out my hand.

She holds my gaze, her eyes narrowing ever-so-slightly. In this moment, I'm reminded of the tiny little spitfire from my youth. With a dramatic huff, she thrusts the panties against my chest, tucking them into my snowsuit.

I try to ignore the heat licking my veins, but it's impossible with her touch—even through my shirt and for only a fraction of a second.

Blair ensures her car is locked and slowly trudges through the snow to where my unit is waiting. Once my suit is zipped, I hand over my helmet. "Put this on."

"I'll be fine," she replies, waving off the helmet.

"No, I insist."

Blair holds still as I carefully place the helmet on her head and tug it into place. Her green eyes stare back at me through the visor, so worried, yet trusting, and I have this sudden urge to kiss her.

What the hell is wrong with you?

My movements are jerky as I sit on the snowmobile and stuff my hands into my gloves. "Get on and hold around my waist."

She places her hands on my shoulders and swings her leg over the machine. Even through the cold air, I can feel the heat of her body as she scoots forward, plastering her front to my back, wrapping her arms around me and holding on tight.

Thank God my snowsuit covers what's happening in my pants, because he is very much aware of Blair's nearness. It might actually be the most uncomfortable ride I've ever had.

I move swiftly yet carefully through the snow, goosing the throttle as I round the corner to head up my driveway. Her scream rattles my eardrum, her grip so tight it's hard to get oxygen into my lungs.

I can't help but smile.

The moment I stop beside my back door, she practically bolts from the machine on wobbly legs. "Did you have to do that?" she demands, pulling the helmet from her head.

"Of course," I reply with a smirk. "Have you never ridden on a snowmobile before?" When she just glares at me, I chuckle and add, "I'll take that as a no. Well, let's get inside, shall we?"

Since I left so quickly to go rescue my sister's friend, I didn't bother to lock the door, and the moment we step into the mudroom, we're both engulfed in warmth. Blair removes her gloves and coat, glancing around for somewhere to hang her stuff.

"There's extra hangers in the closet there," I start, pointing across from the washing machine. "I'm gonna run out and put the snowmobile away. Make yourself at home." I move for the exit but can feel her belongings shift against my chest. "Oh, here." Unzipping my suit, I pull the cosmetics bag and clothing out and hand it over. Just as I go to rezip, a splash of pink catches my attention.

Reaching down to my groin, I pull the pink, lacy panties from where they slid down below my waist. Of course, it's a thong. It's a damn pink thong that leaves absolutely nothing to the imagination. "I believe this belongs to you."

Blair snatches it out of my hand, her face burning red with embarrassment, and I'll be damned if that heat flaring in her eyes doesn't do something to me. Something I have no business even thinking about with my sister's friend.

Not tonight.

Not ever.

I turn and escape the small room, desperately needing to cool off. The snow looks to be letting up a little but according to the forecast, shows no sign of stopping until the early morning. Honestly, it'll be a hell of a lot easier to move what I can of the snow tonight, but something holds me back. Perhaps it's the beautiful woman in my house. The one whose incredibly sexy thong I just pulled from my snowsuit.

Sighing, I glance up at the night sky. "You're testing me, aren't you."

It's not a question, but a statement.

I get the snowmobile put in the garage and grab the shovel. Maybe a little extra manual labor will help clear my head. The last thing I need is to go inside and make Blair uncomfortable by obsessively watching her, because something tells me seeing her in my space is going to fuck with my brain.

Majorly.

After clearing the walkway, I go back to the garage and strip off my snowsuit. I put my gloves and helmet back on the shelf, lock everything up, and return to my house.

As soon as I step inside the door, I can feel the difference. There's a sweetness hanging in the air, something fruity and much different than the drywall dust, paint fumes, and wood stain I'm used to smelling. It's recognizable, yet so unfamiliar at the same time, probably because I know it's her scent.

Blair.

Kicking off my boots and leaving them beside her little ankle ones, I head to the kitchen where I find my sister's friend. She's looking at the cabinets, her hand gliding easily over the freshly finished wood. "These are gorgeous," she whispers, wrapping her arms around herself.

"Thank you."

She turns and faces me, her head cocking to the side very slightly, as if in deep thought. "There was pride in your response. You made them?"

I nod. "That's why it has taken me three years to finish the kitchen," I reply with a grin.

"Three years?"

"Which further explains why the floor isn't complete yet," I state, nodding down to the subfloor. "My job doesn't award me the luxury of a lot of free time, so I have to squeeze in working on this place when I can."

"What do you do?"

I meet her gaze, wondering how much my sister has talked about me. Obviously not enough if she doesn't know what I do, or where I work. I know there are some issues between Blair and her father, so it doesn't really surprise me much if they don't discuss the happenings in her former hometown.

Deciding not to go down that particular rabbit hole, I notice her shiver and opt to change the subject. "If you come with me, I can show you upstairs."

"Yeah, thanks. I think I need a hot shower. My toes are numb," she replies with a chuckle.

She follows me up the stairs. I bypass the first door, which will eventually become a guest room. Unfortunately, it's one of the last rooms on my remodel to-do list, so for now, I use it to store building material and tools. The second door will eventually be the guest bathroom, but it lacks some of the key elements like a tub, sink, and toilet. The third door on the right is my home gym. Ultimately I'll update that room too, but for now, I don't need anything fancy for free weights, a treadmill, and a rowing machine.

That leaves one singular door on the left side of the hallway. "In here," I state, stopping outside the door and indicating for her to enter.

She steps inside my bedroom and stops. After a few moments, she mutters, "This is your room."

I swallow hard and nod. "Yeah. This is where you'll be staying."

Hot woman sleeping in my bed?

Shouldn't be a problem.

CHAPTER
Three

Blair

His scent. It's everywhere.

The moment I breach the threshold, something rich and musky wraps around me and steals my sanity. It's strong, more pronounced here than it was in the rest of the house. I'm so transfixed on the sight of the king-sized bed sitting in front of me that it takes me a few seconds to realize I'm in his room.

His. Bedroom.

Where he sleeps.

"What do you mean?" I ask, slowly turning and finding Gabe standing in the doorway. His hands are stuffed in the pockets of his joggers, his long-sleeved T-shirt tight around the upper arms in the most delicious way. I've never been an arm girl before, but...holy hell.

He shrugs and leans against the doorjamb. "I only have one room finished, so I'll take the couch for the night."

Well, that doesn't sit well with me. "What? No."

"It's fine, Blair. Really, I only have the one bathroom completed, so it makes sense to have you here."

"No, I can't take your bed," I insist, ignoring the way my heart seemed to beat a little harder when he referred to me being here.

"Listen, we could argue about this all night, but it won't do you any good. I don't mind the couch. It's a sectional, and to be honest, I've fallen asleep on it many nights." He chuckles, and there's something so magnificent about that sound.

"I don't feel right about it," I whisper, downright hating the fact I'm kicking the man out of his own bed for the night.

"Stop, Blair. Take the bed. Unless you want me to run you back to your car? I'm sure you'll have plenty of room in the back of that Kia," he teases, his mouth turning upward in a slow grin.

Be still my heart.

His smile is breathtaking.

"Okay," I whisper, turning away from his mouth before I do something drastic like kiss it.

"Great. Come on," he says, removing his hands from his pockets and heading for the empty doorway. "Bathroom is in here."

Following, I join him into the most luxurious bathroom I've ever seen. "Holy shit."

Gabe chuckles. "Uhh, thanks."

The gorgeous tile shower and floor, the dark stained cabinetry, and the rich dark blue accents, it's like my dream bathroom come to life. "Oh my God, is that a whirlpool tub?" I ask, moving to where the tub is sunken into the floor.

"It is. Feel free to use whichever you want to help you warm up. There might even be some bath salts in the linen closet," he says, pointing to the closed door.

I don't ask why there would be salts in the closet, but perhaps I should. I don't recall Hallie mentioning her brother getting married, but that doesn't mean he's not in a relationship. Realization hits me like a sledgehammer to the chest. Not only have I been lusting over a taken man, but I could be kicking her out of her own bed.

Nice, Blair. Real nice.

"I'm sorry, but do you live alone?" I blurt out, catching him off guard.

His eyebrows draw together as he replies, "Yes."

"But is there...well, is your girlfriend okay with me crashing in your bed?"

He gives me a blank look for a moment. "I don't have a girlfriend."

"You don't?"

"No."

"Oh," I reply, relief helping calm my rapid heartbeat. "Okay. Good." A single eyebrow shoots heavenward. "What I meant was, I'm just glad I'm not kicking someone else out of your bed," I state with an awkward chuckle. "I'll be the only one there."

When my own words register, there's no way to draw them back.

The blush is intense, the desire to have the floor open up and swallow me whole even greater. "N-not that I'll be there with you. Just me. Alone in your bed. No you."

Kill me now!

"Anyway," he says slowly, "I'll leave you alone. Feel free to use anything you need." When he gets to the door, he stops and turns back around. "I was getting ready to heat up some soup for a late dinner. Are you hungry?"

"Oh." My stomach chooses that exact moment to growl, reminding me that I haven't eaten anything but a bag of peanut M&M's since my road trip began. "I suppose I could eat something," I add with a snicker.

Another panty-melting grin is flashed my way, making me a little wobbly in the knees. "I'll get something ready. Come on down to the kitchen when you're done." Then he turns and leaves, closing the door behind me as he goes.

I take a deep breath and survey my surroundings. That huge walk-in shower has two heads, one coming from the ceiling, but that jetted whirlpool tub is what calls my name. It takes me a minute to figure out the controls, and before long, I have hot water filling the massive tub.

My socks were still damp from the snow that seeped into them from the bank I stepped in, as are parts of my leggings, so to strip those off feels amazing, especially with the warm steam filling the room.

Just as I go to climb in the tub, I remember his comment about the bath salts. How long has it been since I indulged in a soothing bath? Too long, that's for sure.

Inside the linen closet, I find a new box of lavender salts and dump a small scoop inside the tub. The amazing aroma fills the room immediately and relaxes my stressed out muscles the moment I slip into the water.

This is heaven.

A girl could really get used to this.

I pad down the stairs, my nose following the spicy scent of chili filling the air. As soon as I step into the kitchen, I find Gabe at the counter, stirring a large pot of something at the stove. He doesn't hear me enter, which gives me a little time just to watch. It's been years since I've seen him. Hell, besides the casual mention of his name during a conversation with Hallie, it's been years since I've really thought about him. Gabe aged well, that's for sure. He clearly takes care of himself, if the defined arms I saw earlier are any indication. He's always been good-looking, but I think it's safe to say he's a total hottie now. Why he's single is beyond me.

But really, that's none of my business, and I'd do better to remember that.

I must have made a noise, because when I look up, I find Gabe's eyes on me. Not my face, on my body. There's a...hunger there I wasn't expecting, one that takes my breath.

"You made yourself at home, I see."

His words catch me off guard, but only for a fraction of a second. Instantly, realization sets in. It's not hunger swirling in his blue eyes, it's annoyance.

"Oh, uh, yeah. Sorry about that, but apparently, when I grabbed a stack of my clothes, I didn't grab anything to wear to bed. All I have is a sweater and some skinny jeans for tomorrow," I say with an uncomfortable chuckle. "I peeked in your closet and saw this crewneck sweatshirt and joggers on the shelf and grabbed them. I hope that's okay." I bite my lip, waiting for him to say something about the fact I'm wearing his clothes without his permission.

He visibly swallows hard before averting his eyes and concentrating on the pot on the stove. "Yeah, of course. Fine. Dinner's ready." His tone is gruff, his words jerky, which makes me sigh.

Why the hell didn't I pay closer attention to the clothes I grabbed? I managed to make sure I had plenty of underwear, but didn't think about having something to sleep in. Brilliant.

"I hope you don't mind spicy food. It's white chicken and corn chili, but I always add a little extra kick to it." Gabe retrieves two bowls from one of his gorgeous cabinets and fills them both with the mouthwatering soup.

"I don't mind spicy," I confirm, taking the offered bowl and walking over to one of the barstools in front of the counter. "Thank you."

He sort of grunts his reply before turning his attention to the fridge and filling two tall glasses with milk. "This'll help," he says, sliding a glass in front of me.

We eat in silence, the only sound is the clanking of our spoons against the bowls. I have to admit, this soup is really good, and when he returns to the stove to refill his bowl, I actually consider having seconds myself. But I stop myself. It's already so late, and the last thing I need to do is stuff myself and have horrible indigestion. Wouldn't that be my luck?

When we're all done, I head for the sink to rinse my bowl. "You can leave it," he says, speaking for the first time since before we started to eat.

"I don't mind cleaning up after myself. It's the least I can do," I insist, turning to face him. "You rescued me from the snow, let me take over your bathroom and bedroom, and then fed me delicious soup. I really appreciate all you've done."

He shrugs and turns away, as if uncomfortable, but he doesn't say anything else while I finish cleaning up some of the kitchen mess. When it's all done, he tosses the washcloth into the mudroom hamper and flips off the light. "It's late," he says unnecessarily.

"Yeah." I rock back on my heels, taking the hint. Before I even step out of the kitchen, he already has the lights out, except for the single canned light above the sink.

I head to the stairs, taking a quick peek into the living room. Gabe's large sectional does look comfortable, but I still feel terrible kicking him out of his own bed. "I can't take the—"

"Don't say it. I'll be fine, Blair. Just head upstairs and go to sleep. We'll deal with your car and everything in the morning." He seems almost mad, which makes my guilt feel a thousand times worse. I hate that I'm putting him out the way I am, all because I decided to surprise his sister with an early visit without paying close attention to the weather report.

A lump in my throat makes it hard to swallow, so I just nod, willing the onslaught of tears to remain at bay. The last thing I want to do is cry in front of Gabriel Rhodes. So instead of apologizing again, I turn and head up the stairs. When I reach the top, I risk a glance back. Gabe is standing there, hands on his hips, and his head hanging. He looks like he's breathing heavily, which only makes me feel even worse. I've completely upended his life—or at the very least, his night.

First thing in the morning, I'll call for a tow to get my car out of the snow. Then, I'll walk back and leave Gabe's house forever. He won't have to worry about me or my taking over his space any longer than necessary.

Tomorrow morning, he can forget all about me.

CHAPTER *four*

GABE

I can't sleep, and it has nothing to do with my comfort level on my couch and everything to do with the woman upstairs. The one responsible for this erection I can't seem to get rid of, no matter how much I try. There's only one thing left to do, and I'm not sure that's my best option right now, considering I'm in my living room.

Yet, it might be the only way I get any rest.

Just as I go to move my hand beneath the waistband of my pants, I hear my bedroom door open. Moments later, she tiptoes down the steps, trying to be as quiet as possible. Too bad for her I'm already awake and watching.

The moment her feet hit the floor, she pivots to head to the kitchen. "What are you doing up?" I ask, my voice deep and raw.

Blair startles and spins around, her hand covering her heart. "Jesus, Gabe. You scared the shit out of me."

I opt not to stand up, considering the problem I've been having in my pants—which is now more pronounced again with her sudden appearance. "Sorry."

"I didn't mean to wake you," she insists, taking a step into the living room. Her eyes go to the small tabletop Christmas tree my sister bought me last week after she heard I didn't have one. The softest smile plays on her lips at the sight of the white twinkling lights.

"You didn't. I was awake."

"Oh." She glances back over her shoulder toward the kitchen and adds, "I was just grabbing a glass of milk."

"Help yourself," I reply.

She doesn't move toward the kitchen. Instead, she steps farther into the room, her fingers gliding across the arm of my couch. Her touch is gentle, yet seductive, and does nothing good for my erection. In fact, I'm a little worried about permanent damage at this point. I don't recall anyone dying from a ruthless hard-on, but perhaps I missed that case study in medical school.

"Would you mind if I join you for a bit?"

Her question surprises me, since I know I haven't been warm and fuzzy toward her, but that doesn't stop me from replying, "Sure."

Blair takes a seat beside me. Even though she's not too close, I can feel the warmth of her presence, smell the calming scent of the lavender clinging to her skin. It makes me want to drag my nose across every square inch of her skin, memorizing the way she smells, feels, and tastes.

What the hell is wrong with me?

I scrub my hands down my face, feeling completely out of my element. Perhaps it's the fact there's a woman in my house. The first one since my wife left three years ago. Or maybe it's the fact she's a small piece of my past, someone connected to my childhood. Or it could be because she's simply beautiful and she's looking at me like I'm an ice cream cone on a hot summer day. Combined, it's a recipe for disaster.

"I'm sorry for messing up your night. I'll be out of here as soon as I call someone to dig my car out."

I sigh and lean back, closing my eyes for a moment. "There's no rush, honestly. I'm sorry I'm not the most hospitable host. I'm not used to having guests," I confess, risking a glance her way and finding those green eyes watching me intently.

Electricity buzzes in the air, slowly starting to stifle me, making it hard to breathe. Suddenly, all I can see is her, all I can feel is her presence mixed with the sexual tension hanging over us. Her green eyes transform right before mine, those emerald orbs darkening and swirling with desire. There's also no missing the hitch in her breath as she glances down at my lips. My cock jumps eagerly in my sweats, my hands burn to touch her skin.

Then, she moves. Or I do, I'm not sure who moves first, but the result is a clash of mouths and hands. Before I even realize what's happening, Blair is straddling my lap, her arms wrapped around my neck, her lips plastered to my own. She tastes like honey and heaven, all sweet and intoxicating, and every single reason why this is a bad idea evaporates into thin air.

Because there's no way something this good could be wrong.

My tongue delves deep into her mouth, sliding and tangling with hers, as she rocks her hips against my erection. White-hot lust floods my veins. I grasp her ass and try not to come completely undone right now in my pants.

"Gabe?" she asks, swirling her body against me, plastering her chest to mine.

"Hmm?" I mutter, nipping at the soft skin below her jaw.

She sits back slightly and places her hands on my chest. "Will you help me take off my pants?"

My answer is to pick her up and help shed the oversized joggers she found in my closet from her petite body. I don't know what I expected to find beneath those pants, but nothing wasn't it. She's completely bare, and my mouth waters to taste.

Unfortunately, that's going to have to wait, as her hands quickly slide into my own joggers and grip my cock through my boxers. A guttural groan spills from my mouth, her strong hand stroking me from root to tip.

Clothes start flying moments later. The crewneck sweatshirt, my own T-shirt, and anything else until we're both naked and panting. My mouth claims hers once more as I lay her back on top of the couch, her legs wrapping around my waist. My cock throbs between us, but before I take this any farther, I know I need her confirmation once more.

I pull back and meet her gaze. "You sure?"

She responds by rocking her hips, her wet folds gliding along my shaft. "Oh, I'm definitely sure. Now hurry before I die," she whispers, reaching between us and guiding my cock to her entrance.

All it takes is one thrust.

One amazing, surreal thrust, and I'm gone.

Overwhelmed.

She feels too good, too perfect, and even though I try to retain control, the way her body squeezes me doesn't help. It's no use. I pull out and rock forward, filling her completely once more.

Her nails dig into my back as she arches up, drawing me even deeper inside of her warm, tight body. It's all I can do not to lose it right here and now, but somehow, I manage to hold off my release, at least for a few more minutes.

I know instantly when Blair's orgasm hits. My name flies from her lips as her internal muscles grip my cock so tight it triggers my own release. A tingle races up my spine just as my balls draw up tight, and even though I want to close my eyes and ride out the waves of euphoria, I don't. Instead, I focus on the woman below me, the one squeezing the life out of my dick and scratching at my shoulders as she mumbles my name over and over again.

My arms seem to give out, my entire body sated and spent. I roll her to the side, pinning her smaller body between mine and the back of the couch. Blair stretches out beside me, dislodging my cock and creating quite a mess in the process. That's when it hits me.

"Shit, uh, Blair?"

"Mmm," she mumbles, sliding a leg over my hip and curling into my chest as slumber pulls at her.

My heart pounds in my chest. Hard. "We didn't use any protection."

Her eyes open and she gives me her complete attention. "I'm on birth control. I have an IUD, and I was tested earlier in the year." A slight blush creeps up her already flushed neck. "I'm not exactly sexually active often, Gabe."

A lump forms in my throat. How in the world does this incredibly beautiful, sexy woman not have men beating down her door? But since that's not a question I can ask, I focus on the conversation we probably should have had before we went at it like rabbits on my couch. "I'm clean too. I have to test regularly through work and haven't been with anyone since my last test."

Blair nods and snuggles my chest once more. I admit, she feels damn good tucked against me. So much so, just lying here with her in my arms starts to put thoughts in my head. Thoughts I haven't entertained since my wife walked out on me, running from this small Wisconsin town so fast her feet practically smoked.

I know I should pull away. I should get up, send her back upstairs alone to my bed, and forget how soft her skin feels against mine...but I know I can't. I won't.

No, I won't ever forget this night.

I won't ever forget Blair O'Connor.

"You ready?" I ask, finding Blair standing at my kitchen window and looking at the snow.

She turns around, coffee cup in her hand, and flashes me a quick smile. But there's something there in that grin. A combination of sadness and hesitancy that almost has me asking her to stay.

But that's crazy.

We don't even know each other.

Blair is here to visit my sister and part of her family for Christmas tomorrow, and then she'll return home to Indiana, six hours away from here. And who knows how long it'll be before she visits again. I know she doesn't have the best relationship with her father, so the likelihood she'll be back in Pine Village anytime soon is not probable.

I grab the grocery bag I gave her to help carry her belongings, ignoring the desire I have to check to see if she's wearing that pink lacy thong I discovered last night, but I no longer have the right, if I ever really had it to begin with.

I take the bag and her hand and escort her out the back door. The walkway is clear of snow, as is my driveway. Once the sun started to peek through the blinds this morning, I reluctantly got up, leaving Blair sleeping soundly—and *very* naked—on the couch. I began clearing the snow from my own property and then set out to dig her stranded vehicle from the snow. Fortunately, the plows were already running, so I was able to get to her car quickly. After another thirty minutes of shoveling, I had her car free and ready to roll.

Blair climbs into the passenger seat of my running truck and I have to ignore how great she looks sitting there. I climb into the driver's seat and slowly back out of the driveway.

"I'm glad we can make the return trip in a truck," she replies somewhat awkwardly.

I nod and flash her a quick grin, my tongue too thick to speak.

I hate this, and I don't know why.

Because you want her to stay.

I pull in front of her car and throw the gearshift into park. We both sit there, neither of us moving for several long seconds. Finally, she speaks. "Thank you, again. For everything."

"You're welcome."

She reaches for the handle and slowly climbs out of my truck, so I do the same, meeting her at the driver's door of her car.

"Make sure it'll start," I state as she digs out her keys.

Is it bad I'm hoping the engine doesn't turn over? It does, unfortunately, so I set her bag in the back seat beside the luggage she left last night.

"Listen, about last night," she starts, gazing up at me from her seat.

I step up to her open door and crouch down beside her. Brushing the hair off her cheek, I reply, "Don't. Let's just leave it for another time."

She opens her mouth, as if she'll maybe argue, but doesn't. To be honest, I fully expect her to, but whatever she was about to say dies on her full lips. Instead, she nods, a sad little smile plays on her lips. "Next time," she whispers, clearly not believing that there will be a next time.

That's okay.

I don't plan to just walk away.

"Enjoy your time in Pine Village with my sister," I say, leaning forward and pressing my lips to her forehead.

"Thank you," she mumbles.

"Next time," I repeat, standing up. Just as I go to shut the door, I quickly add, "Merry Christmas, Blair."

"Merry Christmas, Gabe." That's my cue to shut her car door.

I watch as she collects her bearings, throws her car into drive, and slowly pulls away, tossing me a little wave as she goes. I don't return to my truck until she's long gone, having rounded the bend in the road and on her way toward town. Only when the chill starts to seep through my jacket do I finally jump in the driver's seat and head home.

Blair front and center in my mind the entire time.

I'm not sure what our future has in store, but I know I wouldn't mind seeing her again. Sure, the distance is a big factor, but not completely unmanageable. All I know is our time together doesn't feel finished.

Not even close.

I'm not ready to let her go.

She's pretty remarkable.

Pretty Incredible
Pine Village Series, Book 1

Cover Design by Y'all. That Graphic.
Photographer Sara Eirew Photography

Editing by Kara Hildebrand
Proofreading by Sandra Shipman, Joanne Thompson, and Karen Hrdlicka

Format by Brenda Wright, Formatting Done Wright

CHAPTER
one

Blair

"Five miles to your destination."

I suck in a deep breath as déjà vu hits me square in the face like a cold wind, even though it's the start of summer. My mind goes back to that frigid December night, the blinding snow, and the drift my car became stuck in. The panic that set in when I realized I wasn't going anywhere anytime soon, and my best friend wasn't around to help.

To the man who rescued me.

Gabriel Rhodes.

I've done everything in my power to forget all about that night, short of drinking myself into oblivion, but I doubt my colleagues would have appreciated me showing up reeking of alcohol and possibly still a little intoxicated from the night before. Yoga has been my go-to stress reliever for years, especially during medical school, and even that seems to have minimal effect on helping me relax at the end of a long day.

That's when the memory of him always surfaces. When I'm alone in my apartment or lying in bed. I can still feel his hands on my body, remember every detail of that one night we shared. It's embedded on my brain like a tattoo.

Shaking my head, I dislodge those remembrances and focus on the road in front of me. This time, as I travel the once-familiar roadway leading to my hometown, it's free of snow. The trees are alive with shades of green, the ground covered with a mix of grass and emerging crops. As I drive the winding road, I can't help but roll down my window and breathe in the familiar scents of earth and clean air.

You definitely don't get this in Chicago.

Moments later, I hit the spot in the road where my car became abandoned on my last trip to Pine Village, and my heart starts to kick up a few extra beats. I follow the roadway around the bend and there it is. Gabe's house. The place I took refuge during that horrible snowstorm two days before Christmas.

The house looks the same, or at least it does from the outside. I wonder if he's completed any more renovation projects since my night there. His big truck isn't sitting outside, but it is late afternoon on a Monday. Chances are he's at work, wherever that is.

Over the last six months, I've had to refrain from asking my best friend, Hallie, questions about her older brother, Gabriel. I hadn't asked prior to my previous visit, so my fear was she'd see right through me if I started now. I was afraid she'd see the truth all over my face, hear it in the questions I asked. Instead, I just left what happened between us that snowy night where it belongs.

In the past.

A couple more miles and I hit the outskirts of town. The old, faded Welcome to Pine Village sign sits exactly where it always has, the population part catching my eye. Three thousand residents of the small town I once left, vowing I'd never return except for short visits.

As of today, it's three thousand and one.

At least for a while.

With a big sigh, I head for my best friend's condo, ignoring the nostalgia sweeping through my veins. Now isn't the time to get all sentimental or to question myself again, like I have since I got the phone call. Since I made the promise. Now is the time to say hello to my best friend and prepare for what lies ahead of me.

This trip back home isn't just about reconnecting with my friend. It's about fulfilling a recent promise I made to help my father. The man I've barely spoken to in sixteen years. The man who turned my life upside down the summer before my senior year of high school, resulting in my move away from the only life I'd ever known. An affair, and a very public one at that, wrecked everything in my perfect little bubble, and I've never been able to get past it. I've never forgiven him for the betrayal, because when you cheat on your spouse, it's not just that person you're hurting.

It's your child too.

I pull into the driveway and park my Kia behind Hallie's Jeep Cherokee. It's just after four in the afternoon, and Hallie should be home, considering she's off for the summer as a preschool teacher. Before I even have the car in park, her front door flies open and she's making her way toward me. Smiling, I slip from the driver's seat and shut the door just as her arms wrap around me and squeeze.

"Holy moly, I can't believe you're really here. For six whole months too!" she bellows, pushing me back and giving me a once-over.

"You just saw me last weekend," I tease, referring to the trip she made down to Illinois to help me pack up my things. "And it's *up to* six months."

She waves off my comment. "Seeing you last weekend was different. Now, I get to see you every day!"

It's true. During my time in Pine Village, I'll be living right next door to Hallie. The condo beside her opened up recently, and the owner agreed to let me rent for a six-month period instead of the standard one-year agreement. Otherwise, my options would be

Hallie, who often has Curtis spending the night, or my father, and I'm definitely not ready for that.

"Let's go inside. You can get settled before we go to dinner," she says, leading me toward the front door.

I'll be staying with Hallie tonight and moving next door tomorrow when my stuff comes. I'm very fortunate my employers granted me a six-month leave of absence to handle personal things here, and thanks to the new nurse practitioner hired at the practice, I was able to sublet her my apartment in the interim while she looks for her own place.

Talk about the stars aligning at the right moment.

But now that I'm back here, I'm having serious second thoughts about my decision to help. I've barely spoken to my father over the last decade and a half, yet here I am, after agreeing to come home and help run his medical practice. Pine Village Clinic, the only general practitioner's office in town. The place my father has owned since I was a small girl. I grew up there, spent countless afternoons twirling in the chair in his office after school, and even stole my first official kiss within those brick walls.

That's also where I discovered my father checking his nurse's temperature with the thermometer in his pants.

Not exactly something a seventeen-year-old girl can just forget, despite how much I tried.

"You look stressed. Was the drive okay?" Hallie asks the moment the door is closed behind me.

"I'm fine," I grumble, dropping down on her couch with a touch of dramatic flair. "Just second-guessing myself."

Hallie gives me a tight smile. "Have you talked to him?" she asks, referring to my dad.

"Not really. He called last night, but I told him I was busy packing so we cut it short. Plus, I didn't want him to overexert himself with too much talking," I reason, even though I know it's an excuse.

The truth is my father had a massive heart attack three weeks ago, requiring a triple bypass, and was only recently released from the hospital. However, even though he's home, he has a long road ahead of him in the recovery department. The cardiologist said it could be four to six months before he's able to return to work, and that's after he completes cardiac rehabilitation.

Hallie smirks. "I'm sure that's the reason you wanted off the phone."

"Listen, I know what you're going to say. We have a lot of baggage, but right now, I have to leave it where it belongs. In the past. The only baggage I want to deal with is what's in my car, needing to be brought in."

She reaches over and squeezes my hand. "I'm proud of you. I know this wasn't easy for you, coming back here and working for the man who wrecked your life, but you did the right thing."

I swallow hard over the lump in my throat. "You sound like my mom."

"She's a smart woman, like me," Hallie boasts with a wide grin on her face. When I roll my eyes, she adds, "Come on, let's go get your bags, and then we can go have margaritas at Cantina."

I pull myself off her couch and take her extended hand. "Thanks for everything, Hal."

She gives it a gentle squeeze. "What are friends for?"

"You remember Shay Long, right?"

I dip my warm tortilla chip into the salsa, thinking back to the girls I went to school with. "Mean girl who looked like Britney Spears?"

She points her straw at me from across the booth before sticking it back inside her strawberry margarita and slurping the rest of the slush at the bottom of the glass. "That's her. She's working at the hardware store."

I blink several times, trying to process. "Shay Long is working at the hardware store? What happened to her modeling career?" I ask, recalling how she was hell-bent on getting out of this small town when we were in high school.

"Technically, it's Shay Johnson now. She left for a few years but ended up coming back. Rumor has it she had problems with diet pills and was sleeping with her trainer. Her very married trainer. Anyway, she returned and set her sights on Logan Johnson."

"The quarterback? He was so nice. What the hell did he see in her?"

Hallie rolls her eyes dramatically. "What do all guys think about in their early twenties when a pretty woman shows them her boobs?"

"Wow, didn't see that one coming," I say between bites. "They're married?"

Hallie licks the tomato off her fingers. "Not anymore. It only lasted about two years before he tossed her to the curb. Only problem was, when his dad died and left him the hardware store, he put her name on it as part owner for some stupid reason. Now, they're divorced, and she won't leave. She works there just to piss him off, even though he's tried everything to buy her out of her share. Poor guy can't do a damn thing about it."

I can't help but shake my head. Talk about small town drama. This is definitely one of the things I didn't miss about my hometown. Merrillville, where I finished high school, and then Chicago for college, med school, and eventually, my pediatric physician career, was nothing like Pine Village. You barely knew your neighbors, let alone their entire life story.

"Jeez," I mutter, taking a healthy sip of my drink. My cheeks are warm from the tequila, which is why I will be stopping at one drink. I rarely indulge, and the last thing I need is to get trashed the night before I officially start at my father's clinic. Then, something else hits me. "Hey, didn't you have the biggest crush on him in high school?"

Hallie's own cheeks darken as she waves her hand, trying to play it off. "For like five seconds, but in my defense, everyone had a crush on Logan."

"I didn't," I state, just as our plates of food arrive. "I was immune to his boyish good looks, athletic body, and super friendly personality."

She snorts and stabs a piece of queso-covered chicken with her fork. "That's because you were all googly-eyed over Trent English all through high school."

I flash her a quick smile. "Oh, yeah. Trent. That boy could move on the basketball court."

Hallie laughs. "Amongst other places, from what I heard."

"Whatever happened to him?" I ask, cutting into my chimichanga.

"Got married a few years back," she replies with a mouthful.

"I bet. Let me guess. Skinny blonde with big boobs and a killer smile?" Trent always had a "type" in school, which was why he never so much as batted his eyes my way. He did, however, date Shay off and on the entire three years I was in high school with them.

"Actually," she replies, clearing her throat. "He's married to a man. A black man named Tyson, and he's the sweetest guy ever."

That revelation stuns me. "Wow, really? I never thought he was gay."

"He hid it well, didn't he? But he came home for our ten-year reunion and brought his husband. They live in California now."

I can't help but ask, "How did that go?"

She shrugs. "Mostly okay. There were a few people who made their feelings known, but for the most part, everyone was super cool and accepted them both. I've actually kept in contact with them on social media, and they're planning to come back later this year for the fifteen-year reunion. You'll get to see them, since you'll still be here."

The thought of seeing those I went to high school with again is both exciting and nerve-wracking. I haven't seen these people in sixteen years, since my father and his nurse became the biggest gossip in town. "Who else is still around here?" I ask, pushing those previous thoughts aside.

"Oh, you know Ellie's still here," she says. "She works at the diner and her son, Brody, is almost sixteen now. He plays football for TD, who coaches the varsity team, and is a cop. Plus, Marcus works at the auto shop, Jillian owns the bakery, and Ava teaches fifth grade."

"I haven't seen Ava since I left. She's not on social media."

"Not anymore," Hallie replies. "She had an issue a few years back with parents finding an old photo someone tagged her in. The parents went to the school board and everything, trying to get her fired. It was horrible, so she ended up deactivating everything she had."

"That's terrible. How old of a photo?" I ask, feeling sorry for Ava. She was always so nice to everyone, even Shay, who was the Queen Mean Girl.

"College era. She was at a frat party doing a keg stand, and I don't think she was twenty-one yet. The parents who created the ruckus were mad at her because she gave their son a failing grade on a test because he cheated."

I just blink in response. Really? They tried wrecking her career because of a failed test? "Ava didn't do anything in college we didn't do. Hell, those parents probably did that or worse while underage."

"Oh, I'm sure, but there wasn't digital proof back then."

"I feel terrible for her."

"The person who posted the picture felt horrible. It was her roommate from college, and all she meant to do was one of those sappy, reminiscent posts about friendship. It was so hard. She won't even go near Trainer's Sports Bar now for fear someone will see her walking in and cause more problems."

My food sits like a lead brick in my stomach. This is a prime example of what I hate about small towns. While you know everyone and there's always someone there to lend a helping hand, there are so many reasons why it has its downfalls too. The fact you can't do anything without everyone and their brothers knowing about it is one of the things I miss about the city.

And it has only been a handful of hours.

We finish up our meal and pay the check before walking back to Hallie's condo. She lives just two blocks off the main drag through town, which will be convenient for those nights I want to grab some takeout on my way to crash at home.

I can't imagine Pine Village has Uber Eats.

"Hey, what's Curtis doing tonight?" I ask as we stop by my car and grab the luggage I brought.

Hallie doesn't reply right away, and my senses start tingling like Spider-Man. "Working," she finally says, her tone flat and lifeless as she rolls my big suitcase toward her front door.

When the door is closed behind us and all of my things are set in the guest room, I turn to face my oldest friend. "What's going on?"

She shrugs and flops down on the bed. "I'm not sure. He seems to be working a lot more lately," she says softly.

Hallie's boyfriend, Curtis, is an investment broker in Hudson, just fifteen minutes away. They've dated for about two years, and even though I've video chatted with him a handful of times, I officially met him this past Christmas on my visit to town. He's nice. Perhaps a bit high maintenance, with perfectly styled hair and designer clothes. I'm pretty sure he gets manicures too. But he seemed to make my friend happy, so I was happy.

Now, I'm not so sure.

"Do you want to talk about it?" I ask, turning to face my friend.

"No, it's okay. There's no reason to get into that tonight. You've had a long day, and tomorrow is going to be busy for you. As soon as I get home from running errands, I'll be able to help you get settled next door. Are the movers still planning to be here by three?"

I nod in confirmation. "I'm working at the clinic until two and then will be here."

"Well, you have my spare key, so let yourself in when you get off work."

"Thanks, Hal. For everything," I state, kissing my fingers and placing them on her cheek.

"I'm happy you're here, Blair, and I'll be honest, I'm sort of holding out that I can convince you to stay," she confesses with a big, mischievous grin.

"Fat chance, Hal. Very fat chance," I reply with a laugh.

Her eyes dance a little impish. "We'll see, Dr. O'Connor. We're gonna make you fall in love with your hometown all over again, and you'll never want to leave."

CHAPTER Two

GABE

I've been up before the sun, anticipation racing through me.

Today is the day Blair starts working at the clinic her father owns. The very one I'm also a physician at.

The older Dr. O'Connor suffered a massive heart attack mere weeks ago, and it's been difficult at the clinic, trying to keep up with his patients, as well as mine. We've extended our hours temporarily and keep both his nurse and mine busy. We even brought in part-time office employees to help to work reception and billing to offset the increased hours.

But all that changes today.

Today, Blair joins the practice until her father returns.

To be honest, I'm surprised she agreed to come work there, even in the interim. They don't have a good relationship, despite Frank reaching out to her on numerous occasions. I know he understands why she struggles to forgive him for tearing their family apart, but that doesn't mean it doesn't hurt. He's never dove into their story with a lot of detail, but I've picked up on things over the years.

I know he loves her and has always wanted what's best for her. Which is probably why he hasn't pushed it.

But their relationship isn't my concern, at least not today. I'm a little eager at seeing Blair for the first time since she spent the night at my house six months ago. I'll never forget that night. The snowstorm that left her stranded just down the road, and the rescue that brought her to my house late that evening. Nor the way my empty house suddenly felt alive with her presence. The plan had been for her to sleep in my bed, upstairs, and while that might be how the night started, that's not how it ended.

It ended with her naked on the couch, sleeping beside me after the most memorable sex of my life.

I ignore the way my cock jumps in anticipation of seeing her again. I know the bastard is anxious for another round, but he's just going to have to settle down. That's not happening. I don't even think she knows I work at her father's medical clinic, which might make for our first meeting in six months a little shocking.

I do my best to push all thoughts of Blair and our night together aside. I fill up my travel coffee mug, glancing around the recently completed kitchen. When she was here, I didn't have the flooring done. I can't help but wonder what she'd think of the stone tile I chose for this room, which, I've been told, complements the countertops and cabinets nicely.

Shaking my head, trying to dislodge the memory of her, I straighten my necktie and head for the back door with my coffee in hand. It only takes me a few minutes to get to town, beating the pre-work morning rush, if you can call it that. The streets of Pine Village are busier before eight and right after five during the week, in what we call rush hour.

Fortunately for me, the streets are still somewhat empty this early. With Dr. O'Connor out, I've resorted to going in early to keep myself above water. We currently have one patient in the hospital, which means once I'm done at the office tonight, I'll be heading to Hudson to check in on him. Since our town doesn't have its own hospital, we send all our patients requiring more care than we can provide to the city fifteen minutes away.

It's not always convenient, but that's what you get when living in a rural community.

I pull into the lot behind the clinic and park, noticing I'm the first one to arrive. I let myself in and step into my office, the heavy slam of the steel door securing me inside. My desk is nearly empty, except for an empty Mountain Dew bottle and paper coffee cup from the lounge.

Yesterday was a long day.

I don't make a habit of drinking heavily caffeinated drinks, but sometimes the body just craves the extra sugary jolt the popular soda provides. Tossing the bottle and the empty paper cup in the trash, I unlock my filing cabinet and pull out the laptop and papers I was working on at the end of my day yesterday. Then, I get to work.

By the time the first staff member arrives, I've called the hospital to check on our patient, who is on track for a discharge today, and make sure all of my notes are up to date in patient charts.

"Hey, Doc," Stella Stabler greets when she enters the clinic.

"Morning, Stella."

"I'll get a fresh pot of coffee on," she quickly says, removing her coat and standing in my doorway. "Dr. O's daughter should be here soon."

I nod. "I'll be ready."

We spent a big part of the day yesterday rearranging the schedule. Blair is a pediatrician, and a big part of the patients her father saw were over the age of eighteen. So as of today, she'll take all patients under that age threshold, while I'll see all the ones over it. When reception calls to confirm appointments, they make the patient aware of the change in physician, and so far, all of today's clients have been okay with it.

Within the next five minutes, the rest of the staff arrives, and the office starts to come alive with activity. The first patients are scheduled for eight fifteen, which gives us all a half hour to get organized and ready.

At exactly seven forty-five, my nurse, Makenzie, knocks on my doorframe. "Morning, Doc," the twenty-seven-year-old greets me with a smile.

"Morning."

"Want to come up and meet Dr. Blair O'Connor?"

My heartbeat kicks up a few extra beats per second. "Sure."

Grabbing my coffee, I follow Makenzie down the hallway, past the patient exam rooms, and into the front office. Even though she's surrounded by several employees, my eyes zero in on her immediately. Six months has done nothing to quench the thirst I have for Blair O'Connor.

The ladies are laughing at something when Kyla, our office manager, spots me. "Oh, here he is. Blair, meet our other physician, Dr. Gabe Rhodes."

She turns, offering me a gorgeous smile, but I know the moment realization sets in. Her smile falters, as if she's trying to figure out what's going on.

I step forward and extend my hand. "Good morning, Dr. O'Connor," I state softly. "It's a pleasure to see you again."

Blair steps forward, confusion written all over her stunning face. She places her small hand inside my own, instantly, an electric current sweeps through my veins. I know she feels it too when she immediately pulls her hand out of my own and draws it to her chest.

"You two know each other? We should have known. You're both from here," Stella says with a chuckle.

"Blair is friends with my sister," I say, leaning against the wall of medical files and taking a sip of my lukewarm coffee.

She visibly swallows hard. "Yes. Friends with Hallie," she replies, her voice a little hoarse.

"Well, I'm glad you two already know each other. I'm sure that'll help make this transition easier." Kyla flashes us both a grin. "Are you ready for a quick tour before patients start arriving?"

Blair nods, slowly turning around to face the office manager. "Let's do it." With one quick look over her shoulder, she disappears down the hall, and I struggle to keep my breathing normal.

This has bad idea written all over it.

"I brought you back a sandwich," Makenzie announces, stepping into my office and placing the wrapped sub down on my desk.

"Thank you," I reply, pulling a ten out of my wallet and handing it over, even though she tries to wave it off.

"I'll give you a few minutes to eat. First patient of the afternoon is scheduled in ten minutes," she replies, leaving me alone in the small space I use as my office.

I glance at the clock, confirming it's nearing one o'clock. I've been staring at the files in front of me for the better part of a half hour, but my mind isn't on the task. It's on Blair.

I've run into her several times in the hallway throughout the morning, all passings cordial, but somewhat strained. There was definitely a heaviness between us, an impending conversation I know is coming.

That opportunity presents itself as I'm opening my sandwich. I can feel her presence before I look up and find her standing in the vacant doorway. When my eyes meet hers, she flashes me an awkward smile and holds up her sandwich. "Mind if I join you?"

"Of course not."

I watch as Blair takes the single chair across from my desk and unwraps her sandwich. After her first bite, she finally speaks. "So, a doctor, huh?"

Slowly, I nod. "I've worked for your father since I returned to town."

She takes another bite and chews. "Why didn't you say anything?"

I set my own food down, suddenly not at all hungry. "I knew when you were at my house you didn't have the best relationship with your dad. If I would have told you I worked for him, what would you have done?"

She seems to consider my words. "I don't know."

"It seemed inconsequential at the time."

"But at least I would have been prepared to see you here," she replies, swallowing hard, but not from the food. I think it's as hard for her to be around me as it is for me to be around her.

Interesting.

"To be honest," I start, picking up my sandwich and finally taking a bite. Once my mouth is empty, I finish my statement, "I'm a little shocked you didn't know I was working here."

She snorts a laugh. "You're not the only one. Your sister has mentioned you over the years but not many details. I knew you moved back to Pine Village after college, but she never told me you worked here." She flashes a small smile. "Probably because she knew of my estranged relationship with my father."

Clearing my throat, I ask, "How is he doing?" I've talked to his wife, Patience, a few times since the heart attack three weeks ago, but part of me is curious how much communication Blair has with her stepmom.

She picks at the edge of her bun and pops a small piece in her mouth. "Okay. Patience says he sleeps a lot still, thanks to all the medication he's on, but has asked to speak to me." She averts her gaze for a moment before she adds, "I'm not ready."

"Understandable," I reply before taking a big bite of my food.

We both finish eating in silence, and the moment I ball up the wrapper and toss it in the trash, Makenzie pops her head in. "Dr. Rhodes, your patient is in exam room one."

"Thanks, Mak," I state, turning my gaze to the woman I haven't stopped thinking about since last Christmas. "Ready to get back to it?"

She nods and stands, throwing her own trash in the garbage. "Let's do it."

Together, we head toward the door. "You're out of here early, right?"

Blair nods, shoving her hands into the pockets of her white lab coat. "Movers are supposed to arrive with my stuff around three. Last patient is scheduled for one forty-five."

I grab my own coat off the hanger on the back of my door and slip it on. "I have to run to Hudson to discharge a patient after we close, but I could stop by and help if you need it."

She watches me intently for several long seconds before she replies, "Hallie's going to help me. I'm sure we'll be okay."

Shrugging, I adjust the sleeves of my white button-down beneath my coat. "The offer's on the table."

Blair steps into the hallway and moves toward the exam rooms on her side of the hallway. Before she enters, she stops and glances back. "Thanks, Gabe."

I lift my chin, unable to find words, thanks to my suddenly too-thick tongue. If I thought casual Blair was beautiful, professional Blair is a fucking knockout. Her hair is pulled back in a tight ponytail and she's wearing minimal makeup, but there's something so sexy about seeing her in her element. From the shapeless white lab coat to the basic black slacks, crisp blue button-down, and comfy black shoes she wears on her feet.

The only sight more enticing was the one of her naked beneath me.

"Dr. Rhodes?" Makenzie says, pulling me from my inner thoughts.

I glance up to see her standing there, ready to put my next patient in the next exam room. "Yes, sorry. Just lost in thought," I reply, glancing over her shoulder. "Good afternoon, Gerald."

"Hey, Doc. This damn shingles virus is acting up again," he mutters, rubbing his side.

"We'll check that out in just a few minutes, all right?" I say, giving him a polite squeeze of the shoulder as I pass.

Grabbing the chart for the first room, I knock on the door and step inside.

It's time to get to work.

The afternoon progresses slowly. A handful of sick patients, two broken bones, three employment physicals for the local trucking company, some stitches on a hand, and yes, getting Gerald's shingles taken care of, and I'm ready to call it a day. Unfortunately, I still have to head to the hospital to complete the discharge of one of our patients, when all I really want to do is drop by Blair's and see if she needs anything.

Despite the fact she told me she didn't.

As I'm heading to Hudson, I put in a call to the eldest Dr. O'Connor. "Hello?" the older man answers, his voice tired and gruff.

"Hey, Frank. Just thought I'd check in and see how you're doing," I say, a little surprised he answered. I've only been able to talk to him once since his heart attack. Usually, his wife answers his phone.

"Well, I'm still alive, so that has to count for something," he replies with a chuckle.

"It does, and I'm damn glad for it," I reply honestly. Losing him would be hard on the practice, but personally as well. He's been a good mentor and I've learned a lot from him since joining his practice.

"How's Blair?" he asks after a beat of silence.

"She seemed to do well today. The staff gushed about her after she left, and from what Kyra said, the patients loved her."

Frank sighs. "I'm happy to hear that. Not that I was worried about her, but, as you know, Pine Village is very different than Chicago."

"It is," I agree. I started my residency in one of the suburbs, and the moment I could come back home, I did. Frank took me under his wing and helped me, eventually offering me a spot in his clinic. It's been a long process, and honestly, a dream come true. I always wanted to come back to rural medicine and have found my footing in Pine Village Clinic.

It's home.

Unfortunately, my wife didn't agree.

We met while I was in med school. She worked at the coffeehouse I used to frequent for caffeine fixes and studying. I knew she was interested in me, but I wasn't sure dating my last year of school was in my best interest. However, Amara wasn't to be detoured. She convinced me she wasn't wanting anything serious, which turned out to be a lie. She was very much husband-hunting, looking for someone to get her out of the coffee shop, and a future doctor fit the bill.

I fell for her and her bullshit, hook, line, and sinker.

The marriage didn't last though. She had always pictured us living in a Chicago suburb, our future kids attending some fancy school with a tuition bigger than the mortgage. She'd be a stay-at-home mom, of course, her afternoon spent shopping for the newest fashion trends and drinking the very expensive gourmet coffee she used to serve.

Amara hated Pine Village with a fire of a thousand suns, and when it came down to it, gave me an ultimatum: Return to Chicago together or she was leaving.

I almost left. My marriage was important to me, and even though I felt at home in Pine Village, I was going to make the change to make her happy.

Until I found out she was screwing a heart surgeon from Hudson.

"Keep me posted on how she's doing," Frank says, pulling me back to the conversation at hand and away from the woman I have since divorced.

"I will."

We chat for a few more minutes, until I reach the outskirts of Hudson. "I'll let you go so you can discharge your patient. Call me if you need anything," Frank says, his voice a little peppier now than at the beginning of the phone call.

"Have a good evening, Frank."

"You too, Gabe."

As I pull into the physician's lot beside the hospital, my thoughts return to Blair. It's both a blessing and a curse to work with her every day. I'm excited to see her, spend time with her, and get to know her, but will definitely struggle keeping my hands to myself. Not when I know how soft her skin feels against my palm and how magnificent she looks when she comes.

But I'm not going to rush this.

Baby steps, Gabe.

Slow and steady wins the race, and my endgame is her.

I want to make her mine.

CHAPTER *Three*

Blair

"I'm going to love living next door to you," Hallie proclaims, finishing off her third margarita of the night.

A giggle spills from my lips. "I haven't drank two nights in a row since college. I think you're a bad influence," I insist, refilling our glasses with the remaining frozen liquor concoction.

"Just don't tell my parents," she says, referring to the ones of her young students. "I don't want to end up like Ellie."

"No shit. We should have invited her," I add as an afterthought.

"Next time. I didn't realize helping you settle in was going to involve a quick trip to the convenience store for crackers and tequila," she states before shoving another Wheat Thins in her mouth.

Just then, her cell phone chimes with a notification. Hallie pulls the device from her pocket and reads the screen, her face falling a little. "Everything okay?" I ask as her fingers fly across the screen.

"Oh, yeah. Fine. I was hoping it was Curtis, but it's just my brother, Gabe. He's on his way home from seeing a patient in Hudson and offered to grab pizza if I haven't eaten yet."

I try to ignore the way my heartbeat spikes at the mention of Hallie's older brother, but it's impossible. So is forgetting the way he looked today at the clinic. I've seen Gabe in casual sweats. Hell, I've seen him completely naked too. But watching him move around the clinic today in slacks, a button-down, necktie, and lab coat was a sight to behold. I've never thought the attire physicians wear to be sexy, but seeing him in his work element, laughing with patients and showing his caring side to everyone he encountered, put him in a whole new level of sexiness.

One that made my thighs clench on multiple occasions today.

"Do you want some pizza? We should probably put something else besides crackers in our stomachs," Hallie suggests, her fingers already typing.

Gabe offered to come help this evening after he discharged a patient from the hospital, but I declined. I needed a break from him. Everywhere I went in the clinic, the sterile scent of cleaning products was always overpowered by his earthy, musk scent, and it was a constant reminder of the night I spent with him six long months ago.

Before I can reply and politely decline, she adds, "Okay, he's stopping and grabbing one. Do you still like pineapple and ham?"

"Love it," I reply, my voice dry and hoarse.

"Good. That's what I told him to get, though he's giving me a hard time about it. He hates pineapple and says his meat-lovers half will now be contaminated with the scent of gross fruit," she says with an evil laugh.

"We can get whatever," I insist.

"No way," she says, dropping her phone on the couch beside her. "Serves him right. I never get pineapple and ham, but I told him you loved it, so he had to deal. Do we have anything to drink besides tequila?" she asks, changing the subject as she gets up and heads over to my empty fridge.

"There's bottled water." When I ran to the store for tequila and crackers, I also picked up some water and coffee grounds for tomorrow morning.

At least I have the basics covered.

She returns to my living room with two bottles and hands one over. "Anything else you want to do tonight?"

I glance around my sparsely decorated living room. I didn't bring much with me, knowing I was only going to be in town for six months at most. A few boxes of clothes and personal effects, as well as my living room and bedroom sets. The physician who is subletting my place had her own furniture for those rooms, as well as some of her own kitchen supplies, which made the process fairly easy and painless.

"I don't think so. As soon as the dryer is done, I have to make my bed, but I think that's all I'm tackling tonight."

"Sounds good," she replies, flopping down on the couch and grabbing the remote. Honestly, I almost left my TV behind. I rarely watch it, but sometimes, after a long day, I like the background noise. Plus, some of the streaming subscriptions are somewhat inexpensive, so it's a logical solution.

While she finds something to watch, I use the notes app on my phone to make a grocery list. The fridge is practically empty, and while I rarely had time to cook meals back in Chicago, I'm hoping the slightly slower pace of Pine Village will award me the luxury.

I miss cooking, not that I ever really did it much while in school, trying to survive my pediatric residency, and then being thrust into full-time physician, but I did enjoy those rare evenings where I could open a bottle of wine and cook. Hopefully, I'll be able to prepare a meal or two every now and again.

"Hey, do you want to come over Sunday for dinner?" I find myself asking.

"Sure," she replies instantly. "What can I bring?"

I shrug, unfamiliar with this calmness coursing through me. I'm not sure I've ever felt this...relaxed. At least not since my life upended the summer before my senior year of high school. "I'm not sure yet. I'll get back to you."

"'Kay." She takes a long drink from the water bottle. "Want me to invite Ellie?"

My eyes light up with excitement. "Yes, that would be great. Her son can come too, if he wants."

She nods. "I'll text her." Suddenly, there's a knock at the door, and my breath catches in my throat. "Later, I'll text. Now we eat pizza!" she declares, jumping up and racing to the front door.

I barely have time to collect my thoughts and prepare myself for seeing Gabe again when the door flies open and he's walking into my condo carrying two pizza boxes. The first thing I notice is he's still wearing his professional attire, sans tie. In fact, he's loosened the top button and rolled up his sleeves, exposing hard, toned arms that would make any woman stand up and beg.

"Oh! Let me run next door and grab paper plates," Hallie proclaims before running out the door.

Gabe toes off his shoes and glances around the space before turning those ocean-blue eyes on me. "Hey."

"Hi," I reply, my voice a tad higher pitched than normal. "Thanks for bringing pizza. We were working on drinking our dinner," I add with an awkward chuckle.

He flashes me a grin, one that makes my panties wet and warmth spread like lava through my veins. "I wondered if she was a little buzzed. She called me Gabriel Alan, which she only does when really pissed off or really drunk."

I shake my head, trying my best to ignore the way my heart flutters when he smiles. "Alan?"

He shrugs. "Named after my grandpa. Want me to put these in the kitchen?"

"Oh, yeah. Sorry," I mutter, chastising myself for being a terrible host. "I don't know why we didn't just raid her fridge," I say aloud, though mostly just speaking to myself.

Gabe chuckles again. "Probably because she knew all she has in there is pizza rolls and diet soda. Hal hasn't learned to cook since you left. Her expertise is opening a can of something and ordering takeout."

"I have plates and napkins," Hallie announces as she bursts through my front door. "Thanks for the pizza, big brother."

He places the boxes on the counter and opens the lids. "Had to do something to soak up the tequila."

His sister casts him with a glare over her shoulder as she takes a plate and grabs two slices of pizza. "We had crackers, thank you very much."

He shakes his head before glancing at me. "Go ahead."

I take a plate and one slice, startling when I feel someone lean into me. "Take two. They're small pieces." His warm breath tickles my neck and sends a shiver down my spine.

I grab a second piece, even though I'm not sure I'll eat it. But the combination of his earthy scent and the deep timbre of his voice has me about to combust with desire.

And recollection.

"How come you got two pizzas?" Hallie hollers from the living room.

"So your nasty fruit didn't contaminate my bacon," Gabe states loudly so she can hear. Then, he takes his own plate and slides three slices on it before following me into the living room.

"Sorry I don't have much seating," I state, noticing Hallie took the chair, which leaves Gabe and me on the couch.

And suddenly, I'm peppered with vivid memories of our last time together on a couch...

"Doesn't bother me," he replies, taking one end of the sofa and leaving an entire cushion between us, which I'm grateful for. I'm not sure I'd actually be able to consume my food if he were any closer.

It's not like earlier today at lunch where we were close, but there was a desk between us. Now, it's more of a casual, intimate setting in the place I'll be staying for the next several months. Hell, my bed is just down the hall, and that's the last thing I should be thinking about. Yet, here I am, imagining all the places we could go at it in my sparsely decorated condo if given the chance.

Stupid over-imaginative brain.

I don't know how I make it through dinner without tossing my plate to the side and climbing onto his lap. All I can think about now is the way his sweats looked hanging on his hips, the very pronounced bulge between his legs like a beacon of light in the middle of the night. Even now, wearing black slacks, I find myself completely turned on and doing everything I can not to steal glances between his legs.

Turns out, I was hungrier than I expected. I finished the two pieces on my plate and then split a third slice with Hallie, while Gabe ate like he hadn't eaten in a week, polishing off five slices of meat lover's pizza.

Fortunately, with having a pizza dinner, there's minimal clean up. I combine the leftover pieces into one box and slip it in the fridge. "Take that with you when you leave," I tell Gabe.

"No way. It's contaminated now." The corner of his mouth ticks up as he tries not to smile.

Hallie rolls her eyes. "You're so dumb."

I reach for my purse and pull my wallet out. "How much do I owe you?" I ask.

He waves off my question. "Don't worry about it. Consider it a welcome to town."

"Oh, well, thank you," I reply, replacing my wallet in my bag.

"I'm going to head home," Hallie announces through a yawn. My oldest friend walks over and throws her arms around my shoulders. "I'm so stinking glad you're here."

"Me too," I whisper, returning the gesture. "Thanks for all your help today. I couldn't have done it without you."

She throws me a grin as she steps back. "It was my pleasure." She pulls her phone from her pocket. "I'll text Ellie, invite her to Sunday dinner, and let you know."

"Sounds good."

Hallie goes over to her brother and kisses his scruffy cheek. "Thanks for the pizza, bro."

"You're welcome," he replies, pulling her into his large frame. "Good night."

"Night, guys," she replies, throwing a wave over her shoulder as she heads for the front door.

"Night," I respond, suddenly realizing I'm alone with Gabe.

"I can let you get settled," Gabe announces, shoving his hands in his pockets. "Need anything before I go?"

"No, I'm good. All I have left tonight is to make up my bed and bathroom."

"I can help," he seems to blurt out, almost too spontaneously. His outburst seems to catch even himself off guard and makes him blush. "I'm sorry. I'm sure you don't need my help making a bed," he adds with an awkward chuckle. "I'll go."

"Well, I mean, if you want to help. Those fitted sheet corners can be tricky." I have no idea why I said that. I've been making my bed for probably two decades without needing assistance.

Without saying another word, I hurry to the dryer and retrieve my now-cool sheets. Usually, I'd restart the appliance to fluff them up, but at this point, I'm not sure if I'm in a hurry because he's about to be in my bedroom or because I'm anxious to get him out of it.

"It's this way," I state when I return to where I left him standing in the living room. Why I said that, I'm not sure. He probably knows the way, considering this condo is the mirror image of the one his sister lives in.

Gabe follows behind me. Even if he didn't make a single noise, I'd still know he was back there. His presence is like its own living, breathing entity. I can feel it.

Neither of us speaks as I find the pesky fitted sheet in the mess of material and toss it on the bed. Gabe takes one side, while I take the other. Together, we easily cover the mattress with the clean, light blue sheet, and before I can grab the top one, Gabe is there. He throws it on the bed, both of us adjusting the sides to make sure it's somewhat even, before he moves to the foot of the bed and tucks it in.

It's been a while since I've had a man in my bedroom, and I admit, it's a little unnerving. Maybe because it's this man. Gabe. My best friend's brother. And the fact I slept with him a handful of months ago, and if the slight throb between my legs is any indication, I wouldn't mind taking that ride for another spin.

But that's not going to happen.

We work together now, which I still find shocking.

When I left, Hallie was pretty much the only person I kept in contact with, but back then, we never discussed family. We talked about boys we had crushes on, clothes, movies we'd seen, and everything else teen-girl related. We didn't discuss her older brother, unless she was complaining about him eating all of the good snacks when he was home from college. It never came up about his career path, and probably because my friend didn't want to tell me. Not that I blame her for forgetting to mention the fact her brother worked for my father, but a little heads-up would have been nice.

"You okay? You seem to be thinking awfully hard over there," Gabe says, pulling me from my inner thoughts.

I look up from the pillow I was stuffing into the case and smile. "Sure. Fine. Sorry, I guess I'm just a little tired."

He nods, making sure my comforter is perfectly positioned on the made bed. "You've had a long day. I'll get out of your hair," he says, turning those gorgeous blue eyes away from me. Except, when they do, they land firmly on the spot I toss my pillow.

His gaze returns to me once more, his eyes dark and dilated. There's a hunger evident, one I remember from that night. One I'll never be able to forget.

But as quickly as it appears, it's gone. Gabe swallows hard and looks down at his feet for a moment. When his eyes return to me, the desire I saw—the desire I *felt*—is gone, replaced with friendliness.

"Thank you, again," I state, my own voice a little wobbly.

"Of course. See you at work tomorrow?" It comes out a question, even though we both know it's not.

"I'll be there."

He nods once before turning and leaving my bedroom, taking the warmth and pleasure with him as he goes. I follow behind as he opens the door. "Make sure you lock this when I leave," he instructs. His tone reminds me of the Gabe I met when I arrived at his house. No nonsense, by the book, and full of authority.

"I will."

He doesn't say another word, just pushes through the screened door and heads to his truck parked on the side of the street. I close the door and make sure it's locked, but peek through the side of the curtains as he climbs into his truck. He sits there for a few minutes, and because of the darkness, I can't tell what he's doing. Maybe he's texting his sister to make sure she's okay before he goes, or hell, maybe he's texting a girlfriend. He didn't have one six months ago, but a lot can change in that amount of time.

Either way, I have no business lusting after my friend's brother, who is also a coworker.

Forcing myself to step back, I drop the curtain and turn off the television. There are several boxes I need to unpack in the kitchen, but right now, I think I just want to dig out my bathroom supplies, find my tablet in my suitcase, and get ready for bed. Tomorrow starts my first full day at the clinic, and I need to be ready.

As I turn down the hall, I hear his truck start and it makes me pause. Something inside my chest flutters, and I wish he weren't leaving.

But I push that thought aside because there's no reason for him to stay. Even if our one night together was pretty incredible, there's no future for us. He lives here, and while I do temporarily, I'm not staying. Eventually, I'll be returning to Chicago, to my old life.

Back home.

Away from Pine Village.

Why does that thought cause an unmistakable pain in my chest?

CHAPTER *four*

GABE

"Dr. Rhodes, we received a call from Ellie Daniels that Brody cut his hand at work. She's bringing him in right away," Makenzie announces the moment I step out into the hall.

I nod at her before turning back to the patient exiting the exam room. "We'll send in your prescriptions, and you'll be able to pick them up shortly. Call the office if you have any questions," I say to the man following me out of the room and make sure he's being taken care of at the front counter before I turn my attention back to my nurse.

"First up, send in these scripts for Roland," I say, handing over his file. "Okay, what's up with Brody?"

"Apparently, he was stocking shelves and the box cutter slipped and sliced his hand."

"Did she say how bad it was?" I ask.

"She thinks he needs stitches for sure," she replies.

Nodding, I instruct, "Get the suture kit ready in the procedure room and bring him in as soon as they arrive. When Blair comes out of her exam room, have her come to my office."

Makenzie vocalizes her understanding and takes off down the hall toward the reception area. I step into my office and head to the mini fridge. I contemplate grabbing one of the caffeinated bottles of pop but opt for the water instead.

Just as I'm taking a drink, I feel her presence before she speaks. "Makenzie said you wanted to see me?"

Recapping my water, I turn to give her my attention. "We have a fifteen-year-old boy with a hand injury on his way in. Mom thinks it's deep enough to require stitches."

She straightens. "Okay."

"They'll take him to the procedure room when they arrive so we can assess the injury," I state, placing my water back in the fridge. When I do, I pull a second bottle out and extend my hand.

"Thanks. Is he your patient normally?" she asks before taking a drink.

"Yes, but I know you can handle it. Actually, you went to school with his mom." When her eyebrows draw together in question, I add, "Ellie Daniels."

"Ellie? Really? Hallie is going to invite her to dinner Sunday," she says, almost absently.

"Doctors, Ellie and Brody are here," Kelly announces.

"We'll be in in just a moment," I state, turning my attention to Blair. Once Kelly is gone, I ask, "Ready?"

"Yes."

I wave her to proceed, not even bothering to hide the fact I shamelessly steal a glance at her ass. I don't care that it's covered up with her jacket. I can visualize it as if I just saw it yesterday. It's burned into my retinas, etched on my brain, and keeps me company late at night when I'm all alone.

Blair knocks on the doorframe of the open procedure room before stepping inside. Her eyes immediately go to Ellie, who throws her arms around her former friend in greeting. "I can't believe you're really here," Ellie proclaims with a sniffle, but I'm not sure if it's from seeing her friend after all these years or if she was crying over her son's injury before we walked in.

"Look at you," Blair says, stepping back and smiling at her friend. "You look amazing."

Ellie blushes a bit and waves off the compliment. "Stop. I look horrible. I've been working at the diner all day and probably smell like greasy food."

Blair just grins, holding Ellie's hand. "I've missed you."

"Me too," Ellie proclaims, throwing her arms around Blair's shoulders one more time. "And Hallie messaged me earlier. I'd love to come over for dinner Sunday to catch up."

"Great. Before you go, give me your cell phone number, and I'll text you the details when I get them figured out."

"So...I'm not gonna lose my hand, right, Doc? I mean since my mom went from panic mode to forgetting all about me?" Brody says, making me chuckle.

"You know how women are," I tease the young man, while taking in the hand he cut. It's wrapped in a towel, which is pretty saturated with blood. "How about we take a look at that hand?"

Kelly goes over to get the tray and sterile suture kit, as well as the saline we'll use to clean the cut, while I unwrap the hand to see the damage. "Wow, that's a doozie," I state, finally catching Blair's attention.

"I'm sorry," she whispers, coming over to stand beside me.

"No worries. I was just discussing with Brody here about how chatty women get," I tease with a wink.

Blair's cheeks turn a delectable shade of pink as she grabs the gauze and saline. "I'm Dr. O'Connor, Brody. It's a pleasure to meet you," she says to the boy with a polite smile as she starts to lay tools out on the table.

"We went to school together until Blair moved away before the start of our senior year," Ellie informs her son, taking a seat beside the exam table her son is sitting on. When she sees the towel and open wound on the side of her son's hand, she turns her head quickly, suddenly a little paler than before.

"You okay, El?" I ask, cleaning the wound.

"Mmhmm," she mumbles, nervously tapping her foot on the floor.

"Kelly, would you grab a bottle of water from the fridge for Ellie?" I ask without looking up from the task at hand. I hear her leave the room and finish irrigating the cut. Fortunately, it's a clean slice, doesn't appear to be too close to bone or severing any tendon. "You got lucky, kid. You cut through the meaty part of the hand. A few stitches and you'll be good to go."

I turn to see Blair start to prep the syringe we'll use to numb his hand so we can stitch him. She knows these steps, even if she hasn't practiced them since she joined her current practice.

When she goes to hand me the needle, I push myself back on the stool. "Go ahead. He's your patient," I advise Blair, getting up from the seat so she can take it.

Kelly drops off the bottle of water while I remove the latex gloves covering my hands. "All right, Brody. I'm gonna leave you in the very capable hands of Dr. O'Connor, but I'll check back in on you in a few minutes, okay?" I ask, holding up my fist for a bump of his good hand. When he taps it, I turn to Ellie, who's sipping water, her hand a little shaky. "You good, Mama?"

She chuckles but it lacks humor. "You know me and blood," she mutters, flashing me an uneasy grin.

I place my hand on her shoulder and give it a gentle squeeze before turning my attention back to Blair. She gives me a subtle nod, letting me know she's got it, so I step out into the hallway and find Makenzie.

"Brody good?"

I nod, taking the chart she presents and recognizing the name at the top. "Sugars come back normal?"

"Borderline, but yes," she confirms. "Same range as last month."

"Thanks," I state before knocking and stepping inside the room where I find Bella Jergeson sitting on the exam table, kicking her feet. "Good afternoon, Bella."

"Hey, Doc."

"How are you feeling today?" I ask, glancing over the rest of her chart to familiarize myself with her previous exam.

"Pretty good. The baby's been kicking up a storm," she confirms, placing a hand on her protruding stomach.

"Always a good thing, unless you're trying to get some sleep."

"That's what Robbie says," she replies, referring to her husband.

"I have the results from your urine sugar test, and they're bordering on problematic still. At this point, we're going to adjust your appointments to every two weeks so we can monitor it. Before you leave, I'll give you information on gestational diabetes, even though you don't technically have the diagnosis yet."

She nods and listens as I go over important details on diet, physical activity, sleep, and what to watch for in case her sugars climb more. Once she understands the information, we continue to the rest of her appointment, including taking a measurement and listening to the baby's heartbeat.

When I'm all finished up, I ask, "Still waiting to find out the sex?"

Bella nods eagerly. "Hopefully we only have to wait two more months, right? We're both anxious to meet him or her."

"Well, you're in the home stretch now. Makenzie will give you the pamphlets we talked about, and if you have any questions, call us."

"I will. Thanks, Dr. Rhodes," she says, carefully getting off the exam table.

"See you in two weeks," I reply, holding open the door and handing her file to Makenzie, who already has the pamphlets I was referring to. When Makenzie escorts Bella to the front reception area, I turn to head to the procedure room to see how Brody's doing.

"How's my favorite patient?" I ask, glancing down to watch Blair tie the final stitch.

"Mom almost passed out again," Brody announces, smiling widely at his mom's discomfort.

"You're grounded," she grumbles, looking at the floor as if it were the most interesting floor in the world.

"We're all finished here," Blair says, removing her latex gloves with a snap.

I check out her work, a bubble of pride swelling in my chest. "Good work, Doc," I compliment, giving her a quick grin.

Before she can reply, a noise echoes down the hallway, followed by rapidly moving feet. We all turn to the doorway just as TD appears in uniform, looking a little frazzled. "What happened?" he asks, his eyes bouncing between Brody and Ellie.

"I cut my hand," Brody broadcasts, holding up his stitched paw.

"Jesus, Brode," TD says, stepping in the room and examining his hand.

"Doesn't hurt now, since Doc O gave me a numbing shot. *That* stung, but I could handle it."

TD grins at the boy and reaches over, ruffling his hair. "And how about your mama? She pass out?"

"Of course you'd remember I don't like blood," Ellie complains.

TD, or Thomas Dexter as his mother likes to call him, was in the same class as Blair, Hallie, and Ellie. He's the local cop, as well as the high school football coach. I've always suspected he's a little sweet on Ellie, even though he's never confirmed my suspicions. It's mostly just an observation, but I do add his appearance today is quite telling.

TD has helped a lot with Brody the last few years, running him home from football practice if Ellie's stuck at the diner or picking him up on his way to weightlifting on Saturday morning. Since Brody's dad isn't in the picture, TD sort of stepped up to be a father figure for the young man, taking him under his wing and providing guidance and friendship.

To Brody *and* his mom.

"I stopped by the grocery store to grab a snack and Evelyn was at the register. She was still worked up and told me what happened,"

TD replies, glancing over at Ellie. "If it's okay with you, I'll stop back by on my way out of here to let her know how he's doing. To calm her down."

"Yes, of course," Ellie says. "Thank you for doing that for us."

He nods in reply before finally extending his hand my way. "Gabe," he says, shaking my hand. Then, his gaze turns to Blair and his eyes light up. "Little Blair O'Connor." TD walks toward her and picks her up, spinning her around as he hugs her. The sound of her laughter is like a cool glass of water on a hot summer day. It's refreshing and exactly what I didn't even know I needed.

But at the same time, I want to rip her from his arms, possessively and with an intensity that scares me a little. I don't, however, because I'm not a caveman.

Also, she's not technically mine.

Plus, I know it's a hug amongst former classmates who haven't seen each other in a decade and a half.

Simmer down, Gabriel.

"We're gonna have to catch up soon."

"Well, what are you doing Sunday? I'm having Hallie, Ellie, and Brody over for dinner. You can join us," Blair offers, and suddenly, I'm a little jealous at his invitation.

Mostly because I didn't receive one.

"Home-cooked food? I'm there. Just send me the details. Ellie's got my number," TD says before turning his attention back to the patient. "All right, I better get back on the streets. Glad you're okay, kid. I'll stop by the apartment when I get off and see if you need anything."

Brody nods. "Thanks, Coach."

TD smiles at the boy before turning to his mom. "Walk me out?" Ellie nods and follows TD out of the room.

"Okay, champ, did you get all the instructions for taking care of this cut?" I ask as Blair starts to cover the wound with a bandage.

"Yep. Doc O told me to keep it dry and covered until tomorrow, and then I can change the bandage and clean it. I'll probably have

Coach help me with that since my mom apparently can't hang with the cool kids," he quips, a big ol' grin spreading across his face.

I chuckle at his comment and squeeze his shoulder once more. "You're a good kid, Brody Daniels."

"We all set?" Ellie asks when she returns to the office.

Blair nods in confirmation. "You're good. We'll have him come back next week to remove the stitches. You can schedule that up front."

"Great," Ellie mutters, "I can't wait to come back for *that.*"

"It's pretty simple," Blair confirms. "Plus, no blood."

"Okay, well, let's get you home, Brode, before the numbness wears off."

Blair walks the patient up front, chatting about Sunday's dinner and potential menu options, while I head to my office and look at the schedule. I know the rest of my afternoon is busy, so I grab a bottle of water and get back to it.

When I step back into the hallway, I practically run into Blair. She's typing on her phone, moving to the office directly across the hall from my own, her father's. "Oops," she says at our near miss. "Sorry. I wasn't paying attention."

"It's okay," I reply, rocking back on my heels.

"I was texting Hallie to let her know I ran into Ellie." She glances up, a concerned look on her face. "Don't worry. I didn't say anything about Brody's injury. I'd never discuss a patient with anyone like that," she insists.

"It's okay, I know you wouldn't."

She seems to visibly relax. "Back at the pediatrics practice I worked at, they were sticklers on doctor-patient confidentiality. It was grounds for immediate dismissal for anyone, including office staff, if it was ever found out."

"That's not a bad policy to have in place. We may discuss patients amongst ourselves, but we don't talk about them outside of the clinic. This town is too small for that."

She flashes me a smile. "Very true. There's a big difference between Pine Village and Chicago."

"Fact," I reply, noticing Makenzie step out of my exam room, indicating our hallway chat time is almost up. "Well, I better get down there and see my next patient."

Blair nods and steps into her father's office. "Oh, and Gabe?" When I turn back around, she continues, "I'm having a few people over Sunday for dinner. If you're not doing anything, you're welcome to join us. It's nothing fancy, and probably not nearly as delicious as that soup you made last Christmas, but it should be edible," she says with a snicker.

She remembers what I made for dinner that night?

Why does that make me feel all warm and excited on the inside?

"Sure, I can come. I don't think I'm doing anything Sunday."

Way to be casual, man.

She nods and smiles. "Okay, good."

I turn and head for the exam room, mentally fist pumping myself the entire way.

An hour later, I've just finished a workman's comp exam from a man who stepped on a nail at a home construction site when I hear voices out front. It's not uncommon for patients to be chatty and talk to all the staff, but there seems to be a lot of extra laughter coming from the front area.

When I leave the patient with Makenzie to get his tetanus shot, I barely step into the hall before a young voice hollers, "Blair!"

I instantly know who's here, and I can't help but worry.

Patience has arrived, Blair's young stepmom, and with her, her five-year-old daughter, Aggie.

Blair's half sister.

CHAPTER
five

Blair

I give my sister a smile. "Good afternoon, Aggie," I reply, walking toward her outstretched hands and taking the hug she's offering.

"We went to the park, and I got to play with Sierra and Cooper on the swings," the little girl with sand in her hair and a smudge of dirt on her knee says. The tiny pink glasses perched on her nose are slightly askew from her afternoon play session.

"That sounds like fun," I reply, ignoring the presence of my stepmother.

"Mommy said you were here finally. I've been waiting *foreverrrr*," she groans, drawing out the last word.

I chuckle at her dramatic exaggeration, shaking my head at her antics.

It's still a little hard for me to believe I have a sister. Aggie is five and is the perfect combination of our father and her mother. She has her mother's blond hair and tall, skinny frame, with the same green eyes and round face I stare at every morning in the mirror. She has worn glasses for a while to help correct amblyopia, or a lazy eye, in her right eye.

When Aggie was born, I kept my distance. The last thing I wanted thrust in my face was my father, his mistress turned wife, and their new baby. I didn't want to meet his new family when he so easily threw away the original one.

It took me a little time to realize my anger was at him and Patience, not Aggie, so last Christmas, when I was staying with Hallie, I reached out to them and requested to meet my sister. I was invited over to their house, but I didn't feel comfortable going there. He lived in the same house I grew up in until the day my world turned upside down. So we settled on the diner.

Dad didn't come. One of his patients was in labor, so he was off delivering a baby, but Patience came. I haven't seen the woman just seven years older than me in more than a decade. Once, they showed up in Chicago unannounced when I was in medical school, trying to buy my affection and time. It didn't go well, and I asked them to leave me alone. Since then, they've obliged. In fact, when I called Patience, asking to meet Aggie, she seemed completely shocked to hear from me.

Fortunately, she granted my request, and since then, I've been in communication with my half sister. We video chat weekly using Patience's phone, and we've even sent each other small things through the mail. She colors me pictures for my fridge, and I send her Barbies and fun things to craft. We've gotten much closer in the last six months than I ever expected, and even though I'm still hurt and angry at her parents, I know it's not her fault.

"I just got here," I tell my sister, giving her a grin.

"Can you come over and play after work?" she asks, hopeful green eyes gazing up at me.

I open my mouth, ready to decline, but it gets caught in my throat. I don't want to deny her, but at the same time, I'm not sure I can go to the house.

"Agg, I'm sure Blair has to get settled into her apartment. Let's give her a few more days to get organized, and then you two can schedule a playdate," Patience says to her daughter before turning to face me. "Hello, Blair."

I'm polite as I nod and reply, "Hi."

"Tomorrow?" Aggie asks, turning pleading green eyes my way.

I can't help but give in. "How about we go have pizza tomorrow when I get off?"

"Yes!" she bellows, facing her mom. "Can we?"

Patience smiles down at the child. "As long as Blair says it's okay."

My sister turns wide, hope filled eyes my way. I can practically feel the begging spilling from them. Before she can ask, I nod. "I can take you home after we eat."

"Yay!" Aggie bellows, the sound echoing off the walls, as she starts to do a happy little jig.

"You're so silly," Patience laughs, her attention turning to Gabe. "Hi, Gabe. Frank said he talked to you for a bit yesterday."

"He did. He kept me company as I drove over to Hudson to discharge a patient."

"He's so anxious to get back to work, yet in no condition for it. I think talking to you helped. He felt like he was kept in the loop better than he has since the heart attack," she says.

I can't help but feel sad for my dad, who has always been so active in his work. I'm sure going from working seven days a week to laid up in a bed, recovering from a massive coronary episode, is tough on him. Heaven knows I would struggle with it, and I'm only thirty-three, about half his age.

"I'll try to keep calling him every now and again and discussing his patients with him, as long as you're okay with it."

I almost roll my eyes, as they continue to converse as if long lost friends. And I guess, in a way, they probably are. Gabe has worked for my father for a few years now, subsequently getting to know Patience and my sister along the way.

With Aggie happily twirling in the middle of the hallway, I'm able to take in Patience from the profile view. Her long blond hair is pulled back in a stylish ponytail, her hazel eyes shining brightly beneath the fluorescent lighting. Her cheekbones are high, her makeup flawless. Honestly, she doesn't look a day over thirty, despite having celebrated her fortieth birthday a few months back.

It's not fair, really. I'm seven years her junior and often look like I just woke the morning after a night of binge drinking. I show every sign of exhaustion or stress, usually on my face. Though, I have noticed, since arriving in Pine Village this time around, I feel a little more refreshed and relaxed. I'm not on call two nights a week, as well as one weekend a month, often taking phone calls into the wee hours of the morning or dealing with patients in the hospital. Even though I love the hustle of city life, I can appreciate some of the slowness this rural community has to offer.

"Well, we'll get out of your hair. Aggie just wanted to stop by for a quick visit," Patience says, offering me a polite smile, one I actually return.

"I'm glad you did," I reply, crouching down in front of my sister. "I'll see you tomorrow?"

Aggie nods eagerly as she pushes her glasses up her nose. "I like cheese pizza with lots of salad."

"Then we will get cheese pizza and lots of salad," I confirm, earning yet another big smile. It feels good to see so much excitement, so much innocence from a young child.

My stepmother takes her daughter's hand, stopping in front of me. "You can text me when you're about finished, and I can run her up here."

I nod, unable to get the words of appreciation past my lips.

Kelly steps up and grabs my attention. "We have an eighteen-month-old on her way in with breathing trouble."

"We'll let you get back to work. See you tomorrow," Patience says, leading her daughter back down the hallway toward the front entrance.

"Bye, Blair!" my sister hollers, waving like crazy.

I wave back and smile, grateful for the little reprieve in my day. It's short lived though, when I see Makenzie bring a woman and her child back to my exam room. Gabe turns and follows them in, as Kelly hands me the chart. "Little Gwyneth had pneumonia this past winter and your dad diagnosed her with RAD," the nurse informs me. I'm familiar with RAD, or reactive airway disease, as I had a few cases of it while working at the clinic in Illinois.

"Thank you. Get her vitals, and a breathing machine ready," I state, following the nurse into the room.

For the next thirty minutes, Gabe and I work together to calm both Gwyneth and her mother and get the necessary dose of steroid and albuterol into the young girl. Once that's complete, she's able to settle enough so we can send them to Hudson for a chest X-ray to confirm my suspicion another bout of pneumonia has settled into her lungs.

"The radiologist will call as soon as he reads the X-ray." Gabe's voice startles me. I spin around in my dad's office, finding him leaning against the doorjamb. He looks relaxed, but the slight stress lines around his eyes tell another story. He's worried about the child.

That's evident in the way Gabe communicates with the patients who walk through the clinic. He knows them, lives amongst them. He sees them when he goes to the grocery store or helped shovel their sidewalks when he was a teenager. Chances are he went to school with either the patient or their parents. Once my patients leave the office, I don't see them until their next appointment. It's another huge difference between us.

It takes another hour before I get the call about Gwyneth. As soon as I have her admitted, I head across the hall to Gabe's office to let him know the news. He's typing away on his laptop when I peek my head in, hand raised to knock on the doorframe.

However, it stops before connecting with the wood. I take a moment to appreciate the beauty that is Gabe Rhodes. He has a pair of black-framed glasses perched on his nose as he studies the screen, a thoughtful expression on his handsome face. It reminds me a little of the grumpy look he wore when I was a short-term guest at his house all those months ago.

That one remarkable night.

As if sensing my presence, he glances up, the seriousness in his eyes evaporating quickly. "Hey, what's up?" he asks, his voice gravelly and deep.

"I heard from Dr. Puite at Hudson Memorial. He confirmed fluid in both lungs. It's not horrible, but with her history, I'm having her admitted. I'm going to head over there in a bit."

Gabe nods. "I'll go with."

My spine stiffens. "You don't think I can handle it?"

He pulls the glasses off his face and drops them on the desk, his gaze intense and penetrating. "Of course I do. I thought I could help you find your way around and introduce you to the staff. She's your patient, Blair, and I have full confidence in your abilities. Your dad wouldn't have asked you to come here if he didn't believe in you. We both do."

I swallow hard, hating how defensive I still get sometimes. "I'm sorry," I reply, swallowing hard.

Gabe stands up and stretches. "Give me ten minutes and we can go," he says, slipping his lab coat off and tossing it over the back of the chair.

I stand here, as if my feet were stuck in concrete, and watch as he loosens his tie and releases the small buttons at his wrists. He looks up again and our eyes meet, a heavy electricity pulsing through the room. Gabe doesn't speak, just holds my gaze while he rolls up the sleeves on his crisp, white dress shirt. My mouth is dry, my blood zinging through my veins. The weight of desire settles between my legs, one I wish I could ignore, but can't.

The same need stares back at me. I can see Gabe's Adam's apple bob, his eyes slightly dilated. I wonder what he's thinking about. Is he recalling our night together, replaying it over and over again the way I am? Remembering the feel of his skin against mine, the way he hovered over my body as he pressed inside me?

"We're going to head out," Kelly announces from the doorway, dousing our intimate moment with a proverbial bucket of ice water.

Gabe clears his throat and looks down at his desk. "Thank you, Kelly. We'll see you tomorrow."

She flashes him a knowing smile before turning and exiting the clinic through the back entrance with some of the rest of the staff.

I glance over at my father's office. "I'll gather up my things and be ready to go in a few minutes," I state before practically running across the hall and shutting the door. Once it's closed, I lean against it and exhale, closing my eyes as my head rests on the hard wood.

"Get it together, Blair," I mumble, trying to push all thoughts of Gabe out of my mind. "You have a job to do."

And that doesn't involve *doing* Gabe.

Even if my brain and lady parts are totally on board.

Ten minutes later, I'm riding in the passenger seat of Gabe's big truck, heading to Hudson. A country station plays softly on the radio as we leave the city limits of town and start our trek to the nearest hospital.

"So, what was with the reaction to me offering to go with you?" he asks, breaking the silence.

I know exactly what he's talking about, but that doesn't stop me from pretending I don't. "What reaction?"

Gabe glances over before returning his gaze back to the road. "When I offered, you instantly got a little defensive. I'm wondering why."

I contemplate how much to disclose. We're not really friends, but we do have a professional work relationship to maintain. It's not necessarily a big secret I'm trying to keep, but it's a tad embarrassing to confess. "When I was hired at the pediatric clinic, one of the owners, Dr. Mehta, was an older gentleman who wasn't really interested in hiring a new physician in the first place, let alone a woman. He was constantly questioning every decision I made, forcing me to second-guess myself all day."

"That sucks."

"It did. They definitely needed the additional physician, which is the only reason he finally agreed to my hire, even though I found out from one of the nurses, Dr. Mehta was pushing for a different male doctor. The other two owners, Dr. Lewis, a forty-year-old man, and Dr. Ambrose, a forty-six-year-old woman, both voted for my hire, and even though I had their confidence behind me, it was stressful. Dr. Mehta was always looking over my shoulder, waiting for me to fail so he could chastise me in front of the other staff, of course."

"Damn, Blair," he responds, shaking his head. "I can't imagine not having support at work like that."

I lift a shoulder in a shrug. "The other two supported me, which was the only thing that kept me there. I think Dr. Mehta was really hoping I'd just quit, but I refused. I'm not a quitter. Plus, I knew he was approaching his retirement, so if I could just hang on a little longer, he'd be gone."

"And is he? Gone?"

I nod. "He retired at the beginning of the year, thankfully. He's still part owner, but he's not there on a day-to-day basis."

"Good. You don't need that kind of bullshit in your life," he replies, and the disdain in his voice is evident.

"We have three nurse practitioners who help too, which makes it a little tight at the clinic, but it works."

The corners of Gabe's mouth turn upward just a hint. "So definitely a little different than the Pine Village Medical Clinic."

I snort a laugh. "Uhh, yeah. Much different," I confirm, even though he already knows.

A few minutes later, we're pulling into Hudson and making our way to the hospital. I've been here before, but many years ago, so I try to pay close attention to the route he takes. Gabe pulls into the physician's lot and parks in the first available spot. I retrieve my lab coat from the back seat and slip it on, noticing Gabe doing the same from his side of the truck. He meets me at the front of the truck and straightens his tie, transforming himself from casual to professional in a matter of seconds.

"Ready?" he asks, giving me a small grin. Even that slightest gesture could melt the glaciers in Antarctica.

"Let's do it," I reply, taking a step, but then stopping in my tracks. The sexual innuendo isn't what I meant, but I quickly realize it's not that inaccurate. Ever since seeing Gabe a few days ago, for the first time since last December, my brain has been inappropriately lodged in a place it has no business being.

He reaches out and gently grabs my elbow, guiding me toward the hospital entrance. "Yes, let's do it," he replies, a naughty little smirk on his face, and even though my cheeks are flushed with embarrassment, I know a part of the warmth is from his statement.

His agreement.

These next few months may very well be the most difficult I've ever experienced. Far worse than dealing with old Dr. Mehta and his constant judgment and scrutiny.

My kryptonite will be working alongside Gabriel Rhodes.

CHAPTER
six

GABE

By the time Sunday dinner rolls around, I contemplate actually going. I've discovered I really enjoy spending time with Blair, despite the fact we're at work. She's funny, caring, and a fucking brilliant pediatrician, and I find myself completely drawn to her like a moth to a flame. Her smile, the light in her eyes, the way she nibbles on her bottom lip when she's in deep thought. I even find her eye rolls attractive as hell, especially when I know they're aimed at me.

Which is why I could use another day sans Blair to get myself under control before I do something stupid like kiss the hell out of those sweet lips. The very mouth I've thought about constantly since I saw her standing in the clinic in her lab coat. Hell, I've jacked off more in the last five days than I have in the last month. The last thing I need is to embarrass myself by acting on this attraction in front of my sister and friends.

Yet, I know I'll go. She's the drug I crave, and I'm too weak to fight the pull.

After a quick two-mile run and a shower, I'm dressed in khaki shorts, a blue T-shirt, and an old pair of flip-flops I found in the back of my closet. I think Amara, my ex-wife, bought them a few years ago for the Caribbean cruise we never went on. She left me three weeks before we were to set sail.

Retrieving the beer from the fridge and the cookie bars I baked, I lock up my house, despite the fact Pine Village is pretty safe, and head for my truck. The drive into town to Blair's condo is short, and when I pull onto her street, I find some familiar vehicles. TD's truck is there, as well as Ellie's car, and a truck I know to be Logan Johnson's.

I park in my sister's driveway and hop out, grabbing the beer and dessert bars from the back seat. The warm sun beats down on my face as I walk across the yard toward Blair's front door. Before I reach it, I can hear the laughter spilling from the open entrance and spot familiar faces through the screen door.

"Knock, knock," I announce, catching everyone's attention.

"Hey," Blair replies with a smile as she approaches. She releases the lock on the screen door and holds it open for me. "Come on in."

"Thanks for inviting me," I state lamely, holding up the bag with the six-pack.

She takes the bag, but her eyes are locked on the container in my other hand. "What's that?" she asks, her eyes twinkling with excitement.

"Oh, uh, chocolate chip cookie bars."

"You bought me some cookie bars?" she asks with a happy little chuckle. "Did you know they are my favorite?"

I follow Blair into her kitchen where everyone else is gathered. As I nod across the room at TD and Logan, I say, "No, I made them."

Blair stops in her tracks, and if I wasn't paying attention, I would have run into the back of her. "You made them?" she asks, seemingly completely shocked by this news.

"Made what?" my sister asks, taking the container from my hand. Her eyes widen as she peeks inside. "Are these chocolate chip cookie bars?"

"Give 'em to me," Blair demands, reaching out her hand.

"No way. Gabe makes the best cookies and bars," Hallie insists, setting them on the counter and popping the top off.

"Stop it. Those are for after dinner," Blair declares, hip-bumping my sister out of the way and reclosing the lid. "Come on, everyone. Let's head out back."

I say hello to Ellie, TD, and Logan as we all head to the back door and am instantly pulled into their conversation about the upcoming Summer Family Festival over the July 4th holiday. I try to pay attention to what they're discussing, something about who to hire to perform at the street dance, but my eyes are glued on the hostess. Blair goes over to a brand-new propane grill and lights the burners.

"I was going to make something like lasagna or chicken parmesan, but it's such a lovely afternoon, I thought I'd grill instead," Blair announces to no one in particular.

"I love a good burger. You get no complaints from me," I reply, going over to where she stands. "New grill?"

She nods in confirmation. "I don't have the opportunity to use one much in Chicago, but I'm hoping I can here. I love grilling almost as much as cooking at the stove or oven." She tosses me a quick smile, one that's relaxed and full of eagerness.

"Hey, Coach! Will you play catch with me?" Brody asks from the middle of the yard.

"Sure," TD agrees quickly, setting his beer bottle down on the table, "but if you split open those stitches, you're dealing with your mom."

I glance over at Ellie, who's now sitting at the table with Hallie. She has a worried look on her face. "Is this okay? He's supposed to be taking it easy."

"It should be all right, as long as he doesn't use that hand to catch the ball. It'll hurt like hell if he hits it with the football," I state, watching the young man and his coach carefully toss the ball back and forth.

"Don't worry, Mom. We have two docs here," Brody says with a cheesy grin.

"Let's not need to use them, okay?" she grumbles, sipping from a bottle of water.

"How's Frank?" Logan asks, coming up to stand beside me.

"Getting along. He's starting therapy this week to start working on cardiac and physical strength."

He takes a drink from his beer. "It's a good thing Blair was available to help, huh?"

"Yeah." It was damn good, actually. I'm not sure what I'd do if I had to see his patients, as well as mine for any extensive amount of time. It was incredibly difficult to manage in the short time between his heart attack and Blair's arrival, even more so than being one of two physicians caring for an entire town.

Of course, not all residents come to our clinic for medical care. There are some that choose to take the short drive to Hudson to see one of their primary care physicians or specialists, but for the most part, we see the majority. Especially for minor injuries and ailments. We're quick, convenient, and know every patient.

"Honestly, I'm shocked she's here," Logan mutters softly as to not be overheard.

"Me too. They haven't had the easiest relationship."

Logan snorts. "No shit. I can't imagine walking in and seeing your dad with his nurse. Then for them to get married a week after his first marriage is dissolved," he adds, shaking his head and leaving the rest of his statement unsaid. He doesn't need to finish it. I know and agree. I can't imagine what it was like for her to witness that, to have her entire life uprooted at the age of seventeen.

"All right, is medium well okay for everyone?" Blair asks as she returns to the back patio, a platter of raw burgers in her hand.

When everyone agrees, she starts to arrange them on the cooking surface and lightly seasons each one. I can't help but notice they're not the pressed patties you buy from the grocery store in town. These are freshly made and are more than just ground beef. "I see green pepper and cheese, but what else do you have stuffed in those patties?"

"These have green peppers, onions, and cheddar cheese in them, and this row is mushroom and Swiss," she replies, using the spatula as a pointer. "And these are just cheese."

"Damn, woman. Will you marry me?" Logan asks, dropping to his knee with a hearty laugh, which makes her giggle at his antics.

I'm, however, *not* laughing.

At all.

A bubble of jealousy worms its way into my chest with a vengeance.

"You're nuts," Blair states, shaking her head.

"My next wife is going to know how to cook," he points out.

"Yeah, let's talk about that for a second," Blair says, turning her attention to her former classmate. "Shay Long? Really?"

Logan sighs as he stands up and takes a drink from his bottle. "Temporary insanity is all I got, Blair," he says.

"Someday, you'll tell me the story."

Logan chuckles. "We'll need a lot of tequila."

"Done." Blair lifts the lid on the grill and checks the food, and even though I tell myself to look away, I can't. I'm drawn to her in a way I've never been, even with my former wife. Maybe it's because she's the first woman I've found incredibly attractive and have a bit in common with since the dissolution of my marriage more than three years ago.

Sure, I've tried dating since. Last year, I took a nurse from Hudson out, following months of obvious flirting on her part. It's not that I didn't want to go out with her, but I wasn't interested in mixing business with pleasure, so to speak. If we did end up dating for a while and then broke up, I'd have to see her often when I visited the hospital.

But over the weeks leading up to our date, she slowly wore me down until I asked her out. We met at a steakhouse in Hudson, and while the evening started off pleasant enough, it didn't exactly end that way. Turns out, she's a very picky diner, meaning she nitpicked everything brought to her, from the salad without a cucumber slice to the steak with too much seasoning, despite being cooked to perfection.

And don't get me started on the dessert, where the rhubarb crisp clearly spent too much time under a heat lamp.

Her words, not mine.

She had no problems monopolizing much of the conversation, which usually I don't mind, but most of it revolved around her ex-boyfriend, who stole her car and her cat when he moved out of their shared apartment. Then, when we went to leave, it started to rain, and she had no problems telling me I should have looked at the weather forecast and brought an umbrella to walk her to her car.

I found my first big date post-divorce to be rather anticlimactic and disappointing.

From that point on, I realized dating just wasn't my thing. I have plenty of conversation during the day and spend enough after work hours seeing patients at the hospital that it leaves little room in my life for the opposite sex.

Yet, I can't stop thinking about what it would be like to have Blair beside me, woven into the fabric of my life. Working beside her every day. Coming home to her every night. Lying beside her as we drift off to sleep, whether it be in a king-sized bed or on the sectional sofa, like last December.

It's a thought that has resurfaced multiple times over the last six months, even more so since I found out she was coming back to Pine Village to work beside me.

"How's the house coming along?"

Blair's question pulls me from my inner thoughts. "Excuse me?" I ask, trying to piece together the question.

"Your house. Last time I was there, you were working on the kitchen," she says, though I swear her cheeks start to flush a little.

Clearing my throat, I reply, "Actually, I've completed the kitchen. Floors and the island are done now. You'll have to stop by and see it," I suggest.

And maybe get naked with me again on the couch...

"Yeah? That's exciting. Maybe I'll do that," she replies, averting her eyes and trying to hide the blush.

"Do what?" Hallie asks, nosing right on into our conversation.

"See Gabe's kitchen," Blair states, opening the lid to flip the burgers.

"Yeah, he finally finished it," my sister goads, elbowing me in the gut. "The guy spends years working on the kitchen, but suddenly, after Christmas, he's determined to complete it. I didn't see him for weeks while he sanded, stained, and finished wood floor planks, and then installed them. I don't know what in the world came over him. I swore he was doing it to forget about a woman," she adds with a laugh.

My stomach? Oh, that dropped onto the concrete floor at my feet.

"A woman? Gabe?" Logan asks, obviously enjoying a tease at my expense. Usually, I wouldn't mind, but with Blair standing directly in front of me, the weight of her green eyes penetrating me like a missile, it feels a little too personal. Like I'm exposed.

"You have a secret girlfriend, Gabe?" Ellie asks, attention turned from watching her son and TD toss the ball to where we're standing and visiting.

"No," I insist with a chuckle, taking a drink of my beer to keep myself from saying anything else.

"Blair, did you see anything when you stayed with him?" Hallie asks, ignoring me completely.

"Wait, Blair stayed with Gabe?" Ellie inquires.

My sister nods. "Over Christmas. She came to town a day early but got stuck in the snow outside of town. Curtis and I went shopping and got stuck there because of the weather, so I called Gabe to go rescue her."

"That Dr. Rhodes is such a sweet guy," Logan joshes.

Yeah. Sweet isn't exactly the word I would have used that night.

Apparently, Blair doesn't quite agree either, judging by the pink color of her cheeks.

"Speaking of, where's Curtis tonight?" Ellie asks my sister, moving the conversation away from the quicksand it was moments ago.

Logan goes off to toss the football with TD and Brody, and as much as I'd love to catch up on the boyfriend drama surrounding my sister, I opt for door number three. "Can I help?" I ask Blair, stepping up beside her as she checks the meat on the grill once more.

"Can you keep an eye on these for a few minutes? I'm going to run in and get the rest of the food ready to serve." When I nod, she adds, "I'll only be a minute." Then, she disappears into her condo.

The backyard is sparce. In fact, I'm pretty sure the table and chairs sitting on the patio belong to my sister, which would make sense, considering Blair's only going to be here for a handful of months. That thought doesn't sit well with me. The same draw, that incredible pull I felt toward her, is still very much alive. I just have to figure out how to approach it with her.

A quick look at the meat confirms it's about ready, so I shut the lid and make my way to the back entrance. Pulling open the door, I pop my head in and state, "Meat's ready."

Blair startles and whips around, her hand covering her mouth.

Realization sets in, and I couldn't stop the smile from spreading across my lips if I tried. "Whatcha doing?" I ask in a singsong voice, stepping into her kitchen.

Her hand still covers her mouth, but I can clearly tell she's chewing. Toss in the fact the lid to the cookie bars is askew, and it's obvious what I busted in on. "Nothing. Just getting everything ready."

I'm surprised she doesn't spit cookie all over herself as she talks and busies herself with the food. Walking over to the cookie bars container, I reseal the lid and narrow my eyes at her. "You stole a cookie bar."

"I did not," she insists, wide green eyes full of guilt.

I can't help but laugh. "You're the worst liar ever, Blair. You ready for the burgers?"

She nods stiffly and grabs the platter. "I can get them."

Waving off her comment, I take the large plate and move to the door. "I got 'em. You finish up in here." Before I step outside, I turn back around. "Oh, Blair?" When she faces me, I brush my fingers over the corner of my mouth and add, "You've got some cookie right here."

Blair gasps before she laughs, frantically wiping at her face to rid the evidence of her stealing cookie bars before dinner. The last thing I hear as I exit is the rich sound of her sweet laughter. It's a glorious noise, one I'll replay over and over again the rest of the night.

I don't know what it is about her.

I can't get enough.

CHAPTER
seven

Blair

"Good morning. I brought you coffee."

Glancing up from the file on the desk, I offer Gabe a quick smile, taking in his early morning appearance. His dress shirt is crisp and white, the tie around his neck red and blue. He's wearing navy blue dress pants and tan shoes that may be built more for comfort than style, but on him, they look pretty good. Top it off, his jaw is scruffy, as if he didn't bother shaving this morning before work. I actually think I prefer the stubble.

It reminds me of last Christmas.

Of our single night together.

"Thank you," I state hoarsely, reaching for the offered paper cup of yummy coffee and sipping the contents. "You seem awfully chipper for a Monday morning."

Gabe shrugs and takes the empty chair across from my desk. "Actually relaxed a little yesterday," he replies, the corner of his mouth tipping upward in a lazy grin.

"Yeah, me too, which is a rarity." After another sip of coffee, I add, "Thanks for coming over last night."

"Thanks for the invite. I had a great time." Those cool blue eyes follow my every movement, causing little shivers of excitement to race across my skin. He takes in the file on my desk and asks, "Whatcha got there?"

"Lillie Darth's paperwork. She was admitted yesterday when she fell off the deck at a relative's pool. She hit her head fairly hard on the wooden edge and knocked herself out. Fortunately, her older brother and a cousin were right there and dragged her out of the water before yelling for help. She came to on the ambulance ride to Hudson Memorial, but they've been monitoring a pretty big knot on the side of her head and some swelling."

"Shit," he mutters, taking the report I hand over and reading the first page. "I hadn't heard. Did you go over last night?" he asks, his penetrating eyes focused solely on me.

"No, the attending said it wasn't necessary. He faxed over the reports bright and early, including the latest from the neurologist. She's still complaining of double vision and, fortunately, the vomiting has stopped. They kept a close watch on her overnight."

"I have a break in my schedule at noon if you want company going over and seeing her."

I nod, appreciating the offer. "Thanks. I may take you up on that." I ignore the voice in my head telling me it's because I want to spend more time with him, not because I need assistance going to check on a patient.

"Well, I'll let you get to it," he says, slapping his knees before standing. Gabe retrieves his coffee cup from the desk and heads for the door. "Oh, I brought the remaining cookie bars and put them in the break room. If you want one, you should get in there before the others come in. Those four women have a sweet tooth, and they'll be gone before the first patient arrives." With a wink, he disappears across the hall to his office.

I sit there for a moment, trying to ignore how potent his wink is and the power of his smile. It makes me want to do things—*naughty things*—with a coworker inside the walls of my workplace. Even when we were discussing something as serious as a patient injury, I couldn't ignore the heat of desire licking at my skin.

By the time the rest of the staff arrives, I've made sure to grab a couple of cookie bars from the break room and hide them in my desk drawer—after I had one with my coffee, of course. As patients start to arrive, I find myself very busy for a Monday. I treat a bee sting on a six-year-old, who broke out in hives, as well as dealt with a sprained wrist on a twelve-year-old following a fall off her trampoline.

As I sit and chart my morning appointments, I get the phone call I was waiting on from the hospital. "Good morning, Dr. O'Connor, this is Phillip Angelo, the attending physician seeing Lillie Darth. I have good news to report this morning. Lillie has kept food down today, and her CT scan doesn't show any swelling or bleeding. She has a severe concussion, but I'm confident with rest, she'll be good to go very soon."

"Happy to hear that. How long will you keep her?"

"We're going to discharge her later today. I'm recommending she follow up with you at the end of the week."

"Sounds good. I'll be sure to call the nurse and check on her before she's released."

"That's good of you," he replies, a smile evident in his voice. "You remind me a lot of your father."

My throat thickens and suddenly, it's hard to draw air into my lungs.

"Well, I'll let you get back to it. Thanks for taking my call."

Clearing my throat, I reply, "I appreciate you reaching out to me."

"Have a good day."

"You as well." I hang up the phone, my mind still reeling from his statement.

When I was little, everyone liked my dad. He was the epitome of a caring physician, and I was so proud of him, even at a young age. I knew when I was six, I wanted to follow in his footsteps. He bought me my first play doctor's bag, complete with stethoscope, thermometer, plastic band-aid, syringe, and blood pressure cuff, all in a plastic blue carrying bag, and I nursed everything from my stuffed animals to the kid down the block back to health.

I'd spend hours at the clinic, soaking in his knowledge and pretending I was the one treating the patients who walked through the door. During my teen years, everyone expected to see me there, and in most cases, humored me when it came to discussing their health. I was in my element, working hard in school because I understood the commitment it took to follow in my dad's footsteps.

Then it all changed.

The day I arrived at the clinic and found his arms wrapped around and his lips plastered to his then-nurse, Patience, was one of the worst days of my life. The man I loved more than anything, the one I hoisted high on that pedestal, was nothing but weak, a mere mortal.

I tried to change my major. Really, I did. After the divorce, I looked into every field you could think of that was on the far end of the employment spectrum from medical. But deep down, it was in my blood. I knew I wouldn't be happy doing anything else, so I relented. I went to school and studied my ass off, determined to be a better physician, a better person than the man I once watched, my mentor.

A throat clears, pulling me out of my own head. "Sorry to interrupt. I heard Hudson was on the phone?" Gabe asks, his warm and concerned eyes seeing right through me.

"Oh, uh, yeah." I relay the details of the phone call, noticing the relief that settles in his features.

"That's good news. I was a little worried."

"Me too," I confess. I worry about all my patients, even in the bigger clinic where I see dozens of kids a day, but there's something about this town and the people who live in it that just speaks to my heart.

Gabe reaches up and grabs the doorjamb above his head, and I try to ignore the way his forearms flex and his white button-down molds to his body like a second skin. "Since you no longer have to make a trip to Hudson, care to join me for lunch at the diner?"

I glance at the clock, noticing it's just past noon. My heart flutters in my chest with eagerness, which is probably exactly why I should decline the offer. The last thing I need is to get used to spending extra time with Gabe Rhodes, even though my body seems to be fully on board with the notion.

Before I can reply, he goes in for the kill. "They're serving bacon-wrapped meatloaf and cheddar mashed potatoes for their special."

I almost groan aloud. "I'm in."

Gabe chuckles and taps on the wall. "Holler when you're ready."

I open the desk drawer and grab my purse before hanging my lab coat on the back of the door. The moment I step into the hallway, Gabe is there and waves toward the back exit. The sun shines high in the sky, the June air warm against my skin as we walk around the building to the sidewalk. The diner is just down the block, so it only takes us a few minutes to get there. We're both quiet, but it doesn't feel uncomfortable. In fact, it feels natural, as if we can both co-exist without forcing conversation twenty-four seven.

When we reach the familiar glass door of the diner, he reaches out and pulls it open, the familiar sights and sounds of Frannie's Diner surrounding me. As soon as I step inside, I hear a very recognizable voice. "Hey, guys! Have a seat wherever," Ellie hollers, delivering two plates of food to one of the booths on the far side of the room.

I glance around the room and find an open booth near the big windows. "That okay?" I ask Gabe, who quickly nods in agreement.

He leans closer, his earthy scent infiltrating my senses. "Wherever you pick is fine."

Ignoring the way my stomach flutters, I slip into the booth and mentally remind myself this isn't a date.

Even though it feels a little like one.

"Is that little Blair O'Connor? I was wondering when I'd run into you."

That voice. It's familiar and annoying, like nails on a chalkboard.

I turn just as Shay Long—or I guess, Shay Johnson—struts over to our table. That's the only way to describe her walk. She has a wide grin plastered across her heavily pink-stained lips. Her hair and makeup are flawless, of course, like she's prepared for a photo op at the drop of a hat. Then there's her outfit. Tight little jean shorts that barely cover her ass cheeks and an equally tight fitted T-shirt with the logo for the hardware store plastered across her ample chest.

Those are clearly new since I last saw her.

"Hello, Shay," I reply, giving her a pleasant smile, even though I don't really feel that friendly.

"Oh, hello, Doc," she states, sugary-sweet, as she runs her red nails across the logo on her shirt. I want to roll my eyes at her brazen act of drawing attention to her double D's, and then climb out of the booth and rip the blond extensions right off her head.

"Shay," Gabe replies, offering a polite nod as he reaches for the menu in the holder behind the napkins and ketchup bottle.

"I wasn't expecting to see you so soon," she practically coos with a giggle.

"No?" he asks absently, his eyes searching the menu as if he's studying it, despite already knowing what he's having.

"Not yet, anyway. My appointment is at three. It's time for my annual exam."

My stomach clenches as she flashes a bright white smile, but it's not the actual grin that causes my distaste. It's the exam. As a woman, I'm all too familiar with exactly what an annual exam entails, and the thought of Gabe *there* brings out a side of jealousy I wasn't prepared for.

"Well, I'll see you then," he says, throwing her another small grin, and I quickly notice it's doesn't quite reach his eyes.

Shay straightens her spine, thrusting her too-big boobs straight out. "Oh, I look forward to it."

The girl who was fairly mean in high school doesn't say anything to me as she saunters away, doing all she can to draw every set of male eyes to her as she exits the café.

"Ugh, what did that viper want?" Ellie asks, setting two glasses of ice water down on the table.

"Just to overshare about her upcoming appointment with Dr. Gabe," I grumble, taking a long sip of the cold water in hopes it cools the heat flowing through my veins.

Gabe glances at me over the menu, humor laced in the wrinkles around his baby blues.

"Eww, I hope you wear gloves and a mask," Ellie mutters, making us both laugh.

"I definitely wear gloves, Ellie. Always. Now, how about we stop talking about what I get to do later this afternoon and ask Saul to whip me up some meatloaf and mashed potatoes," Gabe says.

"I'll have the same," I add, winking at Ellie as she jots our orders down on her notepad.

"Anything else to drink?" she asks.

When we both opt to stick with the water, she turns to place our orders with the kitchen.

"I forgot how great this place was," I say, almost absently, taking in the old, yet familiar diner. Everything is the same, except maybe some fresh paint on the walls and recovered vinyl seats. The tables are still the ones they put in when the diner opened in the seventies, and the décor is straight out of the fifties. There's something nostalgic and comforting sitting here, just as I did back when I was a kid and would come up for fries after school or root beer floats on a hot summer day.

Gabe glances around, as if taking it in through my eyes. "When I moved back home, it was the first place I came. Nobody cooks the way Saul does."

"I can't believe he's still alive," I mumble, hoping no one around me hears. Saul was old back when I was in high school, but the man was committed to the diner. He is Frannie's older brother, and everyone used to say he'd probably die here, just like his sister.

"Alive and still fixing the best food, though he only works three days a week now, breakfast and lunch, so make sure you come on Monday, Wednesday, or Friday. The others are good, but nothing beats Saul's home cooking."

"I'll remember that," I reply, taking another sip of my water. While I do, I study the man sitting across from me. It's only a brief observation, but I watch the way his Adam's apple bobs as he takes a drink and the way his jaw is already covered with prickly stubble.

I remember exactly how that very stubble felt against my neck, my chest, my thighs.

"You okay?" he asks.

"What?" I ask, clearing my throat and looking anywhere but at him.

"You're a little flushed."

"Oh, uh, yeah," I stutter finding the right response without sounding like an idiot. "I was just going over my afternoon schedule," I add.

His eyebrows draw up, and the look on his face lets me know he doesn't believe me. Thankfully, he doesn't call me out on the lie. Instead, he leans back in his seat and stretches his arm across the back of the booth. He looks so casual, so relaxed, and to be honest, so very unlike the man I first met in December.

Then, he was cranky, his demeaner slightly off-putting, at least in the beginning.

Now, I understand a little more about that night he set out to rescue me from the side of the road. He was just getting off work after a long day of seeing patients at both the clinic and the hospital and ready to relax for the night.

"What are you thinking about?"

I glance up, meeting his gaze, and decide to be honest. "I was just recalling how grumpy you were that night you rescued me from the road," I reply with a smile.

Gabe chuckles a deep, throaty sound that vibrates my lady parts. "Sorry I was so hostile," he says with his own grin.

I shrug. "Understandable. If anyone gets it, I do." I've figuratively taken patient cases home with me at the end of the night, unable to leave the job behind at the office. "Besides, it wasn't all bad," I confess, and know he'll understand the meaning of my statement.

Gabe blushes, that coy grin playing on his lips. "No, not at all."

Before either of us can say anything else, our food arrives, and we dive in. Even though we don't further discuss our night together, we're both thinking about it. I see it in the glint of his blue eyes and the way his teeth graze across his bottom lip, as if he's nibbling on...well, me.

My entire body heats with desire.

Working beside Gabe Rhodes—and keeping my hands to myself—may very well kill me.

CHAPTER eight

GABE

Flashes of Blair naked filter through my mind. When I should be enjoying a friendly lunch, I'm fighting to conceal an erection. Thank God I'm sitting down.

"Oh my God, I forgot how amazing his meatloaf is," she mutters, practically moaning in pleasure as she chews.

I clear my throat and take a bite of my own food, hoping it'll help pull me back down to earth. Unfortunately for me, the noises she makes while enjoying her meal do nothing of the sort and only solidify my desire for her.

Sharing a meal with her was clearly a bad idea.

"So, have you spent any more time with Aggie since pizza night?" I ask, scooping up mashed potatoes and gravy with my meatloaf, desperate to find a topic that doesn't make me think about Blair naked.

"Not yet, but I promised her we'd go to the park this weekend. She wants to show me how far she can go on the monkey bars," Blair replies with a chuckle. "So we'll probably do a park playdate and dinner."

After I swallow, I add, "I'm sure she'll love that. She's enjoying getting to know you." I can tell by the way Aggie speaks of Blair the few times she's been mentioned in conversation when I'm around.

Blair doesn't respond right away, her eyes drawn down for a moment. "I'm really enjoying getting to know her too. It's still a little hard to believe I have a sister." A plethora of emotions dance in her eyes as she looks up at me. Happiness, confusion, sadness, and even guilt.

"I imagine it is," I confirm. "I grew up having to deal with a bratty kid sister and her friends." I fight the smile threatening to take over my face, and somehow keep it at bay.

She gasps. "What? I was not a bratty friend," she insists, feigning insult.

"Lies," I argue in between bites. "I know it was you and Hallie who emptied my entire can of shaving cream in the bathroom sink, even though you both adamantly denied it."

Blair laughs the sweetest sound. "I don't know what you're talking about. *If* Hallie and I did that, it was probably only because you were so protective of that can of shaving cream, and we were trying to figure out what the big deal was."

Now it's my turn to chuckle. "It *was* a big deal. I was fifteen and my mom finally agreed to let me shave."

"And we were eleven and told not to touch something. Can you blame us? I mean, hypothetically, of course. *If* we were the ones who did it."

My belly laugh turns a few heads, but I don't care. Laughing and joking with Blair is as natural and easy as the sun rising in the morning. "Of course, hypothetically. I'll just make sure to hide my shaving cream next time you're over."

My statement seems to register with her at the exact moment I realize what I just said. Her gaze meets mine across the table, and before I can open my mouth to try to retract my statement, she grins. "You do that."

We eat the rest of our lunch in relative silence, both lost in our own thoughts. My thoughts are most likely a little dirtier than hers. I'm picturing exactly what I'd do to her if she were naked and wet in my shower, and I had a can of shaving cream. The vivid images of watching foamy suds slide down her delicate body is enough to give me a permanent erection.

By the time we're done eating, I'm, yet again, in no condition to stand up without drawing attention to my groin, so when my old math teacher walks past our table and strikes up a brief conversation, I gratefully dive right in. As we talk about the potential for an extra warm summer, I finally feel the heat ebb from my body. Apparently, talking to an eighty-two-year-old man was exactly what I needed to keep from embarrassing myself.

Mr. Horner flashes a smile to Blair. "It's lovely to see you in town, Dr. O'Connor."

"Thank you, Mr. Horner. It's good to see you out and about on a beautiful summer day," she replies politely.

"I never miss meatloaf day at Frannie's," he states. "My Junie always loved Saul's meatloaf. We'd always take our leftovers home and make sandwiches the next day."

She quickly looks my way, the question written in her pretty eyes. I subtly nod in confirmation before she returns her gaze to the old man. "I'm so sorry to hear of her passing. I used to enjoy visiting with June at the library after school."

Mr. Horner smiles fondly. "She loved anything to do with books and always adored her time there. She often came home and shared stories about the kids who she saw that day, you included. She knew you'd go on to do great things in life."

There's no missing the way Blair's eyes fill with unshed tears. "She was a special lady."

"As are you, Blair. I'm so glad you've returned to Pine Village, and I hope you find everything you're looking for in life while here." Mr. Horner nods to us both before shuffling away.

"He's an incredible man," I state after he has left.

"I didn't have him as a teacher, but I heard all the stories."

"The most caring teacher I've ever encountered. It's a shame you didn't have him. He was the type of educator everyone wanted and needed. Tough, compassionate, and understanding to everyone who entered his classroom."

"His wife was the same type of person. I loved speaking to her in the library," she confirms once again. "How long ago did she pass?"

I clear my throat. "About two years ago now. She had a heart attack. June went to sleep and never woke up. When Mr. Horner found her, he said she looked like an angel lying there, her hand tucked safely in his own."

"That's the sweetest. They always seemed to have a special relationship. I remember seeing them out and about on the weekend. Wherever they went, they were always holding hands."

"Always. They went everywhere together," I confirm, shifting in my seat as the longing settles in my chest. I've always wanted a relationship like the one the Horners had. They were exactly the type of couple you envied, the goal you set in any relationship you had. I thought I found it once, but quickly discovered my marriage to Amara was anything but.

"Can I get you anything else?" Ellie asks as she approaches our table.

"No, thanks. Just the check," I reply, reaching into my back pants pocket for my wallet.

"I've got it," Blair quickly responds, retrieving her own wallet from her purse.

"No way," I argue, but before I can say anything else, she counters.

"Nope, my treat. You brought coffee to work. I can grab lunch." She quickly tosses two twenties at Ellie, even though our total bill won't be half that.

"Let me get you some change," Ellie says, turning to head for the register.

"Keep it, El," she adds, waving off the statement and sliding out of the booth. "And tell Saul it was as amazing as I remember."

Ellie tosses her friend a wide grin. "I'll be sure to tell him. Stop by Friday if you can get away from the clinic. He's whipping up stuffed shells with garlic bread made from Texas toast that's to die for."

Blair looks equally as excited. "I'll be here."

I slide out of the booth feeling a little off-kilter. I know we weren't on a date, but something inside me wanted to get her lunch. "I'll buy next time," I insist, shoving my hands in my pockets.

She shrugs and heads for the door, waving at a few familiar faces along the way. I do the same, recognizing everyone in the place, but keep pace with Blair. As soon as we hit the sidewalk, I move in beside her, letting the warmth of her nearness seep into my skin.

"You know, on Sunday, I was thinking about going for a ride," I state, hoping it sounds as casual as I intended.

She glances over, the corner of her mouth ticking upward as she gazes as me curiously. "What kind of ride?"

"The kind on four wheels," I reply. "I was thinking of taking the quad to the trails for the afternoon."

She doesn't say anything for a few long seconds, and I can't help the bubble of disappointment that pops up. She's trying to think of a way to turn me down, which honestly, I expect. Blair is friends with my sister, and even though we work together temporarily, we're not exactly close, not like they are.

Except...I want to be.

"I don't have any riding gear." Her response catches me off guard, because it sounds like she's considering it.

"You really only need a helmet and boots, as long as you have jeans. You can wear a T-shirt, but I wouldn't recommend shorts. Some of the trails still have thorn bushes that pop up every now and again."

We walk back to the clinic and reach the back door before either of us speaks again. I use my key to let us in, the disappointment now as thick as molasses. I don't know why I thought she'd want to go. Blair has been in the city for more than a decade, and if memory serves me, her wardrobe doesn't exactly scream country living. I'm sure spending her afternoon running dusty, sometimes muddy trails isn't her cup of tea.

I step into my office and toss a quick, "Thanks again for lunch," over my shoulder.

Blair is already on her phone, frantically typing away. She hollers, "You're welcome," as I grab my lab coat off the hook behind my door and slip it on.

I settle at my desk, determined to push Blair's non-committed answer and brush-off away, and pull up my afternoon schedule. Sure enough, there's Shay's name with annual exam practically in bold letters. It's not darker, but for some reason, it stands out more than anything else on the log. Usually, I have no problem with female examinations, but for some reason, hers has me a little flustered. Perhaps it was because I felt like she was using it to flash something in front of Blair's face. Like it was part of some game or competition, which I wouldn't put past Shay.

According to Logan, she's a real piece of work.

Everyone else returns from lunch, and the office becomes alive again with activity. Just as I'm summoned to my first patient of the afternoon, Blair steps into my doorway. There's a hint of nerves on her face as she fidgets with one of the buttons on her lab coat. "So, Hallie says I can borrow her helmet and boots, so let me know what time Sunday."

I'm able to school the surprise on my face before she sees it. "How about one? You can come out to my house, and we can take the quad from there."

She nods.

"You remember how to get there, or do you need to put your car in the ditch first?" I tease, getting just the response I was hoping for.

Blair rolls her eyes dramatically and sighs. "I knew you'd bring that up eventually."

"Blair, your first patient is in room three," Kelly states, drawing our attention.

"Thank you, Kelly. I'll be there in a second." When her nurse walks away, she turns her emerald gaze back to me. "I can be there at one, and yes, I remember how to get there."

I'm unable to stop the smile already spreading across my lips. "Good." When she turns to head down the hall, I quickly add, "Oh, and Blair?" She stops, glancing over her shoulder. "Be ready to get dirty."

The first half of the afternoon flies by. Blair is busier than I am, but that's no surprise. I've learned parents will bring their child to the doctor for about anything, and while we don't see too many sick kids during the summer, we see plenty of bee stings and bug bites, poison ivy, and injuries from playing outside, as well as sports and school physicals.

Adults, however, don't go to the doctor unless absolutely necessary. Something usually has to be broken or hemorrhaging before they decide to seek medical attention. Case in point, a forty-year-old man who stepped on a nail three weeks ago. It got infected, and his answer to fixing it was to slap a bandage on it. Of course, since it was on the bottom of his foot and he wore work boots—in the summer—the bandage wouldn't stay put, so he used the best thing he could come up with to keep it in place.

Duct tape.

Today, his foot started hurting so bad, he couldn't get his boot on. He's lucky he didn't have a bigger problem, because that infection was spreading fast. Not only did it reek horribly and ooze pus, but it was very swollen and hot to the touch. There were even red streaks running away from the puncture wound, which is a huge sign of a problem. Fortunately for him, he received a tetanus shot a year ago from another injury on the job, so we only had to treat the main infection with strong antibiotics. He's off work for a few days until we get it under control, which includes keeping his wound clean and dry.

Work boots aren't exactly conducive for proper healing.

My next patient was a twenty-four-year-old man who fell asleep in the sun yesterday while at a swimming party with friends. Let's just say he's a guy with a fair complexion, who didn't use sunscreen. After an hour, someone finally woke him up, but the damage was done. He's going to be painfully sore and blistered for up to two weeks, but with the topical ointment I prescribed and some extra fluids and acetaminophen, he'll be on the mend quicker. There's nothing worse than sunburns. I can't imagine having one on half my face, the back of my arms and legs, and my entire back.

I'm just stepping out of the exam room when I hear a very feminine voice call loudly down the hallway. "I told you I'd be seeing you again shortly." She flashes me a wide, bright-white smile, one that makes most men's tail wag like a dog about to receive some extra attention. I, however, am close enough with her ex-husband to know what lurks behind that pretty smile, perfect makeup and hair, and tight clothes.

I turn and face Shay, schooling my features to hide the resignation I feel in the pit of my gut. "Afternoon, Shay. Makenzie will get you settled in the exam room, and I'll be with you in just a bit."

She winks—actually winks—as she flashes a coy grin and practically sashays into the room. "I can't wait."

Makenzie stops in the doorway and pins me with a look. All I can do is roll my eyes before slipping my previous patient's chart into the bin beside the door and escaping to my office. I lean against the wall and take a few deep breaths. Usually, I don't mind this part of the job, but when the woman on which I'll be performing a vaginal exam is a viper in designer names I can barely pronounce, who flirts shamelessly from the moment I step into the room until I step out, it makes for a long twenty minutes.

"You look like someone just kicked your puppy."

I open my eyes and meet Blair's. "Sorry, I was just taking a minute before my next appointment."

She glances down at her watch as realization hits. "Ahhh. I see what time it is."

"I couldn't interest you in switching, could I?" I'm teasing.

Sort of.

"Not in a million gazillion years, Gabriel. You're going to have to man up on this one."

Closing my eyes, I take a deep breath. "Figures."

"You know, most men would be thrilled at the opportunity to do what you're about to do."

Standing up, I straighten my tie, even though it's perfectly in place, and face her head-on. "Yeah, well, I'm not most men."

Blair studies me for a few moments before the faintest grin crests her lips. "I'm learning that, Dr. Rhodes. Now, get going. There's a woman with a freshly landscaped pubic area with her legs in stirrups waiting for you." When my eyes widen, probably very comically, she adds, "I overheard her oversharing before the door closed."

I groan aloud and shake my head.

She steps up beside me and playfully grabs my bicep. The touch is electrifying, but I'm able to remain perfectly still and just soak up the contact.

"Go get 'em, tiger."

CHAPTER
nine

Blair

My stomach is in knots the entire time he's in the exam room with Shay. Why? The only thing I can come up with is pure jealousy. I don't like that woman—never have, never will—and the thought of her in there with Gabe, her legs spread in the stirrups, her freshly manicured toes and groomed landing strip on full display makes my vision a little red.

I don't like it. I don't want his hands anywhere near her vajayjay, can't even stomach the thought of him giving her a breast exam. I know exactly what those big, slightly rough hands feel like caressing sensitive skin, and while I wouldn't exactly compare the way he touched me last December with a breast exam, I can confirm the man is magic with his hands. I don't like the thought of those very hands being anywhere near my old archnemesis from high school.

Fortunately, I'm able to push thoughts of what's happening in exam room number four out of my head with paperwork. Also, I have a newborn coming in for his four-week well-baby exam. I love that part of the job. Stealing baby snuggles is what gets me through my day sometimes. Plus, it helps calm the baby- fever that can erupt at any moment. A few cuddles with a newborn, and I'm good to go for a while.

My job doesn't exactly leave me a lot of time for motherhood. Not to mention, there's the missing sperm factor. I almost considered it about two years ago when I was dating Alex Turnstall. He was smart, driven, and had the good genes you'd hope to pass on to an heir. However, our relationship lacked that spark, that heartbeat-skipping attraction you can't fight or deny. A kiss that leaves you weak in the knees and wet between the legs.

And why does my mind instantly jump to Gabe when I think about remarkable kisses?

Clearing my throat, I return my focus on work, finishing the charting I started before I heard Shay walk in the clinic. The task takes me longer than normal because my brain has a hard time staying focused, thanks to the images of Gabe's demanding and very talented mouth. My body hums, a faint burn licks my skin, as if I can still feel it brush against me. It's been like this for months, with no end in sight. No matter how hard I try, I just can't stop remembering everything about our one night together.

Sunday won't help.

I know I'm stupid for even agreeing to go for a ride with him. Growing up in Pine Village, I'm well versed on riding a quad, despite having actually ridden one in a while. I know going for this ride will include sitting behind him on a single seat, my front pressed against his back. My hands will be wrapped around his waist, and my thighs hugging the outside of his own legs. We'll be close. *Very* close.

And I'm ridiculously excited about it.

I'm also waiting for the barrage of questions from my best friend. Hallie didn't hesitate to agree to let me use her helmet and riding boots, but she also didn't ask more questions about why. It's probably because she's clearing out her classroom for the big deep-clean they do every summer, elbows deep in old fingerpaint and broken crayons, and she knows I'm living on the opposite side of her living room wall, so it's not like I can hide from her.

My attention is pulled away from the same chart I've been working on for far too long by an opening door and a loud, annoying female giggle. My eyes roll so hard, I swear I just saw my brain, and despite the fact I really want to get up and peek down the hallway at their exit, I force myself to stay put and chart.

"Thank you *so* much, Gabe—I mean, Dr. Rhodes." More giggles. I can practically see her reaching out and squeezing his bicep through his white coat.

I hate her.

With the heat of a thousand suns.

And the passion of a tarantula hidden somewhere in your bedroom.

A shiver sweeps up my spine at the thought. I hate spiders.

"You okay?"

Startled, I look up and find Gabe leaning against the doorway. With a quick clearing of my throat, I reply, "Yes, of course."

His eyebrows pull together. "You sure? You look like you saw a mouse run across the floor."

"Thought about a spider," I confess, my arms breaking out with goosebumps.

His deep, husky chuckle doesn't help. It moves through my veins like sweet honey, thick and rich and does naughty things to the apex of my legs. It's like a caress without him physically touching me, which is something I've never experienced before.

At least not on this level.

"You survived, I see," I state as he enters my office and drops down on the seat across from the desk. He kicks his ankle up on his knee and leans back, getting completely cozy.

"I did. I won't bore you with the details, but I'm very glad those types of exams are only annually," he mutters, avoiding my gaze. My stomach drops, and the sadistic side of me almost asks for the details he's not willing to share.

Why?

Because I have to know how far she took it. I've known Shay a lot of years, and she's one to go after what she wants. When we were in high school, that person was always in a relationship. She didn't care then, and I can't imagine she cares much now. If that person now is Gabe, there's no doubt she pulled out all the stops during today's visit.

But I also feel like I'm starting to get to know Gabe a little better too, and he doesn't seem like the type of man who easily falls under her spell. In fact, I've gotten the feeling he's more put off by her attention seeking and oversharing than attracted to it.

"Busy afternoon?" he asks, changing the subject.

"Not bad. I have a well-baby exam in about fifteen minutes and end my day with school physicals for a set of twins."

"The Hemover twins," he assumes with another chuckle. "Watch your back. Those two are the most mischievous boys I've ever met. They once put a frog in your dad's lab coat pocket without him realizing it."

I groan at the thought. "Thanks for the heads-up. I'll keep a close eye on my pockets."

Gabe stands up and stretches, the material of his shirt stretching tautly across his muscular chest. "I'd watch my hair too. They somehow slid something sticky and green into Kelly's hair. I'm not saying it was boogers, but..."

My jaw drops at the thought of discovering a green, sticky substance in my hair. "I don't even want to know what it was."

He laughs hard, one of those full belly sounds that makes my thighs clench. "I'm still under the assumption it was some sort of slime, even though Kelly was certain it came from their noses."

Just then, Kelly pops her head through the doorway. "Blair, your appointment is here and waiting in room two." Just then, a loud baby scream pierces the air. "And little Andre is not happy today."

I pop a mint into my mouth and smile. "That's okay. He's not my first screaming infant."

Gabe meets me at the door. "Mind if I join you?"

I eye him curiously. Before I can ask any questions, he quickly adds, "I delivered him and did his two-week checkup. I'd love to just say hello and see how much he's grown." A slight blush creeps up his neck, which I find incredibly sweet and endearing.

"I don't mind," I reply, leading the way down the hallway. Just before I knock on the door, I glance back and whisper, "But if his diaper explodes, you're the one cleaning it up."

His laughter follows me into the room, and the moment we step inside and shut the door, Gabe has baby Andre in his arms. The sight is...wow. To see such a masculine guy snuggling with a baby would surely cause ovaries around the globe to spontaneously explode. The newborn looks tiny, his face still puckered in anger, but the moment he's tucked against Gabe's chest, he starts to calm. The man holding him gently bounces, shushing the little guy until he settles and dozes off, all comfy and cozy in his arms.

Lucky baby.

It's hard to concentrate as I talk to Andre's mom, Betsi, and I'm pretty sure I've got one eye on Gabe the entire time. If he notices, he doesn't say anything, thankfully. Instead, he continues to shower the infant with hugs like he's a long-lost family member.

After a few more minutes, it's time for Andre's exam. It's pretty basic, but still needs to be completed. Gabe walks over to the table and mumbles, "You be nice to Dr. Blair, all right, big guy?"

Andre responds by burping.

I do what I have to do quickly, taking the measurements I need to and checking him from head to toe. He's just starting to get fussy when I finish, so I quickly scoop him up and snuggle him against my chest. I can hear Gabe and Betsi chatting behind me, so I take the opportunity to get in my baby cuddles for the day. I subtly sniff his bald head, breathing in the familiar scent of baby wash and lotion. His tiny head is tucked beneath my chin, and I can't help the longing feeling that settles in my chest as he curls into my boobs.

"Do you have kids, Dr. O'Connor?" Betsi asks, the hint of a grin on her lips.

"Oh, me? N-no," I stammer.

"Too bad. You're great with him," she replies, reaching out and swiping a finger across his wrinkly baby cheek, the look of pure maternal love written all over her face.

"I do love babies, which is one of the reasons why I went into pediatrics," I confess, completely aware of Gabe's stare.

When Andre starts to fuss, I hand the baby back to his mother. "I'm so happy you're here. Not that Dr. O and Dr. R aren't great with kids, but it's so nice to have a pediatrician here in our small town. Too bad you're not staying," she says sheepishly, trying to hide her sad smile behind her baby's head. It doesn't work though. I still see it.

And I feel it too.

The pang of sadness hits me square in the chest. Never in a million years did I picture myself coming back to Pine Village, but now that I am here, I remember exactly why I always loved this small town. The people, the slow pace, the friendliness and generosity around every corner.

And the doctor standing beside me isn't so bad either.

"Unfortunately, Andre is in for a few immunizations today," I report, returning the subject back to solid ground.

"I remember Dr. Rhodes telling me that two weeks ago," Betsi confirms with a deep sigh.

"I'll send Kelly in to administer those. Do you have any questions?"

She shakes her head and kisses her newborn's forehead, as if somehow trying to soothe the hurt she knows is to come.

"We'll see you in four weeks," I state before stepping into the hallway and slipping the chart back in the holder on the wall.

"Thanks for letting me join you."

I glance over my shoulder and find Gabe hovering close. Very close. I can smell a mixture of his cologne and the scent of the diner. "You're welcome." My words come out almost hushed, my lips dry and stuck together.

He walks away, and I follow his movements with my eyes. Specifically, I watch his ass. No, I can't see it because of his coat, but I don't need to see it now to know exactly what it looks like in his slacks. I remember.

Vividly.

With a smile on my face, I head to find Kelly so she can finish up with little Andre.

Then, I'll douse myself in ice water, hoping it'll cool the blaze burning through me.

"Push me higher, Blair!" Aggie hollers, her little legs pumping hard as I push her on the swing.

"You go much higher, and you'll be in the clouds," I tease, giving my sister another heave.

It's a gorgeous Saturday afternoon, and the park is busy. There are dozens of kids running around, digging in the sand, tearing down the slide, swinging across monkey bars, and utilizing every swing around us. I've even recognized a handful of moms as either former classmates or lifelong residents of Pine Village.

"Is it time for pizza yet?" she asks, continuing to pump her little legs as if trying to actually reach the sky.

"Are you hungry now?" I glance at my watch and see it's almost five.

"Yep!" she declares, reaching her foot down to drag on the ground to help slow her flight.

Quickly reaching for the chains, I tell her, "Wait, let me help you before you fall off."

The swing is still moving when she jumps down and falls in the sand, laughing the entire time. "I gots sand in my shoes," Aggie declares, peeling her white sandals off her feet and brushing off the sand.

"Yes, but you're still sitting in the sand, so you're going to have more sand in your sandals when you get up, silly." I walk over and pick up her shoes before helping her stand. "Let's go over to that bench and clean off your feet."

"And then we can gets pizza?"

"If that's what you want," I confirm.

"It is. It's my most favorite, but Mommy doesn't eats pizza 'cause it goes straight to her hips."

I can't help but chuckle as I help my sister sit down on the bench. I wonder how many times she's heard that line in her short five years. Patience has always been concerned about her figure, eating salads and lean, healthy foods. "Well, I say we eat all the pizza then," I state, brushing the sand off her toes and slipping back on the sandal.

"You not care about your hips?"

My grin is wide as I meet her questioning gaze. "I care about eating pizza more."

A huge smile takes over her tiny face, her small glasses slipping down her nose a bit. "Can we gets extra cheese?"

Leaning in, I tap the tip of her nose. "Is there any other way to get it?"

"Let's go!" she hollers directly in my face, her wide eyes eager for me to finish dusting off her feet so we can get moving.

I take her hand and lead her toward Main Street. The pizza parlor is only a block away, and since it's such a nice day, I thought we could walk over. Plus, it's easier to leave my car in the lot where it is than trying to park it closer.

Aggie talks the entire way, waving at a few passing pedestrians I don't recognize. But they call her by name and instantly turn toward each other, as if immediately discussing whatever gossip they've heard about me and my return to town. If there's anything I remember about Pine Village, it's that gossip is their favorite pastime.

I don't have time to dwell on it though because Aggie hollers an energetic, "Gabe!" She pulls against my hand until she stops directly in front of him.

"Agnes O'Connor, how are you this afternoon?" Gabe asks, dropping to a knee in front of my sister.

"Good! We're going for pizza!" she declares, practically vibrating where she stands.

"Again?" he asks with a laugh.

Aggie nods insistently. "You come!"

He glances up and finally meets my wide gaze. "Oh, I'm not sure about that. It's your special dinner with Blair," he tells her.

"You not like pizza, Gabe?"

He can't help but smile. "I do like pizza, Aggie, but you're having a sisters' day. I don't want to interrupt that," he informs, standing up beside her.

My sister snakes her hand through his and turns green eyes on me. "Please, Blair! Can Gabe come eat pizza with us?"

I'll admit, she's cute as hell, with her pink plastic glasses perched on her nose and the pleading look in her eyes. What's a good big sister to do but agree with her imploration, even if I know I probably shouldn't? Especially since I'll be spending a big chunk of tomorrow with him as well. A break from my sexy coworker is probably in my best interest.

"Sure, Gabe can come too."

That's me taking a break.

CHAPTER Ten

GABE

I wasn't expecting this.

As I pull the pizza parlor's door open and step back, allowing Blair and Aggie to enter first, I thank my lucky stars I was walking out of the laundromat at that exact moment. I was rushing to get there and drop off four pairs of trousers to be dry-cleaned before they closed for the weekend. I barely made it, the door locking behind me as my feet hit the sidewalk.

That's when good luck continued to rain down on me.

"Have a seat anywhere," someone hollers from behind the front counter.

Blair lets Aggie take the lead and pick our spot, and thankfully she chooses a booth in the back. The girls take one side, while I slip in across from them. The lighting is low, the red globes hanging in the center of each seating group. The tables are draped in the familiar plastic red and white checkered tablecloth that is as much a staple here as the deep-dish pizza they serve.

"Can I play games too?" Aggie asks her sister, her eyes bouncing between Blair and the small room behind me where classic arcade games are housed.

"For a few minutes, okay?" Blair replies, pulling a few quarters out of her bag before letting her sister out of the booth.

I turn and watch as she runs straight to the pinball machine and moves a nearby stepstool so she can see the game. She eagerly slips a single quarter into the slot and activates the lights and sirens. "I was more of a *Frogger* man, myself," I state, noting how into the game the five-year-old gets, even if her reflexes to hit the ball before it drops aren't all that great.

"*Frogger*? No way. *Ms. Pac-Man* was the best. I had the high score for like three years running," she boasts proudly. "Hell, it's probably still the high score in there."

Before I can say any more, our server arrives. "Hey, Dr. Rhodes."

"Lanita," I reply, nodding politely to the high schooler who works here on weekends.

"What can I get you guys to drink?"

Blair and I each order a water, while she asks for apple juice for Aggie. Once our drinks are delivered, we decide on a large pan pizza with extra cheese on half, sausage, mushroom, and green peppers on the other. It feels so normal, natural to sit with her, ordering food, and it really doesn't surprise me that we like some of the same pizza toppings, even if her first choice is ham and pineapple. I've discovered a lot about Blair over the last almost-two weeks since she's been back in town.

Everything I discover, I like.

A lot.

"You ready?" I ask, scooting to the edge of my booth seat.

"For?" Her interest is piqued.

"To see whose *Ms. Pac-Man* score is higher."

I'm anxious as the clock approaches one. Last night, I left the pizza place with a smile on my face and a giddy feeling in my chest. Spending a random Saturday evening with Blair and Aggie was more relaxing than any day I've had in a while, including last Sunday when I had dinner with friends at her condo.

I've discovered Blair is a closet arcade game junkie, and even though she claims to not have played in years, she beat me easily. She's super competitive and trash-talked like a champ, yet backed off to let her sister win too.

When the pizza parlor got busy and needed our table, we finally left. Blair went left to take Aggie back to her car, and I went right to where I left my truck parked up the street. We went separate ways and then I was back home.

Alone.

I didn't care for it.

Now, I pace my kitchen floor on Sunday, my eyes scanning the road in front of my house searching for her car. I don't even realize my breathing is slightly labored until I see her vehicle turn into my driveway. Then, it's like a weight is lifted off my chest and I can breathe deeply again.

She's here.

I grab the insulated bag I packed and head for the back door. Blair is just getting out of her car as I hit the sidewalk and head for my quad. It's already out of the garage, gassed up, and ready to go, but that's not where my attention is. It's on her.

She's so fucking beautiful.

Blair is wearing well-worn jeans with holes in the knees and a fitted maroon T-shirt with the University of Illinois College of Medicine logo on the front. Her long brown hair is tied at the nape of her neck, exposing that smooth, soft skin on her neck that makes my dick twitch, and the borrowed boots are on her feet. She looks completely casual, so different than what I see on the day-to-day basis, and as much as I like her business doctor look, I think I prefer this.

Or her in nothing at all.

That's a particular favorite of mine too.

"I still can't quite believe I agreed to this," she mutters, shaking her head slightly.

"You don't want to go?" I ask, pausing from strapping the insulated bag on the rear fender rack.

"No, I do," she instantly insists, fumbling with the charm on her necklace. "I just haven't done this in a very long time," she adds with an awkward chuckle.

I finish using the bungie cord to secure the bag and turn to face her. "You don't have anything to worry about, Blair. You're safe with me."

"I know," she replies, still fidgeting. "It's just, the last time I was on one of these things was in high school, and the boy I was dating, Hagen, was showing off and popped a wheelie while I was on the back. I wasn't expecting it, so I fell off and landed on my ass in the dirt."

"Shit. What an asshole."

She barks out a laugh. "That he was. Probably why I broke up with him a few weeks later."

"Good."

Blair turns to grab the helmet out of her back seat, but there's no missing the smile on her lips before her face is hidden. When she shuts the door and meets me at the quad, she says, "I didn't break up with him because he dumped me off the back of the four-wheeler."

"No?"

She shakes her head. "It was catching him with his tongue down Shay's throat that was the final nail in the relationship coffin."

Now it's my turn to shake my head. No wonder she's not a fan of Shay Long. "How about we just enjoy the sunshine and the ride, and I promise, if I'm going to pop a wheelie, I'll give you ample warning to hang on."

Her giggle is low and throaty. "How about you just not pop a wheelie?"

"There's no fun in that," I respond with a wink. "Ready?"

She nods, grabbing her helmet and slipping it over her head. "Ready."

My body was already wound tight before, but the moment she slips behind me and presses herself against my back, I'm a live wire, ready to explode. I ignore the discomfort in my jeans and grab my own helmet, slipping it on and firing up my machine. Petite arms wrap around my waist and squeeze, sending all sorts of dirty thoughts to the forefront of my mind.

Stupid hormones.

I slip it into first gear and slowly move around the garage, heading to the wooded area behind my house. I own a few acres that butt against the Bluff Preserves National Park, a 140,000 acre preserve with designated snowmobile trails in the winter and four-wheeler trails in the summer. This park is what keeps our small town booming in the winter months, thanks to the hundreds of weekenders who visit the national park. It's not the biggest or most popular place to ride in Wisconsin, but it's still busy.

I slip onto the first marked trail and maintain the speed limit. Our trail system is monitored regularly by conservation police, and the last thing I want is a ticket for speeding. We run the trails for an hour, climbing steep hills and crossing a few narrow streams that move water into Bluff Lake. It sits in the heart of the park, surrounded by cabins and cottages you can rent. There are also several hotels and larger cabins along the outskirts of the park that reach capacity in early winter and stay that way until the last of the snow melts.

After a decent ride, I need a break, so I pull off the trail and stop my machine in a small clearing near the lake. Even though we've been surrounded by beauty, I haven't been able to just sit back and enjoy the view like I usually do. Not with Blair pressed against me.

She places her hands on my shoulders and climbs off, removing her helmet once she's standing beside me. "I forgot how beautiful it is back here."

I slip my helmet off as well and nod. "I don't get to ride as much as I'd like, but when I do, it always seems to be just what I needed."

She eyes me openly. "I see what you mean."

Remembering my bag of snacks, I unfasten it from the rack and hand over a bottle of water. "I also have grapes, cheese slices, and some cashews. Oh, and chocolate candies I froze before I left. They should still be hard but give them another hour and they'll be perfect."

Blair reaches for the grapes first and pops a few in her mouth. "You've done this before."

I grab two cheese cubes and pop them in my mouth. "Done what?" I ask as soon as I swallow.

"Wined and dined unsuspecting women with pretty scenery and yummy snacks," she states with a grin.

I bark out a laugh, mostly because she's pretty far off course from the actual truth. "Well, the last time I had a woman on the back of my four-wheeler, she ended up filing for divorce a week later."

Blair looks shocked, angry, and mortified, all at the same time. "Wow, I'm sorry. I wasn't thinking."

I shrug and grab a few grapes. "Don't worry about it. To answer your question, no, this isn't something I tend to do a lot. Usually when I go for a ride, I just want an hour or two of quiet. My life can get pretty hectic, as I'm sure you're well aware, and any time I can steal a bit of time to myself, I take it. My go-to is to work on my house, but after a while, those walls tend to close in around me, so I come out here."

She's quiet for a few long seconds, chomping on a few cashews, but I feel her eyes on me the entire time. Finally, I look her way, instantly pulled into the intensity of her gaze. "She sounds like an idiot."

I snort in agreement. "She insisted that I was one."

Blair lifts a single shoulder and props her hip on the machine beside me. "I imagine it's difficult being married to a physician. Our hours aren't regular nine-to-five, and we can get called away at any point, usually when it's least convenient."

"Very true." I'm transfixed on watching her lush lips as she licks grape juice off the bottom one.

"Do you want to talk about this?" she finally asks.

"Not really," I insist, ready to stop talking about my ex-wife. Not that I'm ashamed or embarrassed to talk about my shortcomings in the husband department, but why sully such a gorgeous day—and my time with a gorgeous woman—with something from my past.

Blair shifts her weight, which just puts her closer to me. I can feel the heat of her skin, feel the brush of her arm against mine. It makes my pulse race and more of those naughty thoughts pepper my mind. I don't know what it is about her. I can't stop thinking about our one single night together and what I'd do if given just a little more time.

This time, when I feel her move, her warm flesh pressed against mine, I close my eyes. It's not the warm sun high over our heads or the calm and serene ambiance around me that pulls my attention. It's the goosebumps on her skin as our arms connect. It's the way her breathing hitches just the slightest, as if she's just as affected by the touch as I am.

When I open my eyes, they automatically seek her out. I find her staring up at me, conflict written all over her gorgeous face. We just watch each other, both lost in our own minds, the unspoken questions dancing around us like fireflies.

I don't know who moves first. Was it her? Was it me? Or did we both just get too tired of fighting this unwavering pull that seems to always be there, like an invisible string neither of us can see, yet keeps us tethered together.

My lips crash hard into hers, my fingers diving into the hair at the nape of her neck. I can taste the sweetness of the grapes and the saltiness of the nuts, as well as some overwhelming taste that is uniquely her. It's just as I remember from December, seductive and powerful, a craving I can't seem to fight.

I want more.

Somehow, we move together without breaking the kiss until I'm sitting on the quad and she's straddling my lap. There's no way to hide what's happening in my jeans. My cock is hard and practically begging to be released from its denim confines. Pleading to slide into the one place he feels at home.

Her.

Blair's nails rake against my scalp, fueling the inferno blazing inside me. Her breasts are pressed firmly against my chest as she rocks her hips, creating sweet friction where we both desire it.

My tongue delves deep into her mouth causing a sweet mewl to erupt from her throat. Everything she does, every sound she makes is like a hit to my system. A drug. That's what she is.

My fucking drug.

I feel the heat of her skin beneath my palms as I slowly glide my hands under her shirt and up her sides. My finger grazes over the lace material of her bra, causing her nipples to pebble into hard little points. My mouth waters, my tongue craves a little taste. She rocks again, grinding against my cock to the point I'm dangerously close to exploding in my pants. I'm seconds away from ripping every stitch of clothing we're wearing from both of our bodies. The need to be inside her has been steadily boiling, ready to blow.

But a noise catches my attention.

I rip my lips from hers and listen, trying to figure out what I heard. Puffs of warm breath hit my cheek as she tries to calm her breathing, her hands still in my hair. The sound of birds in the trees and water against the shoreline seems to be drowned out by the blood swooshing in my ears. I listen, but don't hear anything right away. I'm ready to return my mouth to where it belongs when I hear it.

Four-wheelers.

And they're close.

"Shit. We're no longer alone," I mutter, moving back and trying to adjust my pants. It doesn't help relieve the ache—nothing short of being inside Blair again will suffice.

Blair scrambles off my lap, righting her shirt to make sure she's covered completely as three machines pull into the small clearing we're parked in. The owners slowly move around us, parking closer to the water's edge. I slowly get off my four-wheeler, doing everything I can to conceal my erection from the out-of-towners who have rained upon our private moment.

"We should probably head out," I state, my voice sounding tight, even to my own ears.

"Probably," she replies, picking up the containers of food and slipping them back into the insulated bag.

I peek over my shoulder to the new arrivals, noting they're not paying any attention to us. That spurs me to reach for her, drawing her slender body against my own. She doesn't fight me, just moves until she's tucked comfortably into my embrace. Her lips brush lazily against my chin.

As much as I try to fight it, I just can't. I take her lips with my own, careful to make sure our kiss doesn't get out of control, especially with eyes nearby. It doesn't last nearly as long as I'd like and only makes me want her that much more.

Placing one last lingering kiss on her lips, I whisper, "What do you say we get back out there and ride for a little longer?"

Blair's dilated eyes focus on me. "I'd like that."

I nod, making sure our trash is picked up and everything is secured back on my quad. I slowly climb back on, ignoring the pinch of my jeans against my hard-on, and get settled in my seat. Just as she's ready to climb on, I place my hands on her hips and draw her close. "Do you want to come back to my place and have dinner with me?"

Blair sighs and gives the faintest of smiles. She leans her forehead against mine. "I shouldn't."

No, probably not. She knows what will most likely happen if she does.

"But?" I ask, noting the hesitancy in her statement.

She meets my gaze before answering, "But I want to."

"Good. I want you to."

CHAPTER
eleven

Blair

I'm not sure I've ever had a better day. I'm more relaxed than any time I can remember, and that includes last Sunday's dinner at my condo. Of course, I'm not sure I've ever been this keyed up either, thanks to a certain sexy someone who kisses like a god and has a body designed for sin.

And don't get me started on his hands...

My hands, at this moment, are wrapped around his waist and itching to slide down to where his erection presses firmly against the zipper of his jeans. Oh, I know it's there. I felt it loud and proud as I was straddling his lap and making out with him like a teenager. It made me want to do things I haven't done since my Christmas visit to Pine Village.

Still makes me want those things, even after we spend another hour on the back of his quad, riding trails and taking in the sights.

By the time we get back to his house, it's late afternoon and I feel like I'm covered in a thin layer of dirt. That's the downside about riding. It's fun, but dirty. Gabe parks his machine in the garage and hops off, reaching for my hand to help me down. Only when my feet are back on solid ground does he take off his helmet and set it on the bench.

I do the same, setting my borrowed one beside his, and trying to flatten the crazy helmet hair I no doubt have. It's probably sticking up all crazy and will take an hour to brush through the tangles. I'm sure I look a fright.

"You look fine," he says, as if reading my thoughts.

A blush creeps in. "I'm sure I don't," I reply with a chuckle.

He steps forward, his chest almost touching mine, as he reaches over and runs a hand over my erratic flyaways. His thumb lazily glides across my cheek. "Beautiful."

Thousands of butterflies take flight in my stomach, and my hand automatically goes there, as if I can somehow stop their flutter.

"Let's head inside. I have some chicken breasts marinating. I thought about throwing them on the grill."

"Sounds delicious," I reply.

We head inside, and the entire experience is oddly familiar. Except, this time, I feel welcome with Gabe's hand on my lower back. The first time I was here, I could sense his annoyance at having to rescue his sister's friend from the snowdrift. Thankfully, there's none of that this time around.

As I strip off my boots in the mudroom, I can't help but notice how dusty I really am. I feel like my entire body is covered in a layer of dirt, and frankly, it's a little gross. "You know, maybe I should run home and shower before dinner. I feel icky," I say with a chuckle.

Gabe looks up from removing his own boots and scans me from head to toe. It feels like a caress. "I have a shower here."

I swallow over the sudden lump in my throat. "I don't have any clothes."

The corner of his mouth curls upward in the sexiest grin I think I've ever seen. "If I recall correctly, you didn't seem to have a problem finding some the last time."

A slow blush creeps up my neck as I remember grabbing clothes from the suitcase I had to leave in my car but discovering none of them were pajamas. That's why I found myself digging in his closet without his permission to find a pair of joggers and a crewneck sweatshirt to sleep in.

Of course, I didn't end up sleeping in them anyway...

Honestly, I should probably go home and shower, but I know I won't. Not after the way he kissed me out by the lake and the desire that still smolders deep in my chest, begging for him to strike the match.

Without saying a word, I turn on my socked feet and head for the stairs. I'm nearly halfway up when I hear him ask, "I take it you remember where everything is?"

Glancing over my shoulder, I throw him a slow grin. "Oh, I remember everything," I state, feeling his eyes on me as I make my way up to the second floor and disappear into his bedroom.

It's exactly the same. The massive king-sized bed sits in the middle of the room, the bedding neatly made. There isn't much sitting on top of the dresser except a tie pin and some pocket change, and a single book and desk lamp sits on top of the nightstand.

I make my way to the walk-in closet and push open the door, instantly assaulted by the scent of Gabe. My fingers glide across dress shirts and ties, all organized by color. There are shelves with other clothes: jeans, sweats, and several pairs of basketball shorts.

Since the temperature is much warmer than it was during my last visit to Gabe's house, instead of grabbing the sweats, I opt for a pair of his shorts. The problem is I can already tell they're going to be too big. Making a quick stop at the dresser, I dig for a well-worn T-shirt. I find what I'm looking for at the bottom, the material soft and gray and smells like his laundry detergent.

When I step into his gorgeous bathroom, I go straight to the shower this time. As much as I'd love to soak in that impressive tub until I'm relaxed and pruney, today calls for a shower. The water shoots from the ceiling and walls, warm and welcoming, the steam slowly starting to rise. I set the clean clothes down on the vanity and strip off my dusty digs, dropping them in a pile beside the door.

They're definitely going to need to be washed before I put them back on.

Naked, I pad over to the magnificent tile shower, adjust the temperature, and slip inside. I don't even care most of the stall is wide open, with only a skinny piece of glass to keep the jetted water from flying out the back and into the jetted tub positioned behind it. The unit is so big, there's no need to have an actual enclosure.

Once my hair is wet, I grab his shampoo, take a big whiff of the glob I squirt in my palm, and lather my hair. I wasn't going to wash my hair, but the temptation of smelling like him was just too great. It's enough to overlook the fact he doesn't have conditioner, and the tangles are probably going to be horrific.

At least I'll smell amazing.

As soon as I rinse the shampoo, I reach for the bodywash and scrub from head to toe. I had taken care of shaving my legs and some lady-parts grooming this morning on the off-chance there was a possibility of ending up in his bed. Oh, who am I kidding. I was downright hopeful and have thought about nothing but since he invited me to go for today's ride.

When I'm clean, I slip out of the stall and grab a fluffy blue towel. I dry off and head for the clean clothes I left on the vanity, only to find the dirty ones I placed on the floor missing. There's a smile on my lips as I dress in Gabe's clothes, the thought of him slipping into the bathroom to gather my dirty stuff and possibly watching me shower in the forefront of my mind.

I find a comb sitting beside his toothbrush and run it through my hair. Surprisingly, it's not as tangled as I expected. What little eye makeup I wore is gone and my face is slightly flushed, but there's no missing the brightness of anticipation reflecting in my green orbs.

With bare feet, I pad through his bedroom and down the stairs, eager to see what Gabe has been up to. Before I'm halfway there, amazing aromas hit me. It's a mix of grilled chicken, peppers, and cheese. My stomach growls anxiously.

He looks up and smiles, his eyes doing a slow perusal from head to toe. "I see you found something to wear."

I laugh at how ridiculous I look. The shirt is big and the shorts even worse. I have them sinched as tight as the tie would go and still have room to spare. They're rolled up several times at the waist and still hit my knees. "They're a little big," I state unnecessarily.

Blue eyes laced with humor study my appearance, and when they finally return to my face, he says, "If you're not feeling them, you could always just take them off."

A bubble of laughter spills from my lips. "That is always an option," I confirm, taking a seat at the island counter. "You're officially done with the kitchen?" I ask, taking in the now-completed flooring and final touches.

He looks down and nods. "Yeah. After Christmas, I spent a few weeks finishing everything. It was a good way to relieve...stress."

Something in the way he says that last word makes me pause. As if he's not referring to the stresses of his job, but something else that caused him sleepless nights. And suddenly, I know he thought of me as much as I thought of him.

Clearing my throat, I glance down at the skillet. "That smells amazing."

"You're in for a treat, Dr. O'Connor." Gabe adjusts the temperature on the stove and drops the hand towel he's holding on the counter. "I'm gonna run up and shower real quick while that finishes. Make yourself at home."

I watch him go, my eyes glued to his ass until he completely disappears around the corner. I'm torn with indecision as I sit here, alone, my gaze going to the large skillet on the stove simmering. I should sit here and make sure the cheese doesn't scorch to the pan. I know that's the route I should take, yet that's not what I do.

Instead, I jump up and move the pan off the burner, making sure to shut it off. Then I practically run through the kitchen and take the steps as fast as my legs will carry me. When I reach the second floor, I slow my pace and take a few deep, calming breaths. Quietly, I tiptoe to his bedroom door and peek inside. The only sound is the shower running on the opposite side of the bathroom door.

I slip out of the oversized shorts and T-shirt, leaving them lying on the floor, as I creep to the ajar door. When I push it open, I'm assaulted with steam, but that's not what makes my nipples pebble. It's the sight of the man in the shower.

Gabe is leaning his elbows and forearms against the wall, his head dropped on his arms, and the hot water spraying him in the back. And his cock? It's rock-hard and jutting from his body, begging for attention.

I move to the shower and slip inside easily, since there's no door. The moment I touch his back, he tenses, but quickly relaxes, as if realizing who it is. He pushes off the wall and slowly turns to face me, his eyes raging with desire and unspoken need. I ignore the almost too-hot water and hold his gaze, reaching down and grabbing his erection in my palm. Goosebumps pepper his tanned skin, and he closes his eyes when I gently start to stroke him from root to tip.

"Fuck, Blair," he groans, his hips automatically thrusting forward.

The movement makes me drop to my knees, my mouth watering for a little taste. Adjusting my position, I grip his hard length and swirl my tongue around the head, earning me an audible hiss for my efforts. Gabe stands completely still, his cock just as big and hard as I remember. Only this time, I'm going to enjoy more than just the feel of it between my legs.

Ignoring the hard tile beneath my knees, I slowly draw him into my mouth, savoring the salty liquid seeping from the tip. I twist my hand, firmly holding his erection, as I take him as deep into my throat as possible.

"Holy fuck," he moans, trying to hold himself still, but unable to stop his hips from moving. Gabe threads his wet fingers into my hair, holding the now-soaked strands out of my face. The fact he's milliseconds away from snapping his control is what fuels my desire to keep going, to push him over the edge and reap the benefits of my actions.

Because an out-of-control Gabe is truly a sight to behold.

I relax my throat and sweep my tongue across the vein running down his shaft, all while picking up the pace with my hand. His body starts to move, as if on its own accord, his hips thrusting, yet still mindful not to choke me.

When I glance up, I'm locked in the intensity of his eyes, the burning desire mixing with rapture. I can tell he's getting close. His cock swells even more, moisture beading on my tongue. I've never been particularly fond of the taste of a man's release, but I'm eager and excited to take him over the edge.

Unfortunately, Gabe has other ideas. With a growl, he pulls himself out of my mouth with a loud pop and steps back. "Hey, I wasn't finished," I insist as his hands reach down and help me stand.

His mouth is on mine moments later, hard and insistent. I groan as his tongue delves deep, stroking against my tongue. Warmth floods my core like gasoline on a bonfire. He releases his hold on my lips and confesses, "I'm nowhere near finished either."

"But—"

"But if you kept doing that, I was going to come down your throat, and that's not what I want."

My nipples are pebbled as I lean forward, brushing them against his chest. "What is it you want?"

Suddenly, I'm lifted in the air as we spin around. My ankles cross behind Gabe's back as my back is pressed against the cold tile. His mouth descends once more in a bruising kiss, his cock grinding against where I ache for him the most. When he pulls back, he whispers, "Just you."

His mouth is demanding. Claiming. When he pulls back once more, we both greedily suck in hot, steamy air, as his erection nudges my opening. "Gabe," I groan, shifting my hips and taking the head inside me.

He curses and holds me still. "Protection."

I almost groan in frustration. I know we should use it, to protect both of us, but all I can think about his how amazing he feels bare. I've thought of it almost daily since last Christmas. That's why I find myself saying, "I'm still clean and protected from pregnancy, Gabe. No one since you."

An animalistic growl erupts from his throat as he claims my lips once more, but this kiss isn't near as long as I'd like. "Dammit, Blair. I should get a condom, but all I want is to take you bare again."

"Yes. Do that," I pant, very eager for what's next.

He adjusts his hold on me and I feel the head of his cock nudge my opening. "I'm clean too, Blair. No one since you," he parrots, repeating my statement.

Then, he slides home.

That's the only way to describe it.

He feels so...right, as if his body was made for mine. Or maybe it's vice versa, and I was made for him. Either way, it has never felt this good, this perfect before. He holds completely still, his grip on my ass firm with his cock buried to the root. I can feel him flex, feel his muscles tense beneath my palms as he takes a few deep, calming breaths.

"Gabe?" I whisper.

He meets my gaze, his eyes blazing with promise. "Yes?"

"Move."

The corner of his mouth turns up slowly as a wicked smile transforms his face. "My pleasure."

CHAPTER Twelve

GABE

This feeling. It's the greatest feeling in the whole world. Not just the sex. I'm fully aware of the main reason this is so fucking epic.

It's Blair.

I felt it that night all those months ago, as I do right now. Her body molds to mine, made for me.

My hips start to pump completely on their own, and it's still not enough. Blair's nails dig into my shoulders as she holds on, and even though there's a bite of pain, I revel in it. It spurs me on, fuels my need for her. Using the tile wall for leverage, I piston forward, causing her to cry out. Her mouth is open, and all I want is to taste those sweet lips of hers while I'm buried deep inside of her.

The kiss isn't soft or delicate. It's hungry, demanding, and full of passion. Our tongues tangle and match the pace I set with my cock, stroke for stroke. Blair hangs on, her ankles still locked behind my back, her tits pressed against my chest. I want to taste them, to suck each nipple deep into my mouth, but there's no way I can stop to switch things up.

"Gabe," she groans, after ripping her lips from my own.

I respond with a thrust, grinding myself against her. She cries out again, her body tightening around me and almost making me come, but I'm able to hold off. I focus on getting her there, needing to experience her orgasm before I let myself have one.

"So...close," she pants, her nails digging in deep and causing my body to piston forward once more. When I do, it triggers her release, her cries filling the steamy shower with the sweetest sound.

Her internal muscles ripple around my cock as they squeeze like a vise. I'm quick to follow her over the edge, stilling for only a second before pumping hard once, twice, three times before practically collapsing against the wall, her slender body pinned in between.

"I think dinner's ruined," I note, not sure why my brain picked that piece of information to think of.

"Probably," she mutters, kissing up my neck and across my jaw. "That's okay. We'll just skip it and have dessert first," she adds, flexing her internal muscles around my softening cock and causing my blood to hum once more.

"I do rather enjoy dessert," I reason, squeezing the globes of her ass in my palms.

Blair nips at my neck with her teeth. "Oh, I can tell."

I take a few moments to clean us up, turn off the water, and carry her straight out of the shower, water dripping from our bodies as we go. I fall onto my bed, not even caring we're soaking the bedding, and claim her lips with my own. "Now, let's talk more about this dessert."

It's just before one, and I'm finally feeling tired enough to fall asleep. Of course, I think a big part of that contentment is having Blair curled up against my side again. It feels like forever since she was here, yet I can remember every detail as if it were yesterday.

I don't think Blair is sleeping yet. Her breathing hasn't quite evened out enough, and I can practically hear the wheels in her pretty head spinning. She's been thinking for the last few minutes, and considering we just finished round three of orgasm roulette, that's probably not a good thing for my bedroom skills.

"This is going to complicate things, isn't it?" she whispers, finally voicing her concern.

I draw lazy circles with my finger on her bare back. "Probably."

She shifts so she's looking at me. "What do you want?"

Sighing, I fight off the urge to just reply "you" because with that answer comes a lot more questions, and I don't think either one of us is prepared to dive into them. Instead, I decide to go with another honest answer. "I want to fall asleep with you in my arms and wake with you there too, because that one night last December was the best night of sleep I've had in probably forever. I want to take you to breakfast at the diner, because their crepes are even better than I make. I want to enjoy my free time with you, maybe take you to dinner when the opportunity arises, and get to know you better."

"I'm only here until December," she states quietly, the stark reminder like an arrow to my chest.

"I know." Suddenly, it hurts to swallow.

"So, what does that mean? We just...hang out? Date? Have a friends with benefits thing while I'm here?"

"I guess maybe a little of all three? I mean, not necessarily friends with benefits, but I'd like to see you while you're here."

She seems to be considering her options, and I know whatever she decides, I'll respect it. Of course, if she chooses to end whatever this is before it really gets started, I'll be disappointed, but I won't pressure her. Especially with us working together.

"Is sex on the table?" she asks, her eyes widening just a touch.

I reach forward and swipe a lock of hair from her forehead. "Blair, sex is always on the table."

She flashes me a big grin. "Good," she states, pressing her lips against mine. "I happen to be pretty fond of sex with you."

My cock twitches with excitement. How, I'm not sure. The fucker should be pretty well sated for at least a few more hours. "The feeling is one-thousand-percent mutual," I confirm.

With a yawn, she adds, "As long as we both go into this knowing I'm leaving."

My throat is suddenly too tight to draw oxygen into my lungs. "Right," I reply, even though it feels wrong to say.

Blair relaxes against my side, her slender fingers toying with my chest hair as she sighs deeply. "I like hanging out with you, Gabe," she mumbles, placing a kiss against my pec.

"I like hanging out with you too, Blair," I reply, wondering if she can hear the pounding of my heart against her cheek.

Too much. I like her too much.

As she drifts off to sleep, her skin warm and soft against mine, I can't help but wonder if I'm making a huge mistake. I already know letting her go in a few months is going to be hard, but I'm afraid it might be way more difficult than I'm even anticipating. Watching her leave a second time is going to be far worse than the first.

That leaves me with two options. Enjoy my time with her, but keep her at arm's length, or go all-in and pray she doesn't leave.

I don't know which one is better, but I already know which way I'm leaning.

I wake with a start and glance at my clock. When I see the time, I let out a loud groan. It feels like I just fell asleep.

"Sorry, I didn't mean to wake you."

I follow the sound of the voice and find Blair standing in the middle of my bedroom. "You didn't." I throw the sheet back, ignoring the fact I'm naked and hard, and get up, stretching my arms over my head. "My alarm would be going off in five minutes anyway."

Even in the early morning light, I can see the blush creep up her cheeks. "I, uh, wasn't going to leave without saying goodbye."

My eyes slowly peruse her delectable body from head to toe. She's wearing my clothes again—the shorts and T-shirt she had on before joining me in the shower. I can't stop my feet from moving in her direction, my hands from grasping her waist and pulling her body against mine. "Again, I see you found something to wear."

She smiles coyly. "My things are still in the washing machine," she announces, a stark reminder of how everything came to a crashing halt last night. Once we made it to bed, we didn't leave, with the exception of a quick trip downstairs to cut up some summer sausage and cheese for a late-night dinner. The chicken? Oh, that was most definitely ruined.

"I see," I reply, running my hand under the shirt and up her bare back. "And your bra?"

"I have no clue where that's at."

Chuckling, I bend down and kiss her, despite the fact neither of us have brushed our teeth yet. "I like you in my clothes," I confess, her hands slowly moving down my back to grip my ass.

"They're comfy," she replies and then sighs. "I need to get home."

Nodding, I hesitantly release my hold on her. Her eyes drop to my erection, and she licks her lips. "That's not going to get you out of this house before noon, Blair," I counter, my dick ready to play.

She shrugs and runs her finger down the center of my chest. "Perhaps we should just call in sick."

"While I like the way you think, I believe we both have full schedules today," I reason, even though I'd much rather stay here— in bed—with Blair. The reality is we both have a major commitment to the business, the town, and the people who live in it.

She makes a tsk sound in the back of her throat and turns to head for the door. "Then I suppose I'll just have to suck your cock like a lollipop later tonight."

Brain. Explodes.

Before I can even process a response, she grins mischievously, winks, and then walks out of my bedroom, leaving me standing with an erection I'll most certainly have to beat off in the shower to get to subside.

And then have to figure out how to make it through the day without replaying her words over and over again or picturing her on her knees in front of me, taking me as far down her throat as she can.

Yeah, today's definitely going to be the longest day of my life, because all I want is for night to come again.

So we can both come again.

I slip into the bathroom and turn on the shower, making sure the water is scalding hot. Perhaps I can burn her touch off my skin?

It doesn't work. Nothing seems to erase the vivid picture of naked Blair and the feel of her sweet pussy gripping my cock, which is what has me reaching for my dick and giving it a hard squeeze. Sensations flood my veins, my balls achingly heavy with need.

I grab the bar of soap and lather my hand before letting it stray to my erection once more. Gripping the base, I slowly slide it up to the tip. A groan spills from my lips as I close my eyes, my hand starting to move faster and faster. All I see is her. All I feel is her. All I want is her.

When my release hits, it's with the force of a tsunami. I growl her name as waves of pleasure crash into me. My hand doesn't stop moving until I'm sagging forward against the wall, my body too weak to hold itself upright unassisted.

"Jesus, you're like a teenager," I chastise myself aloud, reaching for the soap again. But, I admit, the statement has merit. I'm different when she's around, definitely horny like a damn kid. This isn't how a thirty-seven-year-old man, who has been married and divorced, should act.

But do you know what?

Fuck it. I like it.

And damn, I like her.

The rest of my shower progresses quickly, and within thirty minutes, I'm dressed and ready for work. I head down to the kitchen to make a cup of coffee and smile when I see the pot already on, coffee hot and waiting.

It only takes me a few seconds to pour myself a large travel mug of black coffee and head for the door. The moment I step outside, my phone rings. There's only one person I know who'd call me at seven on a Monday morning.

"Good morning, Mother," I answer cheekily.

"Good morning, Son," she retorts, just as she does every time I answer the phone in that fashion. "Are you at work?" she asks, knowing I tend to get to the office early unless I'm headed to the hospital to see patients before the clinic opens.

"I'm actually just leaving the house," I tell her, getting into my truck.

As soon as it's on, the Bluetooth engages, and my mom's reply comes through the speakers. "Just now leaving? Did you oversleep?"

Images of Blair pop into my head. "Uh, no. I was up before my alarm," I state. It's the truth. I just leave out the part about taking a little longer in the shower.

"Well, anyway, the reason I was calling," she starts, taking a quick sip of her own coffee. I can picture her sitting in the kitchen with her second cup of Joe, waiting on my dad to finally come downstairs for breakfast. "Your sister's birthday is Saturday. I'd like to have a cookout."

"That sounds nice."

"You'll be there, right?"

Backing into the spot adjacent to my driveway, I turn myself around and head for the road. "Of course I will. Unless something comes up with a patient," I counter, even though she knows the drill. It hasn't happened too often but does on occasion. A patient is admitted or being transferred, and I'm needed at the hospital.

"Well, hopefully there won't be any issues. I'm thinking arrive around four, dinner around five thirty. I'll have your dad fire up the barbecue."

"Sounds good," I reply, pulling into the back parking area behind the clinic. "What can I bring?"

"Nothing. I'm not doing too much. Maybe some potato and pasta salads, chips, and some watermelon. Easy stuff I can make ahead of time. Oh, and I'll order a cake from Jillian at the bakery," she confirms.

"Okay, well, if you change your mind, shoot me a text. I can whip something up," I reply, waiting in my truck to finish the conversation.

"Will do. I'm going to message a few of her friends too. Curtis, Ellie and Brody, and Ava."

"Message TD too. If he's not working, he'll come. Hell, even if he is working, I'm sure he'll stop by for a bit."

"Good thinking," she says. I can practically hear her pen writing on a slip of paper. Mom's a note taker, and I'm sure she's jotting down everything we're discussing on one of the many pads of paper you'll find around the house.

"Oh, and Blair. I can't forget about her. It's so weird having her back in town now. How is she doing at the clinic?" Mom asks. The mention of Blair has my blood humming through my veins.

"She's doing well. The patients love her," I confirm, trying to keep the bubble of excitement out of my voice.

"I'm sure they do. If she's anything like her father, I can only imagine what kind of physician she is. It's just too bad their relationship is so strained. Maybe that can be fixed while she's here."

"Maybe," I agree, even though I'm just not sure. There's a lot of baggage between those two, and it would take a major conversation in order to try to sort it. I'm just not sure they're there yet.

"I don't have her number," my mom says almost absently. "Will you invite her for me?"

I'm unable to hide my smile. "I will."

"Perfect. Thank you. I'll let you go. I'm sure you're already at work."

"All right. Let me know if you change your mind and want me to bring anything," I reply.

"I will. Have a great day, Gabe."

"You too, Mom," I say before signing off.

Grabbing my coffee, I turn off my truck and head for the back entrance of the clinic. I've always felt a sense of eagerness to get my day started, but that enthusiasm is even more pronounced now that Blair is part of it. I'm trying not to get ahead of myself here, but I already feel like she's quickly becoming the best part of my day.

And I can't wait for her to arrive this morning.

Especially after spending the night with her.

Keeping myself from mauling her, stripping her naked, and having my dirty way is going to be a challenge, but one I can handle.

I'll just have to act on those particular impulses later tonight.

CHAPTER
Thirteen

Blair

I tuck the white bag under my arm and slip in the back door, anxious to see the man I just spent the night with and saw less than an hour and a half ago. My body is already humming with anticipation, even more so than it was before we spent last night together. Prior, I was constantly thinking about that one night last Christmas. Now, the last twenty-four hours are playing on a continuous loop in my brain, leaving me yearning for more alone time with Gabe.

The clinic is mostly quiet as I move to the office on the right and peek around the doorframe. Gabe is sitting at his desk, his gaze locking on mine. "Good morning," I greet, my voice sounding a little breathy.

"Morning," he croons, that single word like gooey honey on a warm summer day.

I head in his direction, a little extra swing in my hips, which he notices. His eyes are glued to my walk, darkening with desire. "I grabbed you breakfast."

When his eyes finally return to mine, the corner of his mouth turns upward. "Funny, I was just thinking about eating."

My thighs clench, because that one single word—eating—is dripping with dirty intent. "Well, good thing I'm here then, huh?" I ask, taking a seat in the chair across from his desk.

He runs the pad of his thumb across his lips. "Damn good thing," he confirms, a knowing little smirk on his face.

"I take it you slept well, Dr. O'Connor?" he asks as I take the first Danish from the bag and set it in front of him.

"Actually, I slept amazingly well, Dr. Rhodes," I affirm, taking a bite of my sweet breakfast treat.

"Happy to hear," he states, taking a bite of the strawberry Danish. "Good sleep is such an important part of the day. I think whatever you did to warrant such amazing sleep should be repeated tonight."

A giggle slips from my lips. "Doctor recommended?" I quip.

I'm rewarded with a full-wattage smile. "Damn right."

The back entrance door opens and a flurry of voices filter in. "Good morning, Doctors," Kelly greets, followed by a few others.

"Well, I should get ready to start my day," I state, slipping my half-eaten Danish back in the bag.

He shoves the rest of his in his mouth and chews. "Before you go, Mom and Dad are having a cookout on Saturday for Hallie's birthday. They asked me to extend an invite to you."

"Okay, what should I bring?"

His eyes scan my entire body from head to toe. "Just your swimsuit. Preferably a bikini," he replies, his voice low and gravelly.

My nipples pebble hard against my bra. "They still have the hot tub?" I ask, recalling how we'd spend nights sitting in that hot tub, the snow falling around us and the frigid temperatures keeping us submerged in the warm water.

"They do," he confirms.

"Isn't it a little too warm to sit in a hot tub?" I ask, leaning against the doorjamb.

Gabe shrugs his shoulders and throws me a cat that ate the canary grin. "Probably."

Chuckling, I shake my head at his antics. "I'll be there, Dr. Rhodes. Me and my tiny pink bikini."

The last thing I hear as I slip into my office across the hall is his pained groan. I can picture how hard he is, his mind imagining me in the little bikini I referred to, mostly because I'm thinking about him there, wearing trunks with water glistening off his hard chest. Just like in the shower.

I have to cross and recross my legs when I sit at my desk, the hum of desire landing squarely between my legs. I've already had to take care of my own needs in the shower this morning. Apparently, three times wasn't enough to sate my need for him. The moment I stepped under the spray, I thought about waking up beside him, his erection pressed firmly against my ass, had my hand slipping between my folds and getting myself off.

Now, I'm thinking about him again and ready to jump on for another ride.

"Dr. O'Connor, your first patient is here," Kelly announces from my doorway, pulling me back to the present. I have a full day of seeing patients ahead of me. There will be little time to think about Gabe, let alone picture him naked.

Oh, who am I kidding?

There's always time for that.

Hallie: Got time for lunch?

I glance up from my phone to the clock on the wall and notice it's almost noon. Even though I should probably just eat one of the yogurt cups I have in the fridge, I decide some of Saul's home-cooked food is just the ticket.

Me: If you're thinking about Saul's food at the diner, then I can definitely find time!

Hallie: Duh! It's meatloaf day!

Me: I have one patient to go, and then I'll meet you there.

Hallie: Sounds good. I'll go get us a table.

I set my phone down on the desk and get up, stretching my arms over my head. Exhaustion is starting to set in, thanks to a very late night with a certain sexy doctor. I'm sure stuffing my belly full of meatloaf and mashed potatoes won't help, but it'll be worth it. I can go to bed early, right? Catch up on my sleep later.

As soon as I step out into the hall, Makenzie flags me down. "Dr. Rhodes asked me to let you know he had an emergency in Hudson with a patient who was admitted earlier this morning. He went to meet with the cardiologist and their family to discuss options. It's not looking good."

"Oh, I'm sorry to hear that. Is there anything I can do?" I ask, even though I'm certain I already know the answer.

"No, unfortunately. Mr. Holohan has been a patient of Gabe's since he first joined the practice. I think I heard his wife used to babysit him and his sister, Hallie, when they were young."

"I remember them," I reply absently, recalling the couple who attended all of Hallie's school functions throughout our youth. My friend referred to them as her second grandparents. The thought of losing one of them now makes my heart break for Hallie and Gabe.

"Thank you for letting me know. I'm going to head down to the diner for lunch after this patient, but you can call me if something comes up," I tell the young nurse.

"I will. Emma Morrical is in room four," Makenzie states before heading back down the hall to where the nurses' station is positioned.

I pull the chart from the door and give it a quick scan. A medication refill, which will involve a quick assessment of the seven-year-old. The appointment takes less than fifteen minutes, and the moment little Emma and her mom head out, I wave goodbye to Kelly and Makenzie and grab my purse to head to the diner.

Hallie is sitting in a booth, sipping sweet tea when I arrive. "Sorry I'm late," I say as I slide into the bench across from her. The moment she meets my eyes, I can tell something's wrong. "What?"

She sighs loudly. "So much."

"Hey, Blair. What can I get you to drink?" Ellie asks with her usual friendly smile plastered on her face.

"Just an ice water."

"Okay. Are you both getting the special?" she asks, referring to the amazing bacon-wrapped meatloaf I've been thinking about since Hallie invited me to lunch.

"Yes," Hallie and I both reply at the same time.

With a chuckle, Ellie says, "All right. They'll be out in a few."

As soon as we're alone, I lean in. "Okay, what's up?" I ask quietly, hoping no one around us can hear.

The sadness in her gaze tugs at my heart. "It's been a rough morning. My brother called me a bit ago and said Kenny Holohan isn't doing well. His family gave him permission to call me and my parents. He was admitted this morning with the end stages of congestive heart failure. When he gets released, he'll go home with hospice care," she mutters, her crystal blue eyes filling with tears.

"I'm so sorry, Hal," I reply, reaching over and squeezing her hand.

"Thanks." She sniffles and takes a sip of her tea. "Throw in Curtis drama and it's been a pretty crap-tastic day."

I'm ready to open my mouth when Ellie returns with two plates of piping-hot food. "Do you need anything else, my friends?"

"No thank you, Ellie. This looks and smells amazing," I reply, unwrapping my utensils and ready to dig in. Once we're alone, I ask the burning question. "What did Curtis do?"

Hallie sighs, poking around at her food with her fork. "It's not what he did as much as what he didn't do. He was supposed to come to my house yesterday, but, as always, something came up," she huffs, the tips of her ears turning red with her anger.

"What keeps coming up? It seems like he's canceling time together more than you're actually having it."

"He is. He's canceled four times in the last week alone. Four. And do you know how many times we've actually seen each other in the last two weeks? Once. And that was only because I drove there and forced him to have lunch with me."

I can see the mixture of anger and pain in her eyes. Hallie and Curtis have dated for two years, but it seems like one isn't quite as committed to the relationship anymore, which breaks my heart. I may not have seen much of Hallie over the years, but we've stayed in touch, and I've always considered her my best friend. We've spent a lot of time over the years on the phone talking or texting.

"I'm giving him one last shot," she says, steeling her back where she sits. "Mom called and is having a birthday dinner for me Saturday. If he doesn't come, that's it. I'm breaking up with him."

"I understand your frustration," I state, taking a small bite of my delicious food. "Is he just working? Is that it?" I'm trying to give the man the benefit of the doubt.

"So he says," she mutters, the meaning behind her words loud and clear. Hallie believes something—or someone—else is keeping her boyfriend from her. I hope that's not true, because Hal is one of the best women you'll ever find, and she deserves someone who'll commit to her completely.

"I'm sorry, Hal, really. You don't deserve that. Is there anything I can do? Wanna come over tonight and have wine? I have the stuff to make queso dip. We can gorge ourselves on nachos, drink wine, and watch trashy reality TV."

A wide smile spreads across her face. "Are you sure you're going to be home?" she asks, a knowing little glean in her eyes.

The hairs on the back of my neck stand up and the food I'm swallowing falls like lead in my belly. "Why wouldn't I be home?" I ask, trying to play it cool, but knowing I'm starting to sweat a little in the armpits.

"Probably because you'd be with my brother?" she says, turning her statement into a question. "I mean, if that's who you spent last night with, considering you didn't come home."

I can feel my face heat with the fire of a thousand suns. "What?" I ask, even though I know it's fruitless.

My best friend laughs in my face. "Seriously? You're going to deny it?" she asks, laughing.

"No, I..." I stammer, the words just not coming.

"It's okay," she says, shoving a big bite of her food into her mouth. When she swallows, she adds, "I mean, I don't want to know details, but if you two are, like, seeing each other or something, I'd be on board with it."

"You would?"

She nods. "Yeah. Seriously, you're the best person I know, and even though my brother is totally annoying, he's a good guy. He went through a rough divorce a few years back, and I don't think he's dated much since."

I don't confirm or deny her comment. Anything he says to me will remain between us, unless it's something that would cause him or someone else harm. That's the exact honor I extend to her, and a very important part of any friendship.

"All I'm saying is if you two were to, you know, hang out while you're in town, I'd be okay with it. There are way worse single ladies in this place, like the viper who just strolled in wearing heels to work at the hardware store," Hallie mutters.

I turn to see Shay walk to the counter, giving her signature hair flip as she talks to Ellie. Even though our friend has a smile plastered on her face, I can tell the light in her eyes doesn't quite shine as brightly as normal. Shay's always had that effect on people.

"Like her?" I find myself asking aloud, even though I already know the answer.

"I'd have to kill my brother if he ever brought her home," she mutters quietly before taking a big bite of her food. "Anyway, all I'm saying is it'd be pretty cool if you two were, like, a thing."

"A thing?" I quip, trying hard to hide my smile.

"Yeah, a thing. Except you don't share *any* of the details about...stuff. Got it? No details," she reiterates, pulling a disgusted face.

"Got it," I agree.

After a few seconds she asks, "Do you like him?"

Again, I feel the blush creep up my neck. "Yes, I do."

She smiles widely. "Good. I don't know, maybe you two will really hit it off, fall in love, and you'll stay in town forever."

My heart skids to a halt in my chest. My eyes must resemble those cartoon characters where they bug out of their heads, because Hallie throws her head back and laughs at my shock.

"Calm down. I'm not saying you're going to marry my brother. What I am saying is that would be pretty cool if you did," she states with a chuckle. "So if you're busy tonight, I'd understand."

"No, I have no plans. Let's have dinner and wine," I insist, finishing off my lunch.

"You sure? I don't want to get in the way of you hanging out with Gabe," she replies with a smirk.

I roll my eyes dramatically at her as Ellie returns to our table. "Anything else for you, ladies?"

"I'm good," Hallie says, eating the last few bites of her mashed potatoes.

An idea hits me. "Actually, can I order a special to go, please?"

"Sure thing. Give me a minute to bag it up for you." Ellie turns and scurries back to the kitchen, grabbing an empty glass to refill along the way.

"You hungry?" Hallie quips.

Shifting in my seat, I state, "Your brother has been in Hudson, so I thought I'd have something waiting for him in case he hasn't had the opportunity to eat lunch."

She seems to sober a little, as if remembering exactly why her brother is at the hospital. "Oh, yeah. Good plan. I'm sure he'll appreciate that. Plus, he loves Saul's meatloaf."

I nod in agreement. "You should go over and see them. When he gets out of the hospital. I'll go with you," I offer, reaching over again and squeezing her hand.

"Thanks." She offers me a sad, watery smile. "Maybe on Sunday. I don't think I want to go before my party on Saturday."

"Whenever you're ready, count me in."

"Thanks," Hallie replies as Ellie returns with my to-go order and the check.

I snatch it from her hand before Hallie can grab it. "My treat."

"No way," my best friend argues. "I'm the one who invited you."

Grinning, I pull my wallet from my purse. "You're too slow."

"Fine," she grumbles, reaching into her own purse and pulling out cash. "I've got the tip then."

"Deal."

Once the bill is paid, Hallie and I head for the door, and I admit, I'm a bit grateful Shay is already gone. "What time tonight?" she asks when we hit the sidewalk.

"Six? That gives me time for a quick shower after work. We can order something so neither of us has to cook."

"Sounds like a plan," she replies, pulling me in for a hug. "And about the other thing? I really am okay with you and Gabe. I mean, it's a little weird, but only because he's my brother. Usually I'd want all the dirty details, but in this case, I think I'll pass." She pulls a disgusted face that makes me grin.

"I think I can handle that, but don't get too attached to the idea of us together forever. We've already talked about that, and we're both aware I'm leaving by the end of the year. Six months is my max here. My bosses are expecting me back by mid-December at the latest."

She sighs. "Fine," she grumbles, clearly not happy with that response. "I'll just keep my hopes and dreams to myself about you two falling in love, getting married, and you becoming my sister for real."

Chuckling, I shake my head. To her, it probably looks like I'm just shaking off her comment, but really, I'm shaking off the reaction my heart had at the idea. We definitely don't need that thought taking root in my chest, growing hope and enthusiasm.

"See you after work," I say, turning to head toward the office.

"Bye," she hollers, going in the opposite direction to where her car is parked.

Unfortunately, I realize quickly the damage is done. What would it be like if I stayed here? It's too soon to plan a future with Gabe, but I can't hide the fact he's the first guy in a while to make me want to entertain that idea. Now that the thought is planted, it seems to be monopolizing too much of my brain space. I need to push it clear from my head. The fact still remains, I will return to Illinois. To my old apartment. To the clinic I've called home since I began my career.

I won't be staying in Pine Village, despite the way my heart suddenly yearns for more.

I need to just stop thinking about it.

But I'm not sure I can.

Stupid brain.

CHAPTER *fourteen*

GABE

I'm exhausted by the time I get back to the clinic. It's been an emotional two hours, filled with doctor meetings and consoling Delores Holohan and their two sons, Robert and Douglas. Kenneth will be discharged in two days on hospice care for end-of-life comfort measures. The cardiologist says it could be anywhere from a few days to a few months, just depending on how long Kenny—and his heart—hangs on.

Sitting with the Holohans while they conferred with the best cardiologist at Hudson was at their request. Delores wanted to make sure every step taken in Kenny's care was part of her plan to keep him comfortable and home as much as possible. At least they'll get some time with him before he passes, something not everyone is privileged to receive.

Calling my parents and then my sister was the worst. The Holohans have been a part of our family since Hallie was a baby. I was an ornery four-year-old, who wasn't thrilled to have a newborn baby sister in the mix. Delores started watching us during the day, while our parents worked, and we instantly formed a bond with the older couple. It lasted through our adolescence and into adulthood.

I let myself in through the back door of the clinic and prepared myself to jump into seeing patients. The office staff was able to reschedule the appointments I was missing, but the rest of the afternoon is still booked. The moment I step inside my private space, I catch a whiff of something heavenly. My mouth instantly waters as I search for the source of such an amazing aroma. When my eyes land on my desk, I can't help but smile.

My feet carry me quickly to the white Styrofoam container, my eyes scanning the note scrolled across a slip of paper on top.

Wasn't sure if you'd have time to eat or not, so I grabbed lunch, just in case. -Blair

I set the note aside, open the lid, and groan. Saul's bacon-wrapped meatloaf with mashed potatoes and gravy, and it's still warm. I grab the plastic fork sitting beside the container and dive in. I must finish the entire meal in two minutes flat, which turns out to be all the time I have free before Makenzie pops her head in my office.

"I thought I heard you slip in. Your one thirty is here," she states.

"Give me two minutes," I tell her, opening my desk drawer for my toothbrush.

"No rush. How's Kenny?" she asks, leaning against the doorjamb.

"He doesn't have much time. They've called in hospice," I confirm, even though she probably already saw the report they sent over.

"I'm sorry. I know you are close with his family."

"Thank you."

"Take a few minutes. Donald Smith is in room two."

I nod and head for the employee bathroom inside the break room. After brushing my teeth and using the head, I return to my office and slip on my coat. It's time to get back to it. The emotions of the day will have to wait until later. Right now, I'm needed in room number two.

I pop my head into her office, finally able to talk to Blair for the first time since I returned to find lunch waiting. "Hey," I say, receiving a bright grin the moment her eyes meet mine. Just that one gesture makes all the tightness in my chest ease just a bit.

"Hi."

"Thank you for lunch," I tell her, wishing I could walk around her desk and take her in my arms.

"No problem. I know what it's like to have to run over the lunch hour, so I took a shot that you wouldn't have much time to eat. I figured, if anything, it would make great leftovers for another time," she says, that warm, beautiful smile spreading across her lips.

"I definitely appreciate it. I wasn't able to grab anything on my way back to town, so Saul's meatloaf sure hit the spot."

"I'm glad," she says, leaning back in her chair just a bit. "Listen," she starts but is cut off.

"Hey, Gabe, we have a situation. Harold Foreman is here. He doesn't have an appointment but insisted on being seen. When asked what the problem is, he said his privates are swollen, and to be honest, there's an infectious odor permeating the air," Kelly announces quietly, a look of both concern and perhaps disgust in her eyes.

"Go ahead and take him to a room. How's the rest of the schedule?"

"It will push us back a little, but shouldn't be too horrible," she states. "Makenzie is setting up a patient in room one."

"Okay, go ahead and do an initial assessment, and let me know."

She nods and hurries down the hall.

"An infectious odor? That can't be good," Blair says.

"No, it can't. Especially if his privates are swollen," I reply, mentally running through a short list of things that could be wrong. "Well, I better get going."

"If you need anything, holler. I have a thirty-minute break before my next patient," she informs.

I tap on the doorframe and head off to find out what's going on with Mr. Foreman. Before I can even find out which room he's in, Kelly practically sprints into the hallway looking a little green.

"Oh my God," she whispers, closing her eyes and taking a few deep breaths.

"What's going on?" I ask, trying to keep my voice down.

She grabs my arm and drags me into the employee break room, her left hand covering her mouth. "That's the grossest thing I've ever seen, and I'm a twenty-year veteran on this job, Gabe."

"Tell me," I insist, giving her my full attention.

"He's severely infected. He's uncircumcised, and it's…Gabe, I've never seen anything like it. The smell. Oh, God," she grumbles, swallowing hard and closing her eyes. "It's horrible."

"What's going on?" Blair asks, joining us in the break room.

I give her a quick rundown and watch the horror cross her face.

She clears her throat and turns to Kelly. "Why don't you take a break? I don't have a patient for a bit yet, so I can assist Dr. Rhodes."

"Oh, I can't ask you to do that," the nurse insists.

"You didn't. I volunteered. I think there's a few of those yummy cupcakes Kyla brought left in the fridge," she adds.

Kelly chuckles. "I'm not sure I'll ever be able to eat food again," she mutters, but heads straight for the fridge to grab a cupcake.

"Well, it looks like it's just you and me," I state, noticing how her eyes darken just a bit.

"Lead the way, Doctor," she replies. If we weren't standing where we are, about to do what we're about to do, I might get a little turned on by her teasing, yet professional manner.

It's sexy as fuck.

I knock on the door and step aside, allowing Blair to enter first. As soon as I breach the threshold, the odor hits me, but I school my features and carefully breathe through my mouth as I close the door. "Good afternoon, Harold. How are you today?"

"Well, not bad, Doc, but I got a bit of a situation."

I take a seat on the stool and turn to face the old man. He just celebrated his ninetieth birthday a few months back, and until today, we rarely see him in the clinic. Harold's always been fairly healthy, with very few underlying medical issues, all things considered. He contributes his exemplary health to bacon and beer, and not the light stuff either. Harold drinks Pabst Blue Ribbon, two every night with dinner.

"Harold, this is Dr. O'Connor. She's going to assist me today while Kelly takes a quick break. What's been going on?" I ask, even though I'm pretty certain I already know.

"Well, for the last few weeks, my Johnson has been a little sore. Then, it started to swell up, and now it's oozing."

I keep my eyes focused on the old man in front of me and not on the woman I can sense at my side. "Okay, well, let's take a look, shall we?"

As soon as he opens his gown, I have to force myself not to react. "Have you been cleaning around the head of your penis, like instructed?"

"Of course, Doc. I've been taking care of myself since I was fourteen," the old man quips.

"I'm sure you have. Unfortunately, you have a pretty severe infection beneath the foreskin. Have you had difficulty urinating?"

The old man sighs. "I haven't peed right since the seventies, boy. When you get old, your whole body changes."

I give him a quick smile. "I'm sure you're right. What we're going to do today is get this cleaned up a little. I'm going to prescribe some strong antibiotics and some painkillers to help alleviate the discomfort."

"I have all the painkiller I need," Harold retorts, giving me a knowing grin.

"I'm sure, but PBR isn't good on your bladder or kidneys," I reply, as Blair gets some supplies out of the cabinet.

"PBR has been keeping me alive for the last decade."

I hear Blair giggle as she sets what I need on the tray and slips on a pair of gloves. I don't even have to direct her. She jumps in and starts to clean the infected area.

"You're the first woman to see me naked in twenty-two years, missy. Well, besides the nurse."

Blair doesn't reply, just winks at the ninety-year-old patient and gets him all cleaned up. "I put some antibacterial ointment on there, and we'll send you home with some. Put it on the infected area three times a day," she informs, handing over the small tube of ointment.

"Will do, missy. You married?"

I hear Blair choke on air. "No, sir."

"Huh," Harold replies, leaning back a little. "You know, if I was a little younger, I might have to court you."

Blair looks up at me, her eyes sparkling like emeralds. "I'm flattered."

Harold just shakes his head. "But since I'm old enough to be your grandpa, I'd like to recommend the good doctor here. He's smart, funny, and I've heard the ladies in the coffee klatch group talking about how good looking he is. He's a catch."

Blair chuckles and squeezes Harold's bicep. "I'll keep that in mind. Now, I'll leave you in the good doctor's hands. See you around, Harold."

"You bet you will, missy," he replies, watching her walk out the door. "What'd you say her name was?"

"Blair O'Connor," I answer, smiling at the man who seems as bewitched with Blair as I am.

"Related to Dr. O'Connor?" he asks, meeting my gaze, but I can tell he already knows the answer.

"His daughter."

He slowly nods. "I remember her now. They left town when the affair became public."

"They did," I confirm.

He shakes his head and reaches for his red and white checkered flannel shirt. He wears them year-round, despite the temperature. "I'm glad she's back. How is Doc?"

"He's slowly getting better. Just started his cardiac therapy," I reply, "and I don't think she's staying. She works in a practice in Illinois."

"Illinois, huh?" he asks, slowly getting off the table, not caring his swollen and infected penis is on full display. "Not a fan of that Chicago. Too many people. I prefer a smaller pace, like Pine Village."

"You and me both, Harold. I'm going to leave you to finish getting dressed. Head over to the pharmacy and pick up the antibiotics and the pain relievers. Take them both, preferably with food and without PBR."

"You're no fun," the old man grumbles, reaching for a pair of tighty-whities.

"Let us know if it doesn't get any better in a few days or if it feels worse," I inform him before reaching for the doorknob.

"Will do, Doc. Take care of that pretty youngen', huh? Maybe you can convince her to stay."

And with that, I carefully open the door and slip out, leaving Harold to get dressed. Kelly is in the hallway, waiting.

"Did Blair fill you in on what I want sent to the pharmacy?"

She nods. "She did, and I thanked her profusely for taking one for the team and going in there with you. I definitely owe her lunch soon."

I give her a small smile, switching out Harold's chart for the one she's holding. When Makenzie steps out of the next room, I ask, "Who's on deck?"

"Dylan Jordan," Makenzie says, handing over his chart.

"He seventeen?" I ask, opening the chart to find his age.

"Just turned eighteen yesterday. When his mom called, she said he was insisting he see you, since you're his doctor."

"Okay," I reply, looking over her notes. "His ear is hurting."

"That's what he said," she states, skepticism written all over her face. "He has no fever, and all of his vitals appear normal."

I nod and head for the room across the hall. After a quick knock, I step inside the exam room. "Hey, Dylan. How's it going?" The teenager looks visibly nervous, which puts me on high alert. However, I don't let it show, just casually take a seat on the stool and keep my facial features open and friendly.

"Hey, Dr. Rhodes," he replies, dropping his gaze down to his feet. "It's going."

"That's good. Nurse Kelly said your ear is bothering you?" I ask, propping my foot on the bottom rung of the stool.

"Well, actually," he mutters, still staring at his feet like they're the most interesting shoes in the world. "My ear is fine."

"Okay. Why don't you tell me what brought you here today."

He finally looks up, his eyes laced with panic. "I've been dating Cece Jones, and well, last night, we, uh, had sex," he mumbles. "It was my first time."

I nod. "Did you use protection?"

He replies right away, "Yes. I made sure we used a condom, but then afterward, things were...itchy."

"Okay."

"It's all red and kinda swollen too," he adds, again averting his gaze, no doubt out of embarrassment.

"Does anything else itch or are you swollen only on your penis?"

He nods. "Only there."

"Sounds like you have a latex allergy, my friend."

His eyes go wide. "Does this mean I can't have sex?"

I can't help but smile as I stand up. "No, they make non-latex condoms. They're a bit more expensive, but you should be able to get them at the pharmacy."

"No way am I getting condoms from the pharmacy," he replies, adamantly shaking his head. "I drove three towns over to get those so no one saw me."

"Well, if you go to a large pharmacy or super center, like Walmart or Target, you should be able to find some. Why don't we check you out to make sure it's just a minor allergy, okay?"

He sighs. "So, I have to take off my pants?"

"Unless you know of another way for me to examine the affected area without removing them," I quip.

This time, his sigh is loud and dramatic. He carefully gets up off the table and removes his pants. I can't help but realize this is the second penis I've had to examine in the last thirty minutes. When I thought about becoming a doctor, I didn't exactly think about this being one of the duties.

"Okay, Dylan you can put your pants back on," I tell him, once I've completed the exam. "The good news is it's mild. I'm not going to prescribe you anything. You just need to go to the pharmacy and get an antihistamine, like Benadryl. It's over the counter and doesn't cost too much. Take it as directed for a few days, and it should help clear up the redness and itchiness."

Once his pants are secured around his waist, he nods, but I can tell there's more on his mind.

"Anything else?" I ask, giving him a chance to talk.

He looks up and takes a deep breath. "Do you have to tell my mom?"

"No," I reply evenly. "In the state of Wisconsin, once you turn eighteen, you don't need parental consent to treat, even though you're on their insurance."

He visibly relaxes. "Okay. Good. I just, I mean I know sex isn't the end of the world and everyone does it, but I didn't want to have that conversation with her, you know?"

I can't help but smile, recalling exactly how uncomfortable those talks can be for teenagers and their parents. "I understand. If you don't feel comfortable talking to your mom, perhaps your dad."

He nods. "Yeah, I usually go to him for the guy questions, but he was sleeping last night when I got home and then already gone to work this morning. I didn't want to call him. This doesn't exactly seem like the kind of conversation you can have over the phone."

"I get it."

"What should I tell my mom?"

I take a seat on the stool. "I can't tell you what to do, but I think you should come clean to them. Latex is a pretty common item, so the chances of you coming in contact with it again at some point are good. Just be open and honest."

He nods. "Okay. Thanks, Dr. Rhodes."

"No problem, Dylan," I reply, standing up. "If it clears up, no need to see you for a follow-up, but after forty-eight hours, if it's not any better, call us. Or if you think it's getting worse. If we're not open, you should head to Hudson to be seen in their ER."

He groans. "Let's hope that's not an issue."

Chuckling, I reach over and squeeze his shoulder. "Let's hope. Stop up at the front counter to check out."

"Thank you, Doc."

"You're welcome," I reply, leading Dylan out into the hallway and watching him head for the front counter.

"Everything okay?"

I turn to find Blair standing behind me, her perfectly kissable lips ripe for the taking. I refrain though, considering we're at work. "Yep. Just another day in the life of a doctor," I banter, earning a big smile.

"Some days are definitely more interesting than others."

"You've got that right."

CHAPTER
fifteen

Blair

By Saturday, I'm ready to relax and unwind with friends.

I haven't been able to steal anything more than a few kisses behind closed doors while at the clinic with Gabe, thanks to a few patients he's been dealing with at night at the hospital, so I have high hopes for this evening after the party, and if the dirty text message I received earlier is any indication, we're definitely on the same page.

I pull into my childhood friend's parents' driveway and park in the grass beside the other vehicles. Grabbing the small gift bag in the back seat, I climb from the car and follow the music to the backyard.

"There she is!" Hallie hollers, her eyes a little glassy, as she throws her arms around my shoulders and gives me a hug.

I glance over to where Ellie and the others sit, already reading their expressions.

Curtis didn't show up.

"Sorry I'm a little late. Aggie called over video chat, and it took forever to get her off the phone," I state.

She gives me a lopsided smile, one laced with a bit of intoxication. "She's such a sweetie," she gushes, bringing whatever fruity drink concoction she's drinking to her lips. "Go! Put on your suit. We're getting in the hot tub now that you're here," she demands, turning and strutting over to where the rest of our friends sit.

I take in the small group. Ellie's here, as well as TD, Ava, and Logan. I can't help but notice the way Logan's eyes watch the sway of Hallie's hips as she walks his way, but before his gaze lingers too long, it drops down to the beer in his hand.

Interesting...

"Welcome," Hallie's mom, Debbie, says, coming over to greet me. She wraps her petite arms around my shoulders and pulls me into a hug. The gesture instantly makes me miss my mom, who I've talked to several times since I arrived back in Pine Village but haven't been able to see since she visited me in Chicago earlier this spring.

"Thank you for inviting me."

"It wouldn't be Hallie's birthday celebration without you," she replies, giving me that familiar, warm smile I've come to expect from her. "There's plenty of snacks over on the table and drinks in the cooler. I think the kids are all getting ready to get in the hot tub." She playfully rolls her eyes. "It's eighty-three degrees out here."

Chuckling, I pat the bag under my arm. "I was told to bring a suit."

"You can change in the bathroom downstairs, or if that's occupied, just run up and use Hallie's old room."

"Thank you, Mrs. Rhodes."

"Debbie or Deb," she replies, giving me a teasing glare mom-look.

Smiling, I head for the house, passing the group at the table as I go. "Where's your suit?" Hallie asks loudly.

I hold up the bag. "I'm running in to change."

"Hurry up! We're getting in," she declares as she stands, stripping off a tank top and exposing her bright red bikini top.

I don't miss the way Logan's eyes practically bug out of his head either. "I'll be right out," I state as the others start to strip down to their suits.

When I step inside the familiar house, I find Hallie's dad, Roger, standing at the counter. "Good afternoon, Blair. Good to see you," he greets.

"Hi, Mr. Rhodes. I just came in to change into my bathing suit."

"I think the hall bathroom is in use. You're welcome to run upstairs," he says, pressing fresh ground patties in a burger press.

"Thank you," I say, turning and heading for the stairs in the hallway.

I move up to the second floor and easily find Hallie's old room. It's the first door on the right. After closing and locking the door, I slip out of my shorts and top and grab the little pink bikini. It's one I bought last summer, but have never had the chance to wear.

As I'm slipping it on, images of Gabe filter through my mind. I can't help but wonder if he'll like the suit, even though I'm pretty sure he will. It covers all the necessary parts but doesn't leave much to the imagination. It's a halter-style top, with a keyhole between my breasts. The bottoms cover my ass—a necessity—and has the same keyhole openings on the sides at the hips. It's pretty, yet sexy, and I secretly can't wait to see his reaction.

When I'm ready, I stuff my clothes in my bag and open the door. As soon as I do, a large figure pushes through the doorway. Arms wrap around my waist, and big hands grip my ass. His scent immediately infiltrates my senses, causing my core to flood with wetness and my nipples to pebble.

"Holy fuck," Gabe mutters, quietly closing the door behind him without removing his other hand.

"Well, hello to you too," I tease.

"I've been thinking about you all damn day in a bikini, but this is...wow. You're a vision. A fucking wet dream come to life," he mumbles before claiming my mouth in a passionate kiss.

My fingers instantly slide into his dark hair, curling in the soft locks and giving them a slight tug. The result is a deep groan bordering on painful, but I'm certain it's not from the actual hair pulling. It's from discomfort in his groin, because that erection, it's large and hard and plastered against my stomach proudly.

"I'm not going to be able to go downstairs for a while," he mumbles against my lips, shifting his hips and grinding his cock against me.

"Too bad we didn't have a few extra minutes up here. I could...*help* with your problem."

Again, he groans. This one as distressed as the last. "Fuck, now all I want is for you to drop to your knees. I'm going to be stuck up here for hours. I should just leave."

"And miss soaking in the hot tub?" I tease.

"I'll never make it out of there alive, Blair. I'm going to be so painfully hard; I won't be able to get out ever. I'm going to die in the hot tub with an erection."

I can't help but chuckle at his dramatics. "Poor baby," I coo, sliding my fingers down his bare chest. "You know, I'm not doing anything later either. I could come home with you. You know, *if* you're still requiring assistance."

His hands flex around my hips, his fingers digging into my flesh. "Oh, I'm definitely going to be in need of assistance later. Probably a *lot* of assistance."

With a quick smile, I go up on my tiptoes and kiss his lips in a chaste kiss. "Good. I have an overnight bag packed in my car. Now, I better get downstairs before your mom or dad come looking." With a quick glance down at his groin, I add, "I'll give you a few minutes to wrestle that into submission."

His eyes narrow. "The only wrestling it wants to do is with you."

"Oh, and that will most definitely happen." Again, I kiss his lips. "Later."

The last thing I hear is his loud sigh as I slip out of Hallie's old bedroom and head back downstairs, a wide smile on my face the entire time. Not because I've left him with a rather large problem to deal with, but because in just a few hours, I'll be back at Gabe's house, probably naked in his bed.

I'm rather excited about that.

"Do you remember when Aiden Norris put laxatives in Mr. Kaufmann's coffee? I've never seen a man forty-pounds overweight run so fast for the shitter in my life," TD says with a snicker from the opposite side of the hot tub.

I can't help but pause as everyone else laughs at the recollection. No matter how deep I dig, I come up short. I recall Mr. Kaufmann, the grumpy history teacher, but I don't recall that particular memory. There's only one reason I wouldn't remember something that monumental happening in high school.

It happened our senior year when I was gone.

"I remember vividly, and this is exactly why I don't use any cup that doesn't have a lid," Ava proclaims. "No way do I want any of my students slipping something in my drink."

"Or when Mr. Hamilton grabbed Clyde Hooper by the ear and dragged him all the way through the school to the office?" TD chimes in.

"I'm surprised he graduated. That kid did everything he could to push Hamilton's buttons. I remember when he put an old jockstrap in the women's locker room and told everyone it was Hamilton's," Logan states before adding, "It was a size youth small."

Everyone laughs. As if sensing my confusion, Hallie says with a slightly drunk sheepish grin, "Sorry, Blair. It all happened senior year."

I nod, taking a drink of my margarita. We're on round two of slowly boiling ourselves in the hot tub like a crawfish boil, but no one seems to mind anymore. No one is drunk—well, except maybe the birthday girl, who still hasn't heard one word from her so-called boyfriend—and we've been making sure we're drinking plenty of water in between alcoholic ones.

Except the guys. TD and Logan both stopped drinking beer after dinner, and I'm certain Gabe has too. He's been in the house for the last half hour, helping his parents clean up dishes and whatnot from the party, leaving me and my five friends in the hot tub.

As if sensing he's on my mind, Gabe appears from the house, carrying a bottle of water. "Gabriel! Get in here!" Hallie bellows, splashing water over the side as she turns to get his attention.

Despite the fact he has yet to get in the hot tub, Gabe is still wearing his swim trunks, but he slipped a well-worn T-shirt on at some point. He heads for an Adirondack chair sitting near where the hot tub is. "I think I'm okay here," he states, taking a seat and stretching his long legs out in front of him.

She stands up, swaying just a bit and causing Logan to reach out and grab her hips to help steady her. "Nope. It's my birthday. I demand you get in here," Hallie declares, ignoring the fact Logan's hands are still wrapped around her.

Her brother sighs and shakes his head. "You're not going to let this go, are you?"

"Nope," she replies, popping the P. She slowly turns to sit back down. Logan doesn't drop his hands until she's situated. "I think there's room beside Blair," she adds in a singsong voice.

I feel warmth spread up my neck, and unfortunately, it has nothing to do with the heat of the water. Ellie and Ava both look my way, a knowing smirk laced on both of their faces. I try to hide behind my now-empty margarita glass, but it's no use. I'm sure they both read me like a book.

A smutty, naughty romance book.

Ava slides away from me, making space for Gabe to sit. He swings his legs over the side and carefully slips down into the water.

His entire left side brushes against me, sending electricity shooting through my body and striking me squarely between the legs.

"Did your class ever do anything to Hamilton? The man had to have been teaching PE for two decades by that point," TD asks Gabe.

The man directly to my right casually throws his arm over the back of the hot tub, which just so happens to be at my neck. He doesn't wrap it around my shoulders, but rests it there, his skin touching mine. It takes every ounce of control I have not to lean into his side, to snuggle in, just the way I do when we're lying in bed together.

"Of course, we did. Hamilton was an easy target with those damn knee-high tube socks. One time, a classmate of mine found a fresh pair in his desk drawer when he went to retrieve a football and squirted some Preparation H down in the toes," Gabe says, smiling as he recounts the memory.

"What happened?" Ellie asks.

"He had the sophomores last period, and they said he came out of his office, pulling a face and wiggling his toes. When he realized something was in his socks, he made them all run laps around the gym."

I can picture it in my head, even though I haven't seen Mr. Hamilton in years. He had a horrible comb-over back when I was in school, and always wore shorts a bit too short and tube socks, like he fell out of an episode of *Happy Days*.

"Whatever happened to him?" I ask, referring to the old teacher.

TD's the first one to reply, "He passed away last year."

"Oh," I whisper. "Did he ever marry?" I remember hearing about how he never found his Mrs. Right, as he referred to her.

"Never," Hallie replies.

That one word seems to hang heavily over the group. I can't help but think about the fact we're all in our thirties, and there are two failed marriages between the seven of us. Hell, there aren't even any 'couples' in the group if you take Hallie out of the mix, considering I'm uncertain of the state of her relationship with Curtis at this point.

The mood returns to the light banter it had before, and an hour later, we all finally decide to call it a night.

"I'll take the ladies home, since everyone's been drinking," TD offers, always the voice of reason.

"I'll take Hallie and Blair home, since they're not too far from me," Logan announces after returning from the house to change back into dry clothes.

I risk a panicked glance over to where Gabe stands, slipping his T-shirt on. "I can run Blair home," he says, and I want to cringe. I can tell the moment his words register.

"Don't Blair and Hallie live next door to each other?" Ellie asks, doing everything she can to hide her smirk.

"Blair's going home with Gabe," Hallie announces. "They're going to have more sex, but we don't talk about that. Right, Blair?" she asks, her glassy eyes full of mischief.

"Traitor," I mutter as all eyes turn my way.

"You two are seeing each other?" Ava asks with a big grin.

"We-well," I stammer, my mouth opening but nothing else comes out.

Of course, my best friend takes it as an opportunity to talk for me. "They are, but they're keeping it on the DL, since *someone* says she's returning to Chicago at the end of the year. So, basically, they're just doing the nasty and hanging out." She turns and meets my gaze. "Again, we're not talking about that," she insists with a shiver.

"Okay, so Gabe is taking Blair...home. Ava lives near Ellie, so I'll take them," TD interjects, turning the spotlight away from me.

Thankfully.

"Actually, I'm okay to drive. I stopped a while ago, and even then, I only had two. No offense, TD, but the last thing I need is for my neighbors to see you bringing me home after nine o'clock. They'll either assume I was arrested or we're secretly dating," Ava states, already changed into her street clothes.

"All right, so that leaves Ellie with me," TD announces casually, but I can't help but notice the way his dark eyes automatically seek her out and brighten a little when he sees her.

"Give me five minutes to change into my dry shorts and say goodbye to my mom and dad, and we can head out," Gabe says before he goes into the house to put his shorts back on.

I step over to where Logan stands. "Thank you for taking her home."

He shrugs, shoving his hands in his pockets. "No problem. I'd happily give you a ride too, but it sounds like you're covered," he replies, giving me a big smile. The girls went crazy for Logan in school, and I can see not a lot has changed since. He definitely matured into a hot guy. I'm not interested or attracted in that way, but I can appreciate his dark hair, even darker eyes, and scruffy jaw. Toss that in with a smile that melts glaciers in Antarctica and a body built from manual labor, Logan Johnson is definitely a sight to behold.

"If she gets home and isn't feeling well, will you call me?" I ask. Not that Hallie is trashed, but she's been drinking all night in the sun and heat. We made her drink bottled water throughout, but still, I'm concerned.

He meets my gaze, those black eyes locked on mine. "I won't leave her alone if she's not well, Blair."

I nod. "Thank you," I offer, even though he didn't really answer my question. He didn't say he'd call. He said he wouldn't leave her alone.

Gabe returns, his parents right behind him. They hand over a bag of what I'm assuming is leftovers to Hallie—who is still sporting her bright red bikini, by the way. Once they give her hugs and make sure Logan is okay to take her home, Debbie makes her way over to where I stand.

"Blair, always good to see you, dear," she says, holding out a bag. "I went ahead and put together a small bag of leftovers for you."

"Oh, thank you," I state, taking the bag.

"Please feel free to join us anytime. Even if Hallie isn't here, you're always welcome," she adds, pulling me into a quick hug. "And don't worry about your car. It's safe here until you pick it up tomorrow."

"Thank you," I reply, returning the hug.

"Ready?" Gabe asks, stepping up behind me and placing a hand at my lower back as he takes the leftovers from me.

I nod, not speaking for fear Debbie will be able to hear the pitch change in my voice caused by his touch.

"You two be careful. And have a good evening," she says. If I'm not mistaken, there's a hint of a knowing grin on her face. I turn to the side, praying she can't see the blush on my face.

"Night, Mom," he says, applying gentle pressure to my back and guiding me to the front of the house. No one says a word as I quickly grab the small overnight bag I packed from the back seat of my car.

Our friends all follow suit and wave goodbye as they split off into pairs. Well, everyone but Ava, who heads home by herself.

"Ready?" he asks when we reach his truck, his eyes burning dark with desire and anticipation.

My thighs clench, much like they have the entire evening. I wonder if my muscles will be sore tomorrow. In the good way, of course.

One could only hope.

CHAPTER sixteen

GABE

My truck cab is buzzing. There's an electricity filling the space, hanging in the air like a thick fog. My cock is hard, my balls ache. I'm so keyed up, I can't be certain I won't jump her like an animal the moment I park my truck.

Taking a few deep, calming breaths when we reach a stoplight, I make the grave mistake of looking to where Blair sits in the passenger seat. She's so fucking beautiful, with her hair pulled up high on her head, the tendrils that escaped captivity in back still wet from the water. I know without a shadow of a doubt, I'm in big trouble where she's concerned.

"Light's green." Her words and the humor dancing in her eyes slice through my sex-laced brain.

I stomp on the gas a little too hard, determined to get home as quick as possible. I roll at least one stop sign and take the curve at the edge of town faster than I normally would, but within minutes, I'm pulling into my driveway.

Pressing the button for the garage door, I only pause long enough for my truck to clear the door, and then I pull in. I hear the click of the seat belt before I've even stopped moving, and as soon as I press the brake and slide the gear into park, Blair moves. She lifts the console and climbs onto my lap, her mouth hot and eager as it presses against mine.

Blindly, I reach up and press the button to lower the garage door and then the button to shut off the truck. Only then do I take what I crave. My hands grab her ass as she rocks her hips against my swollen cock. Even through the layers of material, I can feel how hot and wet she is.

"Pants. Off."

Without removing my lips from hers, I chuckle and whisper, "You're sitting on my lap."

Blair pauses and pulls back, her gaze meeting mine. "Good point," she pants, sucking in deep gulps of air.

When she carefully climbs off my lap, I almost reach for her to pull her back against me, but I'm suddenly too transfixed on watching her shimmy out of her shorts. It's a little comical to see, considering she's crammed in the cab of a truck, but somehow, she's able to rid herself of every scrap of clothing she was wearing in a matter of seconds.

She meets my wide eyes and smiles. "You're still wearing your clothes."

Clearing my throat, I tell her, "I was too busy watching the show."

Deft fingers move to the fly of my shorts and quickly tug the zipper down before moving to the button. I lift my hips as she helps remove my shorts, her eyes locking on my cock. "I thought I'd save time and leave them off," I state, referring to my lack of underwear.

"Brilliant," she declares before scooting closer.

Just as I lift my T-shirt over my head, she drops and licks my cock from root to tip. "Fuck, Blair," I mutter, my brain effectively shutting down. I've always prided myself on being a smart man. Valedictorian when I graduated high school and top five percent of my class through college and med school. But seeing this woman naked, and feeling her warm mouth wrap around my cock, is enough to ensure I forget everything I've ever learned throughout my entire life.

She works me over hard, taking almost every inch of my dick like she was made to do it. I gently grab the back of her neck and hold on. I want to close my eyes, to let the euphoric sensations wash through me, but I also don't want to miss one single second of watching her mouth.

When she reaches down and cups my balls in her soft hand, I almost lose it completely on the spot. "Blair," I bite out through gritted teeth, trying to keep myself from coming. When she doesn't respond, I try again. "Blair. Stop. I'm getting close."

But she doesn't stop. Or slow down. She bears down on my cock, taking it deep into her throat and swallowing. The ripples around the head are too much to take. Thinking about her all night on her knees, seeing her in that sexy as fuck bikini, and now, watching her give me a blow job is more than I can handle.

"Blair," I groan, trying to warn her of what's to come, but unable to get the words out. I come hard, finally closing my eyes as hot cum shoots into her mouth. Wave after wave of pleasure races through me, my body moving completely on its own. When the spasms finally subside, my head falls back against the headrest, my body too spent to hold it up at this point. "Jesus," I mutter.

"Thank you, but you can just call me Blair," she says, releasing my cock with an audible pop.

I crack open a single eye and smile down at her. Strands of hair escape the elastic confines, her lips are swollen and pink, and her nipples are hard, making my mouth water. She looks positively delicious.

And I'm suddenly fucking starving.

"Get into the back seat," I demand, reaching for the door handle and stepping out, kicking my shorts off my ankles before I trip. My legs are a little wobbly, but my determination to get my mouth on her as quickly as possible overrides my need to rest.

She climbs over the seat as I open the back door and point. She sits in front of me and lies back. I gently take her hips in my hands and pull her toward me, her ass reaching the edge of the seat. Her legs fall open, her pussy wet and inviting. Sliding my hands beneath her, I lift her up at the same time I lower my mouth and swipe my tongue across her clit.

Her moan fills the space like the sweetest song I've ever heard and spurs me on. My tongue glides across her pussy, swirling around her entrance before plunging inside. Her scent tickles my nose, her taste as sweet as sin against my lips. She's so intoxicating. I need more.

I devour her. That's the only way to describe it. Like a man possessed, I eat her pussy until she's rocking and gyrating against my face, her own orgasm near. Her thighs widen, giving me complete access to her most intimate areas.

Keeping my lips locked on her clit, I slide one hand around and push two fingers into her wet pussy. Instantly, I feel it contract around me. "I need you to come, Blair."

She whimpers at my demand, her internal muscles clamping down on my fingers. As if on cue, she erupts, detonating like a beautiful bomb and coming on my face and hand. My name flies from her lips as she squeezes her thighs around my head, and I swear, it makes me feel better than the orgasm I had myself not ten minutes ago.

The moment she starts to come down from her high, I take her in my arms and pull her against my chest. Her legs wrap around my waist as I lift, carrying her from the truck and shutting the door. Our mouths fuse together, her scent and taste still lingering on my tongue, but she doesn't seem to mind.

I head straight for the house, not stopping until I reach it and enter the code to unlock the door. Thank God we're on my property and no one can see us. Not that I'd care much right now anyway. My cock has had time to recover, and I'm a determined man. I need her in my bed beneath me.

Now.

I march straight through the house, only stopping to make sure the door is locked behind me. I can feel the goosebumps along her skin as the cool air hits our bare skin, sending a fresh wave of lust bolting through my veins. Instead of heading upstairs, the way I intended, my legs carry us to the couch.

To the scene of our first time together.

Laying her down on the couch, I press her into the cushions, framing her body with my own, my mouth never once releasing its hold on hers. She's fucking phenomenal. Incredible. Breathtaking. Everything I didn't even realize I was missing from life, but suddenly want for as long as I'm on this earth.

Which is a problem.

Because she's not staying.

"What's wrong?" she whispers against my lips, her hands gliding up my bare back.

"Hmm?"

"You sighed."

I did?

"Nothing, just enjoying the hell out of having you in my arms," I reply. It's not wrong, but it's also not the truth. Not the whole truth, anyway.

Blair grins against my lips. "Well, perfect, because I happen to like being here." Her delicate hands move down to grip my ass. "Now, show me."

I lather up my jaw and neck and turn on the warm water. Just as I reach for my razor, the bathroom door creeps open and there stands the most gorgeous woman. "Good morning," she says softly, the faintest blush coloring her neck and cheeks as she stands there in one of the T-shirts she stole from my drawer.

"Morning," I reply, the razor in my hand stopping halfway to my neck.

Her eyes take a slow, appreciative perusal of my body, from my bare chest with water droplets still dotting my skin to the gray towel tied loosely around my hips. When her eyes finally return to mine, gone is the sleepiness they held just moments ago, and in its place is a dark desire that makes my dick twitch.

Blair steps inside the bathroom and heads my way. She slips the too-big T-shirt over her head, revealing her naked body, and moves between the sink and my body, wiggling her ass until she's seated directly in front of me. She takes the razor from my hand, but my eyes are locked on her chest. It takes every ounce of restraint I possess not to dip down and suck one of those pebbled nipples in my mouth.

"So," she starts, bringing the razor to my jaw and slowly—and very carefully—gliding it across my skin, "What are your plans for today?"

"You mean later, right? Because I'm pretty sure I'm going to stay right here until you're finished and then take you into the shower to help wash you from head to toe," I quip, even though I'm not joking. Not even a little.

The corner of her mouth turns up, but she doesn't divert her gaze from my face. In fact, the tip of her tongue snakes out just a bit as she concentrates on clearing the stubble from my skin. I can't help but try to recall a single time in my life I've experienced something as intimate as this. Even when I was married, everything was always about Amara and intimacy wasn't one of her strong suits. There's no way she would have sat on the counter and shaved my face for me.

Just another reason why Blair is different.

"I'm taking Aggie for a bike ride through the park. Care to join us?"

"What if I don't have a bike?"

She finally meets my gaze. "The mountain bike hanging in your garage won't do?"

I flash her a full-watt smile. "Oh, that one. Yes, it will probably do."

She shakes her head and goes back to her task, but there's no missing the slight upturn to her lips. "I told her I'd pick her up at three."

"Do you have a bike?" I ask without moving my jaw.

"I'm borrowing Hallie's." She meets my gaze before adding, "I seem to be doing that a lot lately."

"What are best friends for?"

Now it's her turn to throw me a big smile. "Exactly. Now, hold still before I accidentally cut you."

"Yes, ma'am," I reply, holding statue-still while she shaves my face.

Just when I think she's finished, she reaches for the can of shaving cream, shaking it and squirting a hearty amount in her palm. She lathers the white foam between both of her hands and then smears it all over my jaw, moving up and covering my cheeks and nose. My mouth opens to question her when her hands drop to my chest.

A loud rumble erupts from my gut as she wipes the foam all over my pecs, swirling it around my nipples and dragging it through the hair running from my belly button down to my towel. With a quick flick of her wrist, she releases the towel, sending it to the floor. "Why, Miss O'Connor, are you wasting my shaving cream again?"

She gives me a Cheshire cat smile. "Maybe."

I slide my fingers into her hair as my mouth fuses with hers. Our bodies press together, the shaving cream cool and wet between us. She shifts her hips, locking her ankles behind me. The movement lines us up perfectly, and all I have to do is push forward.

So I do.

Slowly filling her, I realize she's become a necessity in my life. Like air, I need her. In such a short amount of time, I've fallen for her.

Hard. And the thought of having to let her go in just a few short months is gut-wrenching.

So I don't think about it.

Not right now.

In this moment, I'll focus on the woman in my arms.

Once I'm completely seated inside her, I reach for the can and give it a shake before squirting a little in my hand. Then, I use it to cover her nipples, lightly pinching and massaging them as I go. Blair arches her back and squeezes my cock from the inside. It's fucking glorious.

"Now look who's wasting it," she mutters, the most beautiful smile curling her lips heavenward.

I pull out until just the head is wrapped in her heat, and then thrust back inside.

"Gabe," she moans, rolling her hips and taking me deeper.

Ignoring the feeling swelling in my chest, I cup her jaw, the white mess smearing all over the place, and exhale deeply. "My God, you feel so good," I whisper, letting my hips do the talking.

We move in unison, as if we've been doing this together forever, not just a few weeks. Her pussy grips me, refusing to let go, and that's okay. I don't want it to. I never want it to.

When her orgasm starts, she grips ahold of my hips and meets my thrusts. Her cries of pleasure fill the room and my soul, rendering me speechless. My body takes complete control, trying to draw out her release before finally tripping my own.

I suck greedy breaths of oxygen into my lungs as my body shakes and convulses, my cock still moving within her. Leaning forward, I rest my forehead against hers, not caring we're both covered in melting shaving cream, and run my hands up her back.

"I'm definitely going to need a shower now," she whispers.

"That's perfect," I mutter, sliding my lips across her skin. "Not only do I need one myself, but I happen to have one behind me."

She glances up and meets my gaze, a slight smile on her lips. "Should we bring the shaving cream?"

"Well, I do have a spare can in the closet. I picked one up, just in case you couldn't help yourself," I tease, running my finger down her cheek and tapping some of the white foam onto the tip of her nose.

She brings her hand up between us and wipes it across my chin. "This was not my fault," she says, unable to hide the smile on her face.

"No? I think you were the one who wiped it on my chest first."

She grins the most glorious, wicked grin. "Maybe I was going to shave your chest," she states, jutting her chin out in an attempt to show defiance.

"Yeah? You want me to shave my chest?" I ask, reaching for the discarded razor.

"No," she hollers, throwing her arms around my shoulders and pressing her chest to mine. "Please don't. I was kidding. I like your hair." She runs her hands down my chest, tangling her fingertips in my hair.

I toss the razor aside, lift her up, and carry her toward the shower. "Come on, Dr. O'Connor. I think we could both use a good cleaning."

CHAPTER
seventeen

Blair

It's hard to believe I've been back in Pine Village for three months now. To be honest, I've enjoyed it. And I'm not just talking about spending time with Gabe. It's everything. It's spending time living next to Hallie and catching up with her every chance we get. Even work is going well, despite the fact I'm spending my days at my dad's clinic. I find I really enjoy the slower pace of rural medicine. Sure, I miss the hectic lifestyle of a suburb clinic, but this is really nice too.

And yes, there's Gabe.

We've grown incredibly close over the last few months, despite the fact I'm leaving. In fact, with each passing day, I start to question whether or not I'll actually be able to go. Every time I think about it, my heart starts to beat wildly and it's harder to breathe. Just knowing I'll be giving up lazy nights with dinner and snuggling at his place or stealing kisses in one of our offices between seeing patients has my anxiety returning. I haven't had issues with it since I was a teenager, moving away from everything and everyone I knew and loved because of a cheating father.

I slip off my lab coat and hang it on the back of my office door. I have plans tonight with Hallie, much to Gabe's dismay. In fact, he spent the last half of our workday convincing me to come over afterward. I do admit, it's tempting, and most likely going to happen.

"Blair."

I look up and find Patience, my stepmother, standing in the doorway. "Patience," I reply, trying not to show any emotion at her surprise visit.

"I'm sorry to just drop by. I was across the street at the deli grabbing some sandwiches," she says, and it's then I notice she's wringing her hands together nervously.

"Is everything okay?" I find myself asking, worry creeping in. Is Aggie all right? My dad?

That last one caught me off guard.

"Yes, of course," she states quickly, offering me a small smile. "Everything and everyone fine." She clears her throat before continuing, "The reason I stopped by is Aggie, she has this thing at the school on Friday."

"A thing?" I ask, slipping my hands into the pockets of my trousers and rocking back on my heels.

She flashes me another tight smile. "Yes, a thing. It's an open house at her school, and the first family reading night of the year. She's been talking about nothing but since they sent home the information." She looks up and meets my gaze. "Aggie is hoping you'd be her guest."

My heart thunders in my chest. Can she hear how loudly it's pounding?

"I know this may be a bold request, but, well, I find it hard to tell my daughter no," she states with a chuckle before squaring her shoulders. "So, if you'd like to join Aggie and me, the event is from six to eight. We'll get to see her kindergarten classroom, followed by a story in the gym. I think there's even an arts and crafts station that coordinates with the book."

There's an awkward pause, as if she's waiting for me to say something. When I don't, she continues.

"I'd understand if you don't want to go. I'll tell Aggie you're busy or working or something, but," she swallows hard, "she'd really like you to go with her. It would mean so much to her, and," again, she pauses, "I'd like you to go too."

Okay. I wasn't expecting that.

I open my mouth, but nothing comes out. My mind is spinning as I try to make a quick decision. Do I want to go? Yes, I realize instantly. I want to be there for my sister. To see her classroom and spend time with her during a family school event. But can I handle being around Patience at the same time?

I think I can...

For Aggie.

"You don't have to answer right away," Patience insists, after my silence drags on for a few extra seconds. "Maybe just shoot me a text by Thursday? I'll understand if you're not comfortable going, and I'll be sure to make an appropriate excuse on your behalf. I would never try to make you look bad to her. I hope you know that, Blair. She loves you and getting to spend time with you has been the best thing for her. I hope that never ends, even after you return to Illinois."

My throat is so thick, it's hard to swallow, and before I can even think any further, I find myself replying, "Yes, I'd love to go."

She smiles widely, a look of relief written across her face. "I'm glad. Aggie will be thrilled," she says, adjusting her purse on her shoulder. "I should go." Before she turns toward the door, she adds, "Thank you, Blair. Truly. I know we have a long way to go, but I appreciate you doing this for Aggie."

I nod.

"We'll meet you at the front entrance of the school at six, if that works for you."

"It does," I confirm.

She gives me a slight nod before slipping out the door and exiting the clinic. I'm left standing in the middle of my office—my dad's office, really—wondering if I made the right decision. I'm sure I could text Patience and tell her something came up. She's a physician's wife. I'm sure she's used to that happening, but I realize I don't want to.

I really do want to go support Aggie at her school.

Even if Patience is also there.

I sit down at the desk and grab the stack of papers I need to review. Just as I give the first document a once-over, I hear, "Everything all right?"

I look up and smile when I see Gabe standing in the doorway, a concerned look on his face. "Yes," I find myself responding honestly.

He walks in and drops into the chair across from me. "I saw Patience leave, and Stella said she came back to talk to you."

I nod in confirmation. "She wanted to invite me to Aggie's open house and family reading night on Friday."

"Wow, are you going?"

"Yes."

His sexy mouth curls into a grin. "Good. I'm sure you'll have fun."

I'm sure he's right.

He leans forward and drops his voice. "Plans tonight still on with Hallie?"

I chuckle and shake my head at the hopeful look on his face. "Yes."

"Darn," he says before adding, "I was hoping she might have cancelled."

"She did not. We're meeting at Shiner's at six."

"Hmm," he says, kicking an ankle up on his knee and rubbing his chin as in thought. "You know, Logan *has* been wanting to get together for a beer."

I can't help but shake my head. "And you are available tonight."

He grins. "I am."

Standing up, I pull my purse out of the desk drawer. "I'm guessing I'll see you later tonight."

My smile spreads wider.

"Possibly."

His laugh is a deep one.

"You know, if I have a few drinks, I'll probably need a ride home."

His smile matches my own. "By all means, have a few drinks. Let your hair down. Cut loose."

"And you'll be there to take me home, Dr. Rhodes"

"Damn right, I will."

"And Hallie?"

"I'd be happy to make sure my sister gets home safely too."

"You might as well just stay with me. You know, since you're in the neighborhood," I quip, adding a little extra sultry to my statement.

"I think you're right. It would be safer than being out on the roads late at night."

"True. A lot can happen after ten in Pine Village," I tease, mostly because it's complete bullshit. This town is fairly safe, especially since he only lives a short drive past the city limits.

"It most certainly can."

"Whatever do you think we should do while you're staying over?" I ask, fighting hard not to smile.

He just gives me a huge grin. "Oh, Dr. O'Connor, I'm sure I can think of something."

Matching his eager smile, I say, "I'm sure you can, Dr. Rhodes. I'm sure you can."

"Did you tell him you were coming up here tonight?" Hallie asks, looking over my shoulder.

I turn and find Gabe walking in, Logan only a few steps behind him. Shrugging, I reply, "I might have mentioned it."

She rolls her eyes. "Fine, but if you leave me up here to go have s-e-x with my brother, I'm going to be pissed," she counters, flipping her long hair over her shoulder and turning back to the pool table. She walks around, takes aim, and fires, missing by a mile. "I suck."

"That's what she said!" Logan hollers as he steps up to where she stands beside the pool table. "And apparently, you haven't improved your pool game either."

She narrows her eyes at him. "What are you doing here, Johnson?"

He offers her a wide grin. "My friend invited me for a drink. I should have known you and Blair would be here. I was so shocked he actually agreed to meet up, I didn't even take into consideration that his woman may be here."

I hide behind my glass in hopes no one can see the blush on my face.

We've never made any declarations or given our relationship status a title, but our friends have gotten used to seeing us together, even if we've kept the entire situation pretty casual.

"We're just saying hello. Come on, Logan. We'll eat at the bar," Gabe says, coming over to stand next to me. I can feel the heat from his skin and smell the clean, manly soap he uses. It goes straight to my lady parts.

Hallie rolls her eyes dramatically. "We were just getting ready to order food. You might as well come over and join us. It'll save me and Logan from having to deal with the two of you sending sad puppy dog eyes to each other all night."

Gabe laughs, while my mouth drops open. "I don't have sad puppy dog eyes."

"Do too," both Hallie and Logan state at the same time.

"Whatever," I mumble, turning around and heading to our four-seater high-top table.

Gabe and the other two are hot on my heels, taking the remaining empty seats. "What are you having?" Hallie asks, plucking the laminated menu out of the condiment holder in the center.

"Wings and curly fries," I reply automatically, my mouth watering in anticipation.

"Me too," Gabe agrees, along with Logan nodding.

"So I'm going to be the only one not getting wings?" Hallie asks, making a face.

"Yes," Logan counters, taking the menu from her hand and flipping it over. He taps it and says, "Wings."

"I was going to get fish."

Logan just blinks at her. "You don't go to a bar to get fish, Hal."

"Why not?" she argues, straightening her spine.

"Because."

She rolls her eyes once more. "Because," she sasses.

When the waitress comes to the table to refill our drinks, we put in a food order too.

"I'll have six wings in sweet chili sauce and curly fries," I tell the woman I don't recognize.

"Same, but make mine a dozen," Gabe says.

"Dozen Cajun jerk and jalapeno poppers," Logan orders when it's his turn.

Hallie's jaw drops. "Seriously? How can you eat all that spicy food?"

The corner of his mouth turns upward and a devilish smirk spreads across his face. "I like it spicy, Hal."

I swear my friend blushes. Even under the dimmer, neon lights, I can tell his statement affected her. She lifts her chin and turns to the server. "The cod sandwich, please. With tartar sauce and regular fries."

"Any refills?" the woman asks in return.

"Two for us. Boys? What are you drinking?" Hallie asks.

"Just ice water," Gabe replies, followed by a quick, "Coke" from Logan.

When our server walks away, Hallie says, "Not drinking tonight? Are you a lightweight, Johnson?" She smirks in a teasing way.

"Nope, just making sure I can drive anyone home who might need it," he says, clearly eyeing my friend as if she's going to need him to drive her home. Funny, because we actually walked the three blocks to get here so we could drink and not have to worry about getting home.

When I look over at Gabe, my eyebrows arched upward in question, he just shrugs and shakes his head, as if he doesn't know what's going on with them either.

"So what was it we were talking about?" Hallie asks me, ignoring Logan sitting beside her.

I clear my throat and meet her eye.

She seems to understand what I'm referring to. Hallie glances over at Logan and then to her brother and sighs. "It's okay. We can talk about it in front of them."

Nodding, I ask, "Is it over?"

She slurps up the rest of her mixed drink and sets her empty glass down on the table. "Yes. It's over."

"What's over?" Gabe asks curiously.

"Curtis and I are officially done," she confirms.

Ever since Hallie's birthday party two months ago, Curtis has been trying to save their floundering relationship, but Hallie just hasn't been feeling it, especially when he resorted right back to making excuses and missing planned time together. She told me last weekend she realized she wasn't in love with him anymore, despite his attempts to reconnect.

"I'm sorry," I state, even though I truly feel she'll be happier without him.

"Don't be. I came to the conclusion during these last two months that if he really loved me the way he claims he does, he would make some changes in his life so there's a little more room for me in it, but he hasn't. He did well for about three weeks, putting me before work and even talked about the future, but then it just dropped off the moment a big client appeared. My calls went to voice mail and my texts went unacknowledged."

"What do you mean he talked about the future?" Gabe asks as our drinks are delivered.

"Marriage. Babies. He suggested I move there with him and get a teaching job closer." She meets my eyes from across the table. "I don't want to switch schools. I love my preschool here in Pine Village, and when I said that, he got all butt-hurt defensive."

I don't miss the way Logan blanches when Hallie said the word marriage. Nor the way he reaches for his glass of Coke when she adds the word babies. Something is definitely brewing there, and a part of me is really excited to find out what.

"Speaking of marriage," Hallie mutters, dropping her gaze and leaning in. "Logan's former betrothed just walked in."

"Motherfucker," he mumbles with a deep sigh. "How the hell did she know I was here?"

"Well, your truck is parked out front," Gabe quips with a snicker.

"Oh my gosh, look who's here!" Shay bellows from across the bar, making a beeline for our table. "I thought you said you were going home to watch the game," Shay says to Logan, reaching out and placing her hand on his arm.

He gently pulls it away and leans back in his chair. "Did I say watch the game? I meant to say none of your damn business."

Shay just laughs. "So testy." Then, her eyes focus in on Hallie sitting beside him. "Aww, are you two, like, seeing each other?" she asks, her tone slightly mocking.

"Leave us alone, Shay," Logan grumbles, lifting his glass and draining the cola, probably wishing he had ordered something a little stronger at this point.

But she doesn't leave. In fact, the blond viper turns her eyes on my friend. "You should know what you're getting into with this one," she starts, pointing her boney finger at her ex-husband. "He leaves wet towels lying around, and his work boots always pile up by the back door so you're constantly tripping over them. He can't cook to save his life and hates PDA. Isn't that right, Logie?" she coos, reaching out and touching his arm once more.

196

Hallie turns to the man sitting at her side, and the corner of her mouth turns upward just a tick. "Oh, I don't know. He seems fine with PDA now, right, Logie?" Hallie asks, a wicked gleam filling her eyes. Before Logan can respond, she leans over and plants a big kiss on his lips.

A gasp comes from someone, and it takes me a few seconds to realize it was me. I feel like I should look away, but I can't. Instead, I watch as Logan goes from shocked and statue-still to taking control of the kiss in a matter of moments. He lifts his hand, cups her cheek, and coaxes her mouth open with his tongue, all while his ex-wife watches.

Gabe clears his throat, causing his friend to finally pull away from mauling his sister. Hallie seems a little dazed and a lot shocked by the kiss, but recovers quickly as she leans into Logan's chest and snuggles.

Logan smiles innocently at his ex-wife, who is doing her impression of a fish out of water. "No problems with PDA," he confirms to Hallie, his arm casually thrown over her shoulder.

Shay huffs out her annoyance, flips her hair, and storms off.

After a couple of long seconds, I finally say, "Well, that got her to shut up."

Hallie's face burns red as everyone laughs. "I can't believe I did that. I'm sorry," she says, turning to face Logan.

He shrugs and removes his arm, reaching for his empty glass. "No harm, no foul." There's no missing the happiness in his eyes or the slight uptick to the corner of his mouth.

Yes, there's definitely something going on there. I don't know if Hallie's aware, but I think Logan Johnson is interested.

CHAPTER
eighteen

GABE

"So, you kissed my sister."

Logan looks over at me. "Well, I think technically, she kissed me."

I snort and take a drink of my water. Keeping my eyes forward and on Blair and Hallie, who are throwing darts, I ask, "Is there something there?"

Out of my peripheral vision, I see him tense for a moment before relaxing into his chair. "She just got out of a relationship. One she's been in for a few years," he replies.

Of course I notice he didn't really answer my question. Instead of calling him on it, I just agree. "She did." When he doesn't say anything else, I decide to switch gears a little. "You don't seem to date much."

Logan chuckles as he also continues to watch the ladies throw darts. "Same could be said for you," he quips, giving me a look as if daring me to challenge him.

I nod in agreement. "I know."

After a few beats, he adds, "Hard to date when you have a crazy ex-wife who shows up randomly when you're least expecting it."

I can't help but snort out a laugh. "I can't imagine." At least Amara isn't still in town, making my life hell like Shay. There aren't a lot of differences between my ex and his, appearance and personality wise, but at least I'm not stuck seeing her every single day, thanks to her owning half my business.

"How about you? Things seem to be going good with Blair," he says, sipping his soda.

"Yeah," I respond, watching the woman I've fallen for laugh with my sister across the room.

"She's still leaving soon," he deduces, his voice low and laced with sadness on my behalf.

My lack of reply is answer enough.

"Does she know when?"

Shaking my head, I answer, "Not yet. The cardiologist overseeing her dad's care said it could be anywhere from four to six months." My throat is suddenly dry and my heart beating a little faster than normal.

He blows out a deep breath, which sounds like a whistle. "Damn. That could be soon then, huh?"

I nod, trying not to think about her leaving at the four-month mark. Or the six-month mark, to be honest. I'd rather she just stay forever, but I know that's not her plan.

But plans change…

I make a mental note to give Frank a call later this week. He usually checks in every week, but I haven't heard from him in almost two weeks. I know he's been busy with rehab and resting, so I try not to bother him too much, but I also know how much he misses being face-to-face with his patients.

"How's the house coming along?"

"Good. I haven't started anything since completing the kitchen," I tell him, even though I'm sure he knows. I order all of my building materials through his hardware store. It's slightly more expensive than driving out of town to a big box store, but keeping my business local is what keeps these small family-owned businesses open, and that's important to our town. "I'm going to start the downstairs half-bath and office next. I'm considering moving a wall and making the bathroom a full one. It would be nice to have a shower downstairs on those days I'm covered with dirt from riding, you know?"

Logan nods. "Makes sense. When you're ready, let me know. The supplier I used for your kitchen cabinets has a bathroom line too. I can order a sample unit for the showroom."

"Thanks. It'll probably be my winter project."

After she's gone.

But I don't say that.

"Just let me know when. It'll take four to six weeks to get it in," he replies before his eyes move back across the room.

We hang out for another hour, watching the pair of women carry on and drink. By the time they finally make their way toward us, they're both rosy cheeked from alcohol and grinning from ear to ear. In all honesty, I think it did them both good to have fun and let loose like this, even if it happened on a Monday night.

And they both have to work tomorrow.

I glance at my watch and see it's just after nine, still early enough. "Hey, guys. I think we're ready to head out," Blair says once they reach our table.

"Let me pay the tab," Hallie adds, turning to head for the bar area.

"It's covered," Logan announces, standing up and sliding his chair in.

"What do you mean?" my sister asks, her eyes narrowing just a bit as she places her hands on her hips.

Logan shrugs, not bothered at all by my sister's ire. "I mean it's covered."

Her eyes become little slits as she stares at him, and a part of me wishes we weren't leaving. Something tells me Logan and Hallie going toe to toe would be quite the sight. She sighs loudly and pulls

Blair into her arms. "I take it my brother is escorting you home?" she asks, making eye contact with me over her friend's shoulder.

"Yes," I confirm.

"Fine," Hallie grumbles. "No loud sex though. I don't want to hear anything through the wall," she adds, pulling a disgusted face.

"I think we're heading back to my place," I state, even though I haven't run it past Blair yet.

"Good. I don't want to be scarred for life," she mutters, making sure her little purse thing is wrapped around her wrist.

"Do you want a ride?" I ask, placing my hand on Blair's lower back and ready to guide her to the exit.

"No, I'll walk," my sister announces, turning and heading that way.

"I'll take you," Logan insists, taking a few quick steps to catch up with her.

Hallie stops. "I'm fine. It's only a few blocks, and it's a gorgeous night." Then she pivots and continues on her journey.

Once we step outside, I notice Logan falls in step with her. My sister turns and looks at him. "What are you doing?"

"Walking you home."

She stops. "Why?"

With his hands shoved in his pockets, he says, "Because it's late, and I'd feel more comfortable making sure you got home safely."

"I'm perfectly capable of walking myself home," she counters.

Blair and I hang back, watching the show. I don't know what's going on with Hallie, but she seems a little more defensive toward Logan than normal. Usually, she barely pays him any attention, but tonight, he seems to be pushing all her buttons, whether intentionally or not.

When he doesn't reply, she sighs. "You're going to follow me home like some weird stalker, aren't you." It isn't a question. "Well, let's go, Johnson. Keep up," she states, turning and heading off in the direction of her condo, Logan hot on her heels.

"Foreplay."

I glance down at Blair. "Excuse me?"

"Those two," she states, pointing to Logan and Hallie's retreating forms. "They're flirting without actually flirting."

We fall in step, heading to my truck. "That makes no sense," I tell her, opening the passenger door so she can climb in.

When she's seated, she turns to face me. "Of course it does. They both like each other, but for whatever reason, neither is willing to take that first step. So instead, they're giving each other grief and a hard time for no reason. Their banter is foreplay."

I think about her words and nod in agreement. "Not that I want to think about my little sister and...foreplay, but I see what you're saying. Ready?" I ask, preparing to shut the door.

"Yes." As soon as I climb into the driver's seat, she asks, "Were you serious about going back to your place?"

"I was, but if you'd rather go home, I'd understand," I reply, pulling out of the parking spot.

"No, I was going to suggest stopping by my place so I can grab the bag I packed."

My eyebrows draw together as I glance her way. When she shrugs, I just laugh.

"What can I say? I was hoping," she says with a shrug and a smile that matches my own.

I pull into the driveway on Blair's side of the condo, both of us noticing Hallie and Logan just down the street, heading this way. "I'll be right back," she says, hopping out and entering her place.

A few minutes later, my sister and friend arrive. She doesn't appear to say anything to him, just walks to her front door, unlocks it, throws me a wave, and goes inside, leaving Logan standing on her small concrete porch.

He shakes his head and laughs before turning and walking my way. I roll down my window. "That went well."

Logan just shrugs. "She's home safe. That's all I wanted," he replies casually.

I spot Blair returning, making sure her door is secure. "Want a ride back to your truck?" I ask.

"Naw, I'm good. It's a short walk. Thanks for calling for that beer. It was great catching up with you." When Blair gets inside the truck cab, he adds, "You two have a good evening," before turning and walking away.

"Does he want a lift?" she asks.

"I offered, but he said he was good." Turning to face Blair, I ask, "You ready?"

When she confirms, I back out of her driveway and head for my house. The moment I pull into my garage, she removes her seat belt and asks, "Are you tired?"

Once the truck is off, I turn my attention to her and answer, "Not really. What'd you have in mind?"

"Care to go for a walk?"

"Leave your bag. We'll grab it on our way in," I tell her.

We hop out of the truck. The moment we're outside in the warm September night, I take her hand in mine and lead her to the backyard where the trails run. This late at night, there won't be any machines running around, so walking should be plenty safe. One of the good things about the Bluff Preserves National Park is the curfew for running machines on the trails.

After a few minutes of walking the trails, the moonlight lighting the path in front of us, she asks, "I still have a hard time picturing Logan and Shay married."

I can't help but chuckle. "Yeah, I think everyone was a little surprised by that one, but he seemed happy, at least for a while. I think the new wore off quickly though, especially when his dad suddenly died."

"I was sorry to hear of his passing. He was always a nice man," she replies. "I have a handful of childhood memories featuring Logan and Ed."

"They were pretty close, and no one was prouder of Logan when he got married than Ed. That's probably why he left the hardware store in both their names, assuming they would be married for a lifetime. Unfortunately, it doesn't always work out like that," I say, not necessarily speaking of just Logan and Shay's failed marriage.

"No, it doesn't," she confirms, squeezing my hand in silent support. It's as if she knows what I'm referring to without even saying a word.

After a few short minutes of silence, I finally decide to tell her more about my past. "Amara and Shay have a lot of similarities," I confess. "Except where Shay stayed and seems somewhat determined to make Logan's life hell, Amara ran off with a heart surgeon she'd been sleeping with."

"Wow, I'm sorry," she replies, giving me another squeeze with her hand.

"It's okay. It was three years ago, and I'd like to think I'm over the betrayal. It took a while though. I was mad at the world, myself included."

She stops and turns to face me. "I can't imagine."

"She didn't exactly fight me tooth and nail during the divorce, but she didn't make it easy either. Amara just wanted it her way, and as long as she got it, things went smoothly. But I struggled with awarding her fifty percent of everything I had after her betrayal, especially since I was on the verge of agreeing to her ultimatum."

"Ultimatum?"

"Yeah, she hated Pine Village and wanted to return to Chicago, where we met. She pictured herself a physician's wife, but not in a little town like this. She wanted the big house in a lush suburb, fancy dinners at the best restaurants, and the prestige that went along with the title of being a doctor's wife. Amara was looking for someone to take care of her, so she didn't have to do it herself. A part of me knew it from the very beginning, but I went ahead and married her anyway, blinded by what I thought was love. Right before I found out about her affair, she told me we needed to move back to Chicago or we were over. I had decided I wanted to work on my marriage and was prepared to tell your father I was leaving. I didn't get a chance though. I found out practically the next day she was sleeping with a surgeon from Hudson.

"So, I decided I couldn't stay married to someone I no longer trusted. She filed for divorce before I could, citing irreconcilable differences, which I found ironic, and demanded alimony for ten years."

Blair's eyes widen comically. "Seriously?"

"Yeah, but my lawyer was prepared for that. Since we had only been married four years, we settled on four years' worth of alimony without extension, unless she remarried before the end, then it would stop. I only had to pay a little over a year's worth."

"Wow, I'm sorry you went through that."

I shrug, and we slowly fall into step once more. "It is what it is. Besides, I learned a little about myself and was able to spend time working on my house."

"Like what? What did you learn?"

"You mean besides my love for woodworking and building? I learned what I really want out of this life and out of a marriage."

We're both quiet for a few seconds before she asks, "Would you do it again? Get married, I mean?"

Meeting her gaze, I stop once more and confess, "In a heartbeat. When I find the right woman."

It's you.

But I keep that to myself.

She nods once before turning her attention forward and continuing ahead. "For the longest time, I didn't know if I wanted to get married."

"That doesn't surprise me," I tell her, as a squirrel chases another across the path in front of us. "You didn't exactly have the greatest experience when you were younger."

"No, I didn't."

"What about now? Do you think you want to get married someday? Have a few kids?" My throat is so thick it's hard to swallow. Hard to breathe.

"Yes," she replies, with a small smile. "The older I get, the more I realize I want to share my life with someone." Her statement is just barely above a whisper, as if she's telling herself this revelation, not me.

I don't tell her I want to be that person. I don't tell her how badly I want to spend all my nights with her, not just a few throughout the week when we find the time in our busy schedules. I want to know she's here, in my house and in my life, when I come home at night. I want to wake up next to her, to feel her skin molded to my own. I want lunches and dinners and snuggles on the sectional in front of a fire.

I want it all.

With her.

But none of that is something I can tell her. Not yet. There's still a lot of unanswered questions in this equation, like what's going to happen when it's time for her to go back to Illinois. Will she consider staying here? With me?

"Ready to head back?" she asks, breaking through my thoughts.

"Yeah," I reply, clearing my throat and bringing her hand to my mouth then placing a soft kiss on her knuckles. "I'm ready."

And I am.

I'm just not referring to our current destination.

I mean my life.

I'm ready...for more.

CHAPTER
nineteen

Blair

I find a parking spot in the back of the lot and climb out. I haven't been to Pine Village Elementary since my own time here. The outside of the building hasn't changed much. The windows and doors appear to have been updated and the landscaping has changed, but the brick exterior and big letters with the school's name over the door are the same.

As I head toward the main entrance, I spot my sister and stepmom. Any time I've thought of the term *stepmom* it was always with a negative response, like it was a curse word or a snake ready to strike me. I hated that word, hated what it represented. But as I watch Patience with Aggie, I can't help but feel warmth spread through my chest. She's a great mom to my sister, much like my mom has always been to me. She's attentive, caring, and there's no missing the love reflecting in her eyes as she watches her daughter twirl like a ballerina.

Suddenly, that term doesn't seem as bad as it has in the past.

I push the thought and the implications it presents out of my head just as Aggie turns and sees me approaching. "Blair!" she hollers, waving widely as she runs toward me.

"Hello, Aggie," I greet, crouching down to give my sister a hug.

"I can't wait to show you my classroom! And my teacher said Mrs. Storytime is reading a book to us! Do you know Mrs. Storytime?" she asks, her pink glasses outlining big, excited eyes.

"I do not, but I can't wait to meet her," I reply, tapping the tip of her nose and helping her adjust the little plastic frames.

"Me too! Come on," she declares, taking my hand in hers and practically dragging me through the front door.

"Aggie, Blair is perfectly capable of walking without you pulling her," Patience says, unable to fight the smile. "Hello, Blair. I'm so happy you could join us, and as you can tell, Aggie is beyond thrilled."

A soft chuckle spills from my lips. "I'm thrilled too." I take a deep breath and swallow. "It's nice to see you again. Thank you for inviting me."

Patience seems a little surprised by my open friendliness toward her but quickly covers it up with a grin. "You're welcome." She glances down at her daughter. "Well, shall we go inside? I think this one's about to burst at the seams to show us her classroom."

We slip inside the small school and fall in line with other families heading toward the classrooms. I spot a few patients and old familiar faces, as well as a handful I don't know, and everyone has the same look on their face. It's happiness mixed with anticipation as the kids pull adults through open doors and parents cheerfully go.

I've missed this level of contentment.

"Here it is!" Aggie bellows, tugging our hands to follow her into the classroom marked kindergarten.

Once inside, I glance around the brightly decorated room. Numbers and letters are everywhere, as well as easy sight words in every color imaginable. There's a large, carpeted area for reading, several hands-on activity areas, and small desks perfect for the little students. The room is fun, yet educational, and I can see why Aggie loves it so much.

"This is where Miss Hanson reads my favorite books," Aggie says, dragging us over to the reading carpet. "We get to sit here and listen to the stories."

"Reading is Aggie's favorite part of the day, isn't it?" a young woman says, offering Aggie a warm smile.

"Miss Hanson!" my sister proclaims, throwing her little arms around the teacher's waist.

"Good evening, Aggie. Who do we have here?" the teacher asks her student.

"This is my mom, and this is my Blair! She's my sister," Aggie announces loudly as she bounces up and down, drawing the attention of a few parents nearby.

Miss Hanson chuckles. "Well, it's lovely to see you again, Mrs. O'Connor, and very nice to finally meet you, Blair," she says, offering me her hand once she's shaken Patience's. "I've heard a lot about you. I think your sister is very taken with you."

"Really?" I ask, a little surprised to hear.

"Oh, yes. Aggie loves to talk about you, especially after you two spend time together. I heard all about your recent trip to the park as soon as she arrived at school," she says with a grin.

But I'm stuck on her words. Aggie talks about me? I knew she enjoyed spending time with me, but I wasn't prepared for the giddiness I feel realizing I've become such an important person in my sister's life. In such a short amount of time.

Guilt sweeps in. For not trying harder where she's concerned before nine months ago. For not putting my anger at my dad and stepmom aside for the greater good of my half sister.

Because she's amazing. This adorable little human, who shares half of my genes, doesn't care about my past, my parents, or the drama that happened years ago. She cares about what's happening now, that I spend time with her, and that she's loved.

By her parents and by me.

Suddenly, that longing I've always experienced when I think about my life before the divorce settles heavy in my chest. I miss my dad. I miss the man I knew from my youth. The one I'm still incredibly angry at, yet for some reason, it doesn't feel as substantial as before.

"Come on!" Aggie bellows, tugging my hand toward the reading rug.

We spend the next twenty minutes being shown every little thing in Aggie's classroom by an extremely excited five-year-old. When we've seen everything, including the broom closet with cleaning supplies, we all head to the gymnasium for the reading program.

"Blair, you sit by me!" Aggie declares when we find seats in the bleachers.

Patience chuckles. "I think we're both sitting by you, Ag. You have two sides."

The little girl stops and thinks. "Oh," she replies with a giggle, her small hands covering her mouth. "Yay!"

My sister holds my hand the entire time, and I'm completely taken by her enthusiasm. Her facial expressions show every ounce of excitement, shock, and happiness she feels as Mrs. Storytime, who is completely dressed the part of the book heroine in full historical dress with bonnet, reads and acts out the book. I'm almost sad when it ends.

"Let's go do the craft," Aggie announces, as everyone slowly makes their way out of the bleachers. Some head for the exit, ready to call it a night, while others move to the cafeteria, where the craft and snacks are waiting.

I follow behind mother and daughter as we make our way to the next part of the evening, and I can't help but notice the similarities of their relationship and that of the one I have with my own mother. She's my best friend, even if I don't get to see her as often as I'd like. She stayed in Merrillville when I went to college, eventually finding a home in the Chicago suburb, but we still talk often. If not on the phone, through text. That didn't stop when I moved back to Pine

Village. In fact, she's been very encouraging through this whole ordeal.

Mom never kept me from my dad. I did that all on my own. Well, my anger did. If anything, she was hopeful I'd be able to get past the hurt and resentment I felt and rebuild the relationship I once had with him.

He called me once my first year of med school. He happened to be in Chicago for a conference, and it was after a particularly brutal test. I studied for that stupid test all hours of the day and passed, earning the highest grade in the class, while several others struggled. I was so excited, so proud of my accomplishment, I answered the phone and agreed on a whim to meet him for dinner that night. Only, when I arrived at the restaurant, his wife was there, and all of the ire I felt for them both came flooding back in spades. I couldn't have just one hour with him without them throwing their happy life in my face.

I told him I wanted nothing to do with either of them ever again, not to call me, and for the most part, he's held up to my request. I still get Christmas gifts, mostly gift cards, but I donate those to Lurie's Children's Hospital. The things I've always wanted from him couldn't be bought with money. I craved his attention, his love, despite the fact I pushed him away constantly, telling him I didn't want or need him.

Funny how that works, isn't it?

As the years went by, I think Mom just got tired of fighting me, resolved to letting me forge ahead on whichever path I took, and that path was paved with bricks made of resentment. Even after he messaged me to tell me I had a sister. The pain at seeing those words on the screen, along with the accompanying photo of the small, wrinkly girl, led me to reply with something cruel and hateful.

Now, I regret those words because I lost time with Aggie. I lost those first four years of her life, and I can't get those back. That's why I'm determined to be part of her life now, because it's not her fault our father robbed me of the life I was expecting.

Aggie finds a spot at one of the many crafting tables set up and dives into coloring the construction paper bonnet featured in the story. As she's coloring flowers around the brim, I ask, "Aggie, do you want a cookie and lemonade?"

"Yes, please," she replies, without taking her eyes off her masterpiece.

"Would you like anything?" I ask Patience, who again, seems a little surprised by my pleasant demeanor. I can't say I blame her. I haven't been very nice in the past.

"No, thank you, Blair," she replies with a grateful smile.

With a quick nod, I head to the large refreshments table and choose a chocolate chip and a sugar cookie from the variety. As I'm grabbing a cup of lemonade, the older woman behind the table says, "Blair? Blair O'Connor?"

I glance up, recognition prickling in my mind but unable to immediately place her. "Yes."

"I knew that was you! You haven't changed a bit." Then she adds, "I'm Mrs. Mars. Do you remember me?"

Once she says her name, I'm immediately thrust back to fifth grade. "Mrs. Mars, yes, of course!" I reply, instantly remembering the woman who worked in the elementary school cafeteria back when I was a student here. Of course, she was a lot younger back then.

She smiles widely. "I heard you were back in town, working for your dad."

I ignore the comment and ask, "You still work at the school?"

She shakes her head. "No, I retired a few years back. I just love to help on these school event nights. My granddaughter is in fifth grade. She's the brunette over there with the pink and white striped shirt," she says, pointing to the opposite side of the room.

"That's very sweet of you to do," I tell her, smiling over at the petite girl with a brown ponytail and striped top sitting with a group of four other girls.

"I enjoy the kids. Oh! That looks like your dad," she says, catching me off guard.

I turn just as Aggie hollers, "Daddy!" and takes off running toward the entrance to the cafeteria. I stand there, completely dumbstruck, and stare at the man I used to adore and idolize. He looks much older than I remember—than he did when he visited me in Chicago while I was in med school. That was the last time I actually saw him face-to-face.

My dad bends down and hugs his youngest child, a big grin on his lips. It's then I notice the walker next to him, and my heart squeezes a bit. I stand here and take in his appearance. He's slimmer and frailer than I remember, but I'm sure a big part of that is due to the massive heart attack and the toll it, as well as the surgery, took on his body.

With legs suddenly made of lead and a lump in my throat the size of Texas, I turn and give Mrs. Mars a small smile. "It was nice to see you again," I say before taking the lemonade and two cookies and heading toward my sister.

And my dad.

As I approach, I see the worry in Patience's eyes when she looks my way. Something tells me she didn't know her husband was going to be making an appearance tonight. I'd like to think she would have mentioned it to me, but perhaps not. Maybe this is her way of forcing us to be in the same vicinity at the same time. Plus, if we're surrounded by people, I'm less likely to make a scene.

But when she gives me a small smile, I know she didn't plan this. I can see it written in her eyes.

I set the cookies and the lemonade down on the table in front of Aggie's workstation. She's returning to the table, holding Dad's hand, and talking a mile a minute. He's walking with a slight limp, dragging the walker behind him, so Patience meets him and takes the ambulatory assistive device and sets it aside. "Do I want to know how you got here?" she asks sternly, and even though she's clearly shocked by his appearance, I can hear the love in her voice.

"Blair."

I slowly lift my gaze and meet his. Words die on my tongue as I take in my father for the first time in years. The sight of such a large, imposing man looking so...old, brings tears to my eyes.

"Why don't you have a seat, Frank," Patience suggests, inviting her husband to sit next to their daughter on the bench.

All I can do is stand here and watch, my emotions all over the place and my mind reeling. Dad jumps right in and helps Aggie hold the bonnet while she finishes decorating it, and then helps her thread the string through the punched holes. Aggie munches on the cookies I brought, while Patience takes photos on her cell phone. When the bonnet is ready, Dad folds the paper along the dotted lines and fits it onto Aggie's head. The moment he has the strings tied together beneath her chin, she turns to me and smiles.

"Blair, look! I'm just like Jaqueline from Mrs. Storytime's book!" she declares with a toothy grin.

"You sure are," I reply, my own smile stretching across my lips.

"Let's take a picture now that it's complete," Patience suggests.

I watch as Aggie runs over to the wall, strikes a pose, and grins up at her mom.

"I'm sorry to just surprise you like this."

His words make me pause. "Then why did you?"

He sighs. "Aggie has been talking about this night all week, and I didn't want to miss it. I've missed too much over the last couple of months." Then he adds quietly, "Over the last several years."

Something tells me he's not referring to Aggie with the last part.

"Daddy, come take a picture," Aggie insists eagerly.

Gingerly, Dad heads in her directly, standing beside his youngest child and smiling for the phone camera.

I walk over to Patience and reach for her phone. "Let me take one of all three of you."

Gratitude flashes in her eyes as she hands over her phone and goes to stand beside her husband and daughter. It's hard to ignore the emotions lodged in my throat, but I manage and take a few different photos. Then, Aggie hollers, "Blair's next!"

Dad and Patience move aside so I can step in. My stepmom takes her phone back and points it at us. I crouch down, wanting to get to her level. Aggie wraps a small arm around my neck and smiles. "Cheese," she says, causing me to grin from ear to ear.

Patience takes a few different snapshots before a woman walks over and says, "Would you like me to take one of your whole family together?"

My heart? It practically stops beating.

"Thank you," Dad says, moving over to where I squat beside Aggie.

I meet Patience's gaze, and I can see the hesitancy in there. I think she knows this isn't expected and is gauging my reaction. Her look lets me know she'd step in and refuse the photo if I wanted her to. I've never—and I really do mean never—been more grateful for her than I am right now.

"Yay! My first family picture," Aggie announces to the entire room of Pine Village residents, and it takes everything I have not to let the tears filling my eyes fall.

Instead, using strength I didn't even realize I possessed, I push them away and paint a smile on my face. For Aggie.

I can do this for her.

I stay down beside my sister and smile. Just as the woman goes to take the photo, I feel a hand on my shoulder. It's familiar, yet foreign at the same time. I don't need to look to see whose it is. I know.

Memories flood my mind. My happy childhood. Sitting with my dad in his office, pretending to see patients in the very clinic I'm currently working. Discovering him and his nurse together in his office and essentially setting off the bomb that blew up my life.

I stand up quickly, needing to get away.

Needing space and air.

I look down at my sister before giving her a big hug. "Thank you so much for inviting me to come tonight. I had the best time," I tell her.

She grins and pushes her glasses up on her nose. "Me too! Can we go to the park soon?"

Swallowing over the lump in my throat. "Of course. I'll get ahold of your mom."

"Okay!" she declares, before returning to her table to clean up her craft mess.

Cautiously, I turn to face the two adults behind me. Before I can say a word, Patience says, "Thank you for coming. You made her night."

I nod, unable to find the words to reply. Then, I look at my dad and see unmistakable pain in the same green eyes that stare back at me in the mirror every day. He opens his mouth, but closes it quickly, leaving me both grateful and sad he didn't say whatever it was he was about to. Instead, he goes with, "Drive safely."

Again, I nod in reply before turning and heading for the door, feeling their gazes on me as I go.

Outside, I suck in deep breaths of oxygen, but it does nothing to calm my racing heart. I head for my car, jump behind the wheel, and drive off. I don't head toward my condo. Not to Hallie's either. Instead, I drive out of town, to the big farmhouse I've come to love.

To a pair of arms I know will be open and waiting.

CHAPTER
Twenty

GABE

I know as soon as she pulls into my driveway, something is wrong.

I had just come out of the downstairs bathroom, taking measurements for the next phase of my remodel, when I heard a vehicle pull into my driveway. A quick glance out the kitchen window confirms it's Blair. Even as the night starts to set in, I'd know her car anywhere.

The moment I open the back door and see her slowly making her way toward me, I feel the sadness surrounding her. It's like that proverbial rain cloud hanging over her head, like you see in those dramatic commercials.

Stepping onto the porch and letting the screen door slam behind me, she finally looks up, and what I see almost brings me to my knees. So much pain and anguish it aches me to see. I'd much rather observe those beautiful green eyes filled with laughter and happiness. Something tells me I already know what's caused this look, and I know, right now, I'd do anything to take all her hurt away.

"Hey," I say as she moves up the steps and straight into my arms. The moment she steps into my embrace, the world seems to right itself once more.

Slender fingers grip the back of my T-shirt as she presses her cheek against my chest. After a minute of just standing there, she finally says, "I'm sorry for just dropping by unannounced."

I slide one hand into her hair and kiss the crown of her head. "You never have to apologize for dropping by. Especially when you're upset."

She gazes up at me, and the look on her face kills me. It physically pains me. "Come on," I say, keeping my arm around her shoulder and guiding her into the house. I keep going until we reach the couch, not stopping to let her kick off her shoes. When I reach the big sectional, I pull her down with me, practically cocooning her with my body. I hold her close, gently stroking the side of her face with my hand as I whisper, "Talk to me."

She takes a deep breath and leans into my palm. That simple gesture makes my heart soar. It's as if my touch brings the comfort she desperately needs in a time of distress. "My dad showed up at the school."

"I figured. How did that go?" I ask, even though I kind of already know that answer too.

"It went...fine, I guess. He drove himself there, even though he's not released to drive yet. I could tell Patience was shocked to see him and probably a little upset he got behind the wheel before he was supposed to."

She sighs, clearly doing some heavy thinking, so I just lie here and hold her until she's ready. "He said my name, and it was like I was ten years old again, sitting in his office, waiting on him to return from seeing a patient. I didn't realize how badly I missed it until that moment."

I can't imagine what this is like for her. Years' worth of heartache that's never healed. It's like a scab being ripped off, only to find an infection festering within.

I've remained quiet where her dad is concerned since she arrived in town. For three months, I've barely spoken of the man I consider a mentor and friend, because I know her feelings toward him are night and day different from my own. Maybe now is the time to ease into that conversation, whether either one of us wants to have it or not.

Before I can broach the topic on my own, she surprises me with her question. "What's it like to work with my dad?"

"Well, it's pretty great. He's incredibly knowledgeable, caring, and attentive. Since I joined his practice, I've learned a lot, and not just about medicine. I learned about the type of doctor and person I wanted to be."

She starts to cry, and the sound guts me. It causes physical pain to hear. "That's what I always thought I'd have."

I sigh against her head, my fingers sweeping across her cheek. "I don't think I'm overstepping by saying this. You could still have that, Blair, but first, you have to forgive him. I know it won't be easy or quick, but you won't be truly happy until you do."

"I don't know if I can," she whispers, and a part of me dies with her statement, because if she can't forgive him, then she won't be able to work with him, and that confirms her being in Pine Village is growing shorter by the day. Like sand in an hourglass, I see our time together slowly fading away.

That really fucking sucks.

"You don't have to decide right now," I tell her, holding her a little tighter than before. The thought of her leaving settles in my chest like a weight, making it hard to breathe.

But you do have to decide soon, I want to add, but don't.

She exhales loudly. "I know." After a few long beats, she says, "I'm sorry I'm such a Debbie Downer."

"You're human, Blair. Even brilliant doctors, like yourself, can falter under the weight of life."

She turns her head and gazes up at me, her brilliant green eyes still filled with emotion, but looking a little lighter than before. She moves, placing her lips against mine. "Thank you, Gabe."

"Anytime," I insist, closing my eyes and just breathing her in.

Blair moves first, climbing on top of me and straddling my waist. My cock instantly gets hard, loving the way her pussy hovers over it. I can feel her heat through my sweatpants. She leans forward, her body pressing against me from shoulders to thighs. "There must be some way I can apologize for just showing up unannounced," she says, rocking her hips and grinding against me. "I mean, you look like you were relaxing."

Bolts of lust zip through my veins as she rolls her hips, making me harder than ever before. "After my shower, I went to the downstairs bathroom and office to take some measurements," I reply through somewhat gritted teeth.

"Measurements, huh? Sounds like you know your next project," she says, running her hands across my hips and dipping them beneath my T-shirt. When she scores her nails across my flesh, goosebumps erupt everywhere.

"Yeah. I'll start it this winter." The words get caught in my throat, making it hard to swallow.

She nods slowly, as if understanding where my mind went. This winter, she'll be back in Chicago, and I'll still be here, working on my next remodel project. Alone. There's no way she's ready to relocate, not if she's still so raw and gets upset from seeing her dad. The fact I want her to stay won't outweigh the years of hurt.

Needing to hold, touch, and show her exactly how I feel, I wrap my arm around her waist and flip us over. Hovering over the top of her, I caress her cheek with my thumb as I lower my lips to hers. The kiss is soft, slow, and intimate, and it takes every ounce of restraint I have not to confess my love for her. In three short months, I've fallen. Hard. Hell, I think I started to fall last Christmas after spending just one night with her in my arms.

Her hands slide up the back of my shirt, gripping my skin. I'll never tire of her touch, of feeling her body against mine. Without either of us saying a word, I strip away every stitch of clothing between us until we're both naked. When I enter her, it's without urgency. In its place is tenderness and passion, both the complete opposite of what happened the last time we came together on this couch.

This time I'm making love to her.

Linking our fingers together, I hold her gaze as I carefully push inside her, filling her completely with one long, slow thrust. I watch in complete rapture as moisture gathers in those stunning green eyes and her mouth falls open. The softest sigh of contentment spills from her lips, and that's when I know I'm truly gone.

For her.

There will never be another Blair O'Connor.

Making love to her is easy. Probably the easiest thing I've ever done, and when we both come, there's no denying the emotion of the moment. Without telling her, I've shown her what's in my heart. I've shown her I love her.

We lie together all night, only getting up from the couch to use the restroom or grab a drink. We hold each other tightly and make love two more times until the sun is starting to rise and the birds begin to sing. Only then do we pass out from sheer exhaustion.

It's the perfect night.

One I never want to end.

For the next four weeks, we fall into a routine. We go to work at the clinic, eat lunch together, and head home around the same time every evening. Sometimes we travel to Hudson together to visit patients or check in with someone recovering at home, but one thing has remained constant: she sleeps beside me at night. Then, we wake together and do it all over again.

I left the office a little early today to check on two patients in the hospital, while Blair stayed behind to see patients and chart. Our plan is to meet up for dinner at my place, which is where I'm headed now. I'll be able to get the grill going and prep the potatoes before they need to go on.

Just as I'm pulling onto the highway to head back to Pine Village, my phone rings. Spotting Frank's name on the screen, I hit the button for my Bluetooth and answer. "Hey, Frank. How's it going?"

His deep chuckle rumbles through the speakers. "Going well. Really good, actually. I have news."

"Lay it on me," I say, watching a car in my rearview mirror quickly approach and then fly around me, as if I wasn't going five over the speed limit.

"I was released to come back to work."

My heart soars and breaks simultaneously. "Wow, Frank, that's wonderful news."

"Dr. Bishop released me to return, effective Monday."

My throat is dry as I ask, "Any restrictions?" I'm hoping there are a few. Perhaps less hours in a day? Then maybe Blair will stick around a little longer.

"None besides the usual take it easy and listen to your body bull. The same line we tell every patient after conducting a physical to release them," he replies with a chuckle.

I don't smile. Not because I'm not happy for a friend who received the incredible news he's been anxiously waiting for, but because this announcement is the one I've been fearing and dreading since I realized I was really going to have to let Blair go. With Frank returning to work, it's certain she'll be leaving.

Probably sooner rather than later.

Clearing my throat and pushing away the fear, I ask, "Have you told Blair yet?"

He sighs softly but doesn't reply right away. I can almost see him sitting there, running his hand through his hair as he used to do when he'd get stressed at work. "Not yet. I was going to go speak with her at the office. It's my understanding she's still there."

I swallow over the lump in my throat. "She is."

"Don't say anything to her, please. I mean, I don't expect you to keep this from her, but if you could give me the chance to tell her first, I'd appreciate it."

Something in his request catches my attention. He knows we've been spending time together. "I won't say anything, but I won't keep it from her either."

"I understand and appreciate that. I'm headed to the office now. I should get there as the rest of the staff is getting ready to leave."

I hate that he's going to catch her off guard like this. A big part of me wants to give her a heads-up of his impending arrival, but I also know they need to talk and him just showing up might force that hand. This slippery slope is one hell of a place to be stuck on.

"I know I have no right to say anything, Gabe, but I like you for her. In fact, you might be the right man to actually make her stay."

I briefly close my eyes before returning them to the road in front of me. "I appreciate you saying that, Frank."

"I sense a *but* coming," he replies with a chuckle.

"But I want her to stay for reasons that are entirely her own, not because I make her," I reply, throwing his words right back at him.

"I understand, and perhaps the word making wasn't the right one. Just think about it. Maybe give her a reason to stay, son. If anyone can do it, it's you."

I don't reply as I approach Pine Village. I spot the place in the road her car became disabled last winter before rounding the bend and seeing my house. I want to keep going, to drive to the clinic to be there when Frank stops by and upends Blair's life once more, but I don't. I pull into my driveway and park in front of my garage, not bothering to put it away right now.

"Well, I will let you go. I just wanted to share my news with you first and let you know to expect me at the office Monday morning."

"I'm happy to have you back, Frank."

"These past four months have killed me. I hate being idle, though I do admit, the rest did me good. Just don't tell Patience," he adds with a laugh.

"Mum's the word. We've got everything covered over the weekend. See you Monday," I tell him.

"Have a good weekend, Gabe."

And then he's gone, leaving me sitting in my truck and trying not to let the overwhelming dejection consume me. In a perfect world, Blair will stay and work with us. Her dad doesn't talk about retirement often, but when he does, he always says he'd want to do it by the time he's seventy so he can spend time with Aggie and be more active in her young life.

He's sixty-eight now.

I think he's always held out hope he'd turn his practice over to his oldest daughter, even though he's never actually said those words to me. I can just see it in his eyes any time he talks about the future. What he always envisioned for his life and his business hasn't quite turned out to happen. While he may have success, there's always been one missing link.

Blair.

With a sigh, I take my keys out of the ignition and slide from the truck. The cool October air is a stark change compared to what it was just a few weeks ago. Fall has definitely set in. With heavy legs, I walk to my house and let myself in, tossing my keys onto the counter and taking a long look around.

When I first started this remodel, it was with the assumption I'd be sharing it with Amara, my then-wife, and maybe a few kids. Since that dream went to shit, I'd settled on living here alone, making the house into something I could keep forever or even sell someday. It's a big place with too much space for a single man, but I've enjoyed spending my free time transforming it with pride and determination.

Then Blair entered my life, and suddenly, that picture of a single guy living in the big house alone changed. I saw her here with me, snuggled on the couch and cooking dinner in the kitchen. I've watched her slowly take this house and turn it into a home, just by being in it.

Fuck, I'm going to miss that.

I walk to my fridge, loosening my tie as I go, and grab a beer. This calls for alcohol. Especially if Blair still comes over after she leaves work. After she talks to her dad.

Something tells me tonight will change everything.

CHAPTER
Twenty one

Blair

"Good night, Blair! See you Monday," Stella hollers from the doorway.

"Have a good weekend, ladies," I reply as they all leave me alone to finish up the rest of my charting and paperwork. Then, I'm off myself, heading to Gabe's for the weekend. I can't wait.

Something catches my attention. A scraping sound in the silence surrounding me. My heart rate jumps as I look up and find a figure standing in the doorway. One I wasn't expecting.

"You look good sitting there," my dad says with a soft smile on his face.

I don't reply right away, just stare back at the man who fathered me. Finally, I say softly, "Thanks."

"May I?" he asks, pointing to the chair across from the desk.

"It's your office."

He chuckles as he makes his way into the office, sans the walker he was using the last time I saw him. I take in his appearance. He looks freshly shaved, his clothes clean and pressed, and his gait much better than it was when I saw him at Aggie's school for reading night. He looks...good. Healthy even, and a wave of relief washes over me.

"How have you been?" he asks once he's seated.

"Doing well," I state honestly.

"I'm happy to hear," he replies, the faintest smile on his face. "You look happy."

I'm not sure how to respond to that. Am I happy? Yes. But I try not to think too deep into the reasons why I'm happy.

"Listen, I'm sorry for just dropping by, but honestly, I was afraid if I gave you a warning, you'd leave before we could talk. I wanted you to know I was released by my cardiologist today and plan to be back to work Monday."

My heart sinks. Even though I knew this day was coming, hearing him say the words is that not-so-subtle reminder that my time here has always been temporary. "Oh. That's good news."

His smile is genuine. "I'm ready. I've been ready for weeks, but the good doc didn't agree. Now, it's time." He sits up, leaning forward just a bit as he holds my gaze. "We have our differences, Blair, but I've heard nothing but positive things since you started here. Everyone loves you. I know I don't have the right to ask, but I'd love for you to consider staying."

"Staying?" I ask, my throat is so thick and dry, I don't know how I can even draw oxygen into my lungs.

"Yes."

"I can't stay," I reply automatically, like a defense mechanism.

He nods slowly. "I understand, but I'd be a fool not to ask. And believe me, Blair, I've been a fool for a long time. I don't deny it, but I'm trying to fix it."

"Fix it? How? You can't take back what you did," I argue, feeling the angry tears building.

"No, I can't," he concurs sadly. "I have a lot of regrets, but never you. I've always loved you and wanted what's best for you."

"Bullshit," I counter, standing up and starting to pace. "If you wanted what's best for me, you wouldn't have ruined our family."

His sad eyes follow my movements as he agrees, "You're right. I've made many mistakes along the way."

"Mistakes?" I laugh, but it holds absolutely no humor. "A mistake is speeding and getting a ticket. A mistake is forgetting to buy milk on your way home from work when you were asked to grab it. A *mistake* isn't an affair with your nurse, who's only a handful of years older than your daughter. A *mistake* isn't going at it on this very desk for said daughter to discover after school. No, *Dad*, the only mistake you made was being so careless you got caught."

His own eyes fill with tears as the ones I've been fighting start to fall. His voice is small and sad as he asks, "Will we ever be able to get past this?"

I swallow hard as I give him an honest answer. "I don't think so."

He sighs and nods solemnly before standing. Suddenly, he looks ten years older than he did when he walked into this office. "I understand and will respect your decision."

"I will be leaving this weekend. I agreed to help until you were back on your feet and returned to work, but there's no reason for me to stay."

Except that's not true.

There's Aggie and my friends.

There's Gabe.

But I push those thoughts out of my head. This has always been the plan. My time in Pine Village was always going to be temporary, even if a piece of me wants to argue.

My dad moves to the door but stops before exiting completely. "You're always welcome here, Blair. Your relationship with Aggie means the world to her."

"I won't abandon Aggie," I counter with a touch of dismay in my tone, wanting to add *like you,* but choosing not to.

He seems somewhat appeased by my words. Then, he holds his head up high and adds, "This will always be your home."

His statement is like a dagger to the heart. "This hasn't been my home since I was seventeen."

He holds my gaze and nods. "I am truly sorry, Blair. For everything. Hurting you was the last thing I ever wanted, and I know that's exactly what I did. But you need to know it was never my intention. I've always loved you. Loving you was the one thing I actually got right, even if I didn't always show you. You are one of my two greatest accomplishments in this life."

Then, he leaves, walking out of the office, out the back door, and out of my life again.

Good. I don't need him.

Yet, something niggling in the back of my mind tells me that's not true. I just choose to ignore it.

My vision clouds as I stand here, silent tears streaming down my face. All of the pain I've felt for the last sixteen years erupts, overflowing like lava. I drop onto the chair and cry hard, angry at him. And angry at myself too for letting it get to me after all these years. I should be over it, shouldn't I? I know there's no timeline for this type of grief, but maybe that's because I've never truly dealt with it.

Oh well.

It's done and over with now.

I sit there, replaying the entire conversation. What makes him think he has any right to ask me to stay? After all these years, why now? Our relationship is past the point of fixing.

But is it?

I can't think about that. What's done is done, and my time here is that.

Done.

I give myself a few more minutes to cry, letting the pain wash over me. One last time. Once I leave here, that's it. I won't be looking back, only forward. Then, I wipe away the wetness on my face, stand up, and prepare to leave. For the last time.

Having everything put away and secured, I look around the room, the office I've called my own since late June, the finality settling in my chest with the weight of a thousand bricks. It's heavy and all-consuming, but I push through it. One foot in front of the other.

Fortunately, I have little in regard to personal effects here. Just my purse, some gum in the drawer, and a few snacks. I walk to the front office and find the framed copy of my license hanging on the wall. I was able to get an Interstate Medical Licensure Compact, which allowed me to cross state lines, once approved, to practice in both Illinois and Wisconsin. Ironically, it's positioned above my father's own license.

I stand here for several minutes and just stare at the three frames hanging on the wall. When I was a little girl, I always expected to see this very display. Well, maybe not Gabe's license, but it's so fitting and perfect there. As a young adult going through med school, I never expected to see this. Not my name anywhere near my father's.

My heart aches as I reach up and touch Gabe's name, tracing it with my fingertip. I'm going to miss him. So much.

Because you're in love with him.

Then, I move my hand to remove my frame from the wall. It feels so absolute and maybe a little wrong. I turn and head back to the office, slipping my license into my purse, and walking toward the door. I stop before actually leaving, turning around and giving the office one last look. With a sigh, I flip off the lights and spin on my heel.

Before moving to the back door, I stop in the doorway to Gabe's office. He left in a hurry today, due to having a patient to see in Hudson, and left a small mess on his desk. Not his computer and files. Those are locked away in the matching fireproof cabinet in his office, but I see the Mountain Dew can and a KitKat candy wrapper.

Even though there is a cleaning service who will come this weekend to take care of that stuff, I find myself walking over and tossing it all in the trash under the guise of being helpful, but I think the real reason is I just wanted to touch his desk one last time. To sit in his chair. The same one he'll sit in Monday morning when he arrives, ready to start his day.

The day I will no longer be in the office across the hall.

Instead, it'll be my dad and everything will return to normal.

How it was before I spent four months here.

Needing to get out, I stand and make my way to the door. I give the office one last look, just like I did with the one across the hall and turn to leave. I set the alarm and push through the heavy door, making sure it's secure before I go. Then, I walk to my car and slide inside, forcing myself to keep my vision focused in front of me. No looking back.

When I turn out of the lot and onto the main roadway through Pine Village, I don't head to Gabe's house as planned. I drive to the condo I've been using since June, knowing I have work to do if I'm going to be moved out as soon as possible. Might as well start on it now. I know I should call Gabe and let him know I'm not coming right away, but I just can't seem to do it. Hearing his voice would break me, and there's no time for that.

I park in my driveway and go inside, even though I really want to see Gabe. I drop my purse and keys on the floor and head straight for the second bedroom. The only things in it are the boxes my stuff was in when I moved here. Since I knew I would be returning home, I kept all of the packing material.

I start in the kitchen, and after making a handful of phone calls, an hour later I'm finishing clearing the cabinets when my best friend finds me. She looks around, her face full of shock and sadness. "No," she whispers, her eyes filling with tears.

"He's returning to work Monday, so my time here is done."

She holds my gaze as she steps directly in front of me. "But is it?"

I swallow hard, fighting off my own tears, as I reply, "Yes. We knew it was temporary. It's time for me to go home."

Lacey Black

She cries and pulls me into her arms, squeezing tighter than I expected her slender frame to. "But I was secretly hoping you'd realize you belong here."

I can't help but chuckle as I sniffle. "I know you did, and my God, you're freakishly strong."

"It's all the wrangling of three and four-year-olds," she states with another sniffle. Then, she holds my gaze and sighs. "I'm going to miss you."

"Me too," I tell her honestly. My heart hurts just thinking about not having her right next door or in the same town. Hell, not in the same state!

"Don't be such a stranger this time around," she says, taking in the stack of boxes and grabbing an empty one.

"You could come visit me again in Chicago," I suggest when she heads toward the living room to pack what little is in there.

"Definitely," she hollers from the other room. After a few minutes, she reappears in the doorway. "Done with that room," she adds with a laugh.

"Yeah, there wasn't much in there."

We both grab empty boxes and head to my bedroom next. Besides the bathroom, it's the only room left to pack. Only bringing the bare necessities I'd need for a four-to-six-month stay definitely helped with the whole packing thing.

Hallie and I both drop the boxes onto the floor and plop down on the bed. She exhales deeply and reaches for my hand. "Gabe was worried about you."

I roll to my side, instantly feeling guilty for not sending him a message. "I didn't mean to worry him," I tell her honestly. "My head was just...well, it was a mess after I left the clinic, and my car just sort of drove here. I think I knew if I went to his house, I'd break down, and I didn't want that."

"I get it, really." She stops and considers what she's going to say, and something tells me I probably won't like what it is. "I'm just going

232

to say this because I feel like I have to. You could stay, Blair. You have friends here. You have Gabe."

It physically pains me to swallow. "I know."

"I'm sensing a but," she says with a small chuckle.

"Yeah, there's a but," I agree. "I need to make sure I'm staying for the right reasons, Hal. And I realized when I was talking to my dad, I'm not sure I can get over the hurt he caused."

"Listen, I know he did a number on you and your mom, and I can't even pretend to imagine what that was like."

"I'm sensing a but here," I say, throwing her words back at her.

"There is. *But* you can't let it control your happiness. That's what I realized when Curtis was doing his revolving door bullshit. One minute he was good, attentive and kind, and the next, I was barely an afterthought. I realized he was controlling my happiness, and I was done letting that happen."

"Now you can find your happiness with someone else," I tell her, trying to hide the hint of a smile on my face. "You know, like a gorgeous guy who owns a hardware store."

Hallie rolls her eyes. "Not happening. There's nothing there, believe me. He's annoying and bossy on his good days," she counters, but her eyes give her away. I can tell there's more there than she's letting on, but I don't call her on it. "Besides, can you imagine having to deal with Shay nonstop? Because you and I both know she'd be all up in Logan's business if he ever decided to date."

I have to agree with her on that point. "Yeah, I'm sure that wouldn't be fun. She has a way of worming her way into everyone's business. Logan's included."

"So, if you're done stalling, what are you going to do about Gabe? I'm not asking because he's my brother, but because I see how much happier you've been since you started spending time with him."

"I like him." A lot. More than I should, considering it's always been my intention to leave when my dad returned to work. When we decided to see each other, we both knew it was temporary. I'd be returning to Illinois.

That didn't stop me from falling for him. Somewhere along the way, I fell in love with Gabriel Rhodes, MD. I don't know how or when, but the thought of leaving him here and moving on with my life back home is like a sucker punch to the throat. I can't breathe.

"For what it's worth, I'm pretty sure he likes you too," she replies, sadness once again filling her eyes.

"I should call him."

"Yeah, probably. I told him you were here when he called me earlier, but I'm sure he wants to hear from you that you're okay."

I nod. "He probably knows about my dad."

"I would assume," she says before pulling me into an awkward hug, considering we're lying on top of my bed. "I love you, Blair. I've really enjoyed having you here these last four months, so just know if it's not working out for you back in Illinois, you're always welcome here."

I hang on extra tight as I return the hug. "Thank you, Hal. I love you too."

"Let's get the gang together one last time this weekend. I know it's last minute, so we can do it at my place," she suggests, climbing off the bed.

I follow suit and stand beside her. "Sounds good. Tomorrow works for me."

"I'll message everyone when I get home and invite them over. Can I invite Gabe too?"

"I'd be sad if you didn't," I state honestly.

With a small smile, she gives me one last hug before heading to the front door. I watch her go before grabbing my purse and pulling out my phone. Guilt settles heavily in my chest when I see three missed calls and a handful of messages from Gabe. Without even reading them, I fire off a quick reply and return to the door, making sure it's locked as I go.

Then, I climb behind the wheel of my car and back out of the driveway, suddenly a little more anxious to see Gabe.

If I'm going to leave in two days, I want to spend as much time with him before I go. I know that makes me selfish, but I can't help it. I want to soak up as much Gabe as I can, so I can carry it with me back to Illinois. Heaven knows I won't ever forget him or the way he makes me feel. Not only about him, but about myself too.

Happy.

Content.

Free.

CHAPTER twenty two

GABE

Blair: I'm sorry. I'm on my way.

I stare down at the message I received only minutes ago, relief washing over me. Even though I knew she was at her condo, thanks to a quick call to my sister, finally hearing from her and knowing she's coming to me goes a long way to settle the anxiety I've felt since I got off the phone with Frank.

It's just after eight, and I'm sure I look like I've been home three minutes, not three hours. I'm still wearing my black trousers and gray button-down, though I ditched the tie as soon as I got here. My hair is probably standing on end, thanks to running my hands through it constantly, and my stomach is growling because I haven't even thought about eating. I've done nothing but pace and worry, especially when Blair didn't show up as planned.

I head to the fridge and pull out a package of ham, a tomato, and a few slices of cheese, tossing them onto the counter. I grab the Texas toast from the cabinet, retrieve the butter, and pull the griddle from the pantry. Just as I'm plugging it in, I hear the sound of a car pulling into my driveway.

As I'm buttering the last slice of bread, I hear the back door open and close. I watch as the most beautiful woman comes into view, slowly heading in my direction. She meets my gaze, and there's no missing the sorrow written in those stunning eyes. It breaks my heart to see.

Without saying a word, I point to the stools across from the island where I'm working. Blair pulls one out and takes a seat, her hands resting on top of the counter. I want to reach over and grab those hands, pull her up and into my arms, but I don't. Part of it is a defense mechanism because I know what's coming. The conversation we're going to have will be one of the hardest I've ever had. Maybe even harder than the one I had with Amara when I found out she was cheating on me and leaving.

"Have you eaten?" I ask, even though I already know the answer. Blair is still in her work clothes too, and the wrinkles tell me she's been working at her condo since the moment she got home.

"No."

"Well, sit back and watch magic happen, Dr. O'Connor," I state, placing the first three slices of bread onto the griddle. The sound of the butter starting to sizzle makes my stomach growl.

Blair doesn't say a word, just watches me place the sliced ham and cheese on top of the bottom slices of bread, followed by the top. When I add the top layer of bread, I grab the tomato and start slicing.

"I'm sorry I didn't reach out to you," she says after setting the first slice on a plate.

"I understand," I reply, because really, I do. "Why don't we talk about it after we eat?" I suggest.

"Okay. Do you want a drink?" she asks, slipping from her stool and moving to the fridge.

"Just a water for me, please."

She returns to the island with two bottles of water, opening the first one and placing it in front of me. Neither of us speaks as I prepare three grilled ham and cheese sandwiches, but the silence doesn't feel heavy or uncomfortable. In fact, it's quite the opposite. That's one of the many things I'm going to miss about having Blair here.

When I pull the sandwiches off the griddle and shut it off, I glance up and ask, "Do you trust me?"

Without hesitation, she meets my eyes and confirms, "Of course I do."

I open all three sandwiches between the layer of ham and bread and add a slice of tomato and some southwest mayo to give it a little kick. Placing one sandwich on one plate and two on the other, cutting one of them in half to share, I walk around to join Blair at the bar and take a seat beside her. Her familiar scent wraps around me, and my dick already starts to respond. It's always that way when she's near.

"This is amazing. I never would have thought to put that flavor of mayo on it," she says, wiping her mouth with a napkin.

"It's my favorite. I could eat ham and cheese with tomato and chipotle mayo every day of the week and never get tired of it," I say, already halfway through my first sandwich.

We eat the rest of our food with her knee gently pressing against mine. I try to offer her half of the second sandwich, but she declines and watches me with the slightest smile on her lips as I devour it. When both plates are clean, I toss the paper plates in the trash, return the cold ingredients to the fridge, and reach for her hand. She comes willingly, walking alongside me as I lead her into the living room. Once we're seated, her tucked closely beside me, I finally start the conversation we're both expecting.

"Tell me about your dad coming to see you."

She takes a deep breath and leans her head against my shoulder. It takes every ounce of strength I possess to not react, to not beg her to stay with me forever. "He informed me he's returning to work on Monday. I take it you already know all of that though, right?" Her tone isn't accusing. She knows I have a strong working relationship with her father, and anything to do with the business most likely has been brought up to me.

"Yes, he called me to tell me the news."

Again, she sighs. "I'm glad, really. I'm happy he's made such a strong recovery. Actually,

it surprised me a little how proud I am of him. Is it wrong that I'm angry at him, yet proud at the same time?" she asks, looking up at me with confusion in her eyes.

"No. I think that's perfectly normal. Just because you're mad, doesn't mean you don't still love him or want what's best for him."

She drops her gaze and returns her cheek to my shoulder. "I guess. Anyway, he showed up at my office—well, his office, actually—and shared the news." Another deep breath, and I can instantly tell what she's about to say will hurt like hell. "I'm leaving Sunday. I've already informed the landlord of the condo and booked the moving company I used in June. They're going to be here Tuesday. Hallie will oversee them, though it won't take long to get it all loaded up. There's not much there."

Sunday.

She'll be gone in less than forty-eight hours.

"Sounds like you have everything figured out," I reply as calmly and evenly as I can, even though my heart is screaming for her to stay.

"Well, I don't know about that, but this is what I've always had planned. This is the way it's supposed to be."

I sense a hint of hesitation in her words, but don't dig into it. Maybe that's to protect myself. Maybe I'm chicken. Maybe it's because whatever it means won't matter in the end anyway. "What can I do to help?"

She stiffens against me, but relaxes so quickly, I almost miss it. "Well, some of the packing is already complete, and what's left, I'll finish tomorrow."

"I'll be there."

She looks up at me once more. "You don't have to."

"Nowhere I else I'd rather be," I tell her, which is completely the truth. I want to spend as much free time with her as I can before she goes.

"Okay. Oh, and your sister is hosting some friends tomorrow night. I hope you'll come."

I finally move, pulling her into my arms and shifting her body so she's sitting on top of my lap. "I'll be there, Blair."

Then I kiss her, trying to convey how much she means to me through this one act. Trying to say I love her. I'll never forget her. I'll never be *me* again.

Because I'm certain I'll never love anyone as much as I love Blair O'Connor.

That's why I don't ask her to stay.

That's why I must let her go.

Because she has to come to that decision on her own. If I influence her and she hates it, she'll resent me, and I can't have that. I won't be the reason she's unhappy. So, I'll stand back and watch as she exits my life almost as abruptly as she entered it.

Until then, I'll hold her. I'll touch her. I'll kiss those soft lips and spend every waking hour by her side, all while, deep down, wishing things were different between us. Wishing for more.

Wishing she'd realize she loves me too and would stay.

"You look like you could use one of these," Logan says as he comes up beside me, handing over a beer.

"Thanks," I reply, opening the top and taking a drink. I told myself I wasn't going to drink alcohol tonight, but I've definitely reconsidered my stance at this point. Watching Blair laugh with her friends has been difficult, because as much as I love the sound of her voice, I know my time hearing it is limited.

Last night, after she confirmed she was leaving, I carried her upstairs and made love to her. I needed her in my bed, her scent soaking into my sheets and pillow. This way, it'll hurt even more when she's gone because I'll continue to smell her. Apparently, I'm a masochist like that.

"Hard to believe she's actually leaving, isn't it?" he asks, his intense gaze gauging me.

"Not really. I mean, it's a shock she's going so soon, but we all knew this was coming," I reply diplomatically. It's the stance I've tried taking since the moment she came over last evening. Does it suck? Fuck yes. But it's not unexpected. We've known all along this would be the outcome, even if parts of us didn't want to believe it.

When he doesn't say anything, I glance his way. I can tell he has something to say, but he doesn't respond. Instead, he just nods and takes a drink of his beer. Finally, he adds, "You could ask her to stay."

"No, I can't."

Logan sighs and bumps my shoulder. "No, I get it, really, and I don't blame you for keeping your mouth shut. I just think you should lay it out there, tell her how you feel and let her make the decision."

Now it's my turn to look his way. With a slight smile, I ask, "And how do I feel?"

"You're in love with her," he states accurately, even though I've never confirmed. "Listen, man, if anyone understands the shit you went through with your ex, it's me, so I get it when you try to protect your heart, but I've seen the way you look at her."

"How do I look at her?" I ask, my voice hoarse and my throat dry.

"Like she hung the moon and all the fucking stars in your sky."

My eyes instantly seek Blair out once more. She's surrounded by Hallie, Ava, and Ellie, while TD and Brody throw the football off to the side, and there's a look on her face full of contentment. Fuck, I'm going to miss her.

"And don't think it's not mutual, Gabe. She looks at you the same way," Logan adds. "All I'm saying is you should throw it out there and let her decide. You might be surprised by the outcome."

After a few long seconds, I nod in understanding, even though I'm not sure I agree. Telling her I love her will cause more harm than good. I'm certain of it.

"We're going to head out," Ellie announces, turning back and glancing toward her son.

"But, Mom, it's not even nine o'clock," Brody argues, clearly disappointed to have to stop playing catch with his coach, despite not having minimal light from the patio.

"I have laundry to finish up for work tomorrow, and I'm opening," Ellie counters through a yawn, that slight edge to her tone letting him know not to argue. When Ellie opens the diner, she's there by five.

"Can't Coach take me home?" Brody asks, his voice full of hope.

"I'm heading out too, Brode," TD says.

"Aww, man," the sixteen-year-old replies, clearly disappointed.

"I'll see you Monday in the weight room, right?"

Brody instantly nods. "I'll be there, Coach."

TD reaches over and ruffles the boy's shaggy hair. "Good."

It's none of my business, but I can tell there's a solid relationship between the coach and athlete that runs much deeper than just on the surface. There's a father/son respect and bond there that neither of them realizes they've formed. We've all watched it form and grow over the years, especially when Brody started high school. TD became the male influence the young boy had been craving, and in return, TD found a son he didn't know he wanted.

If only the man would take the leap where Ellie is concerned.

But that's also none of my business, especially since I'm struggling to take a similar jump with Blair.

Speaking of Blair, her arms wrap around my waist, and it's so easy, so natural to pull her close. "Do you mind if I come home with you? Everything's pretty much ready to go at my condo," she says.

Bending down, I place a kiss on the crown of her head. "I'd be disappointed if you didn't."

She gives me a small smile, one laced with sadness. "Okay. I'll go say good night to everyone and grab my overnight bag."

"Need help?" I ask.

"No, it's already packed," she answers before dropping her arms and walking over to say goodbye to her friends.

"Don't let her go without giving her the facts, Gabe. You'll regret it if you don't," Logan states softly so no one in the vicinity can hear.

I glance his way and nod.

When he seems appeased by my response, he gets this ornery grin on his face. "I'm going to go push your sister's buttons before I leave."

Then he makes his way over to where Hallie stands and announces, "Decent party, Rhodes. Food was mediocre, but the company more than made up for it."

I can't help but grin at the angry look she levels him with as she tells him off for probably the second or third time tonight. You know, I really like Logan Johnson.

"I'm ready," Blair announces as she returns to where I stand.

I reach down and take her suitcase with one hand and her hand with my other and lead her to where everyone is saying goodbye. After tearful hugs and promises to visit again soon, I lead Blair to the front, where my truck is parked in her driveway. She climbs inside while I place her suitcase in the back seat, and a few minutes later, we're heading toward my house.

For the last time together.

The pain in my chest intensifies, but I ignore it. Like I have since Frank called me yesterday. I've disregarded the hurt and the ache as much as I can, which has been a pretty difficult feat. There'll be time to wallow in my misery later.

Right now, I have one last night with Blair.

One last night to hold her, and I'm not wasting another second.

CHAPTER Twenty Three

Blair

The silence that wraps around us is nauseating. It's not uncomfortable, but there's so much hanging over us, it's painful. The sand is officially running out in the hourglass.

As if knowing I need his touch to tether me to the ground, he reaches over and takes my hand. I can't help but wonder if he can feel the slight tremble because it's definitely there. The longer I fight to ward off the tears, the harder it's becoming to keep it together completely. The breakdown is coming, I just don't know when.

We pull into his driveway, and I can feel them welling in my eyes. Somehow, I numbly release my seat belt and climb out of the cab, Gabe meeting me at my side a moment later with my suitcase in hand. We walk together into the house, the cool late-October air chilling me to the bone.

"Come on, Blair," he whispers, opening the door and stepping back so I can enter.

Once we're inside, I kick off my slip-on shoes and step into the kitchen. That's when the first tear falls. This beautiful kitchen. When will I see it again? Will I ever?

Gabe comes up behind me and wraps his strong arms around my shoulders, drawing me into his embrace. The comfort and strength of his body is enough to trigger the rest of the tears. I don't even realize I'm moving until I'm in his arms. Gabe lifts me easily and cradles me against his chest. He walks up the stairs and into his bedroom, gently laying me down on his bed. He covers me from head to toe before finally taking my lips with his.

This is heaven.

Pure bliss.

Gabe slips his thumb between our cheeks and brushes away the wetness. Then he releases my mouth and captures the newly fallen tears with his soft lips.

Without saying a word, he gets up and slowly sheds me of every stitch of clothing I have on. He trails kisses over my skin, touches every square inch as he exposes it, as if he's memorizing me.

When I'm completely naked, I do the same to him. I start with his long-sleeved T-shirt, I lift it up and over his head, my fingers grazing over his hard chest and defined shoulders. Gingerly, they make their way down his abs to where his jeans hang low on his hips. I hold his gaze as I release his belt, unfasten the button, and lower the zipper. He doesn't say a word as I slide the denim and the boxer briefs down his hips, letting them fall around his ankles.

Gabe steps out of his clothes, and it's the first time I've noticed his shoes are already gone. He must have kicked them off in the mudroom too, but I was too busy committing the gorgeous kitchen to memory to realize. He bends down and slips off his socks before taking me in his arms once more and guiding me back to the bed.

My legs spread, my ankles locking at his lower back, and with one small thrust, he's seated completely inside me. We fit so perfectly together, it's the most incredible feeling in the world.

Gabe entwines our fingers together as his hips move. He sets a slow and steady pace, stretching me in the best way possible. Before I even know what's happening, I feel my release building. His cock strokes that place deep inside me over and over until I'm crying out.

I can feel my pussy squeezing his cock, and it only takes a matter of seconds before he follows. Gabe whispers my name as he comes, his fingers stroking my cheek and brushing away the tears I didn't even realize I was crying.

When the tremors start to subside, he turns on his side and tucks me in close. I don't even care we're making a big mess all over his bedding. All I can do is hold on and cry, letting the grief wash over me. Gabe doesn't say a word, just holds me tightly and lets me cry until there's nothing left inside but this numb ache.

Soft lips press against my forehead. "You should get some rest," he whispers. "You have a big day tomorrow." I'm sure he's referring to the drive, but my heart thinks he's talking to it. It knows I have a big day tomorrow leaving. Saying goodbye to my sister. My friends.

Gabe.

"I don't know if I can," I tell him, even though I'm exhausted. Between packing away the rest of my things throughout the day, having the cookout at Hallie's, and then coming here tonight and making love to Gabe, I'm emotionally spent.

I have so much I want to say but don't know how. How do I tell this man how much I feel for him and then leave? That would be the ultimate jerk move, and I just can't do that to him. Or myself, if I'm being selfishly honest. I know I'm not staying, so why make my leaving worse by confessing what's written in my heart. Why tell him I love him, that I'll always love him, and then leave?

I can't do that to him.

I won't.

So, instead of saying what I want to, I brush my lips lightly across his chest and hold on tight. To him. To the memories I'll carry with me when I leave Pine Village tomorrow and return to the big city.

My eyes close on their own accord and I can feel myself relaxing. It helps being in his arms. There's no place I'd rather be, and that might include Chicago.

As I slowly drift off to sleep, it's pictures of Gabe and the life we could have together that accompanies me into my dreams.

"I don't want you to go," Aggie cries, throwing her little arms around me one more time.

"I know, Ag, but just because I'm back in Chicago doesn't mean we won't see or talk to each other all the time," I tell her, even though I know the seeing each other will be a lot less than it was while I was in town.

She sniffles and pulls back, meeting my eyes. Her tiny pink glasses have slipped down her nose just a bit, so I give them a gentle push back up. "You're my bestest friend, Blair."

As hard as I try, I can't keep a few of those pesky tears from escaping. "You're my most bestest friend too, Aggie. I love you with my whole heart," I whisper with a small smile.

She sighs and turns to look at her mom. We met this morning at the diner for breakfast, which was probably the wrong place to meet. Being in public didn't help my emotions. First, there was Ellie, who was clearly upset as she served us food. Then, Hallie showed up and joined us, and even though everyone tried to keep the meal light, there was too much of an emotional charge at our table to be overlooked. Gabe sat on one side of me the entire time, holding my hand or squeezing my leg in silent support. I'm not sure if that helped or made it worse.

Now, we're on the sidewalk down the street by the park where my car is waiting, packed with the few bags and personal items I'm taking with me today. "Can we video call tomorrow so I can tell you about school?"

"Of course you can," I insist immediately. "My hours are a little longer back in Chicago, remember? You can call me like you used to earlier in the year. After your bath and before you read your book at bedtime."

She nods. "Otay," she says with another deep breath.

I stand up, her hand instantly slips inside mine. Turning to my best friend, she gives me the saddest smile I've ever seen. It matches what I feel in my heart. "I'm going to miss knowing you're right next door," she says, stepping up and giving me a big hug.

I release Aggie's hand to return the gesture. "Me too."

"Promise you won't be a stranger. I know this place isn't your favorite, but these last four months have been the best having you here."

It's on the tip of my tongue to tell her this place isn't so bad, but I keep it to myself. Hating this place and what it represented has been my security blanket for so long, I don't know what to do without that anger. "I promise. I'm coming back around Christmas," I tell her right away without even consulting my calendar. We'll still work crazy hours at the clinic in Chicago and with me taking the last four months off for FMLA, I don't know if they'll grant me any more time off right away, but I can pull a weekend away when I'm not on call.

"My spare bedroom is yours," she insists before glancing over at her brother. "Unless you have somewhere else to stay," she adds with a slight grin.

I give her one more fierce hug before turning to my stepmom. She came alone with Aggie this morning. Actually, it was her idea to have breakfast before I hit the road. "Thank you for agreeing to let me form this relationship with Aggie," I tell her, meaning every word.

She replies with letting a few tears fall down her own cheeks and throwing her arms around my shoulders. "You're always welcome here, Blair. I hope you know and never forget that. And if anyone should say thank you, it's me. You agreeing to form a relationship with Aggie meant you were agreeing to form one with me, whether directly or indirectly, and I know it wasn't easy for you. So thank you."

I swallow hard and nod. "I know I have said and done a lot over the years," I start, but she holds up her hand.

"Don't you ever apologize for that. I've done things that hurt you—we both have," she says, and I know she's referring to my dad. "I'm not proud of them, and if you're willing to forgive me for hurting you, even if it happens slowly over time, I'm just thrilled for the opportunity to fix our mistakes."

Again, I nod as the emotions clog my throat and strip me of the ability to speak.

"Now, drive safely," Patience says, taking a step back and swiping away the tears on her cheeks. "If you would, please send me a text when you're home and safe." She turns to step back but stops. "Oh, I almost forgot. I have this for you." She pulls a small envelope out of her purse. "You can read it when you're ready."

The look in her eyes tells me all I need to know about who the letter is from. "Thank you," I whisper, taking the small rectangular message and slipping it into my own bag.

Patience reaches down and takes Aggie's hand, leaving me with one last goodbye.

I turn to look at Gabe, who has a stoic look on his face. He looks so gorgeous in his jeans and hoodie, his hands stuffed in his pockets. His ocean blue eyes look tired and maybe a little sad as he watches me walk toward him. Once I reach him, he removes his hands from his pockets and wraps his arms around me, drawing me in. I can hear him inhale as he settles his nose over the crown of my head.

There's so much I want to say, but I have no idea how to get the words out. They're a jumbled mess, like a word search, and when I try to sort them, it just makes it harder to try to separate them.

"I don't know what to say," I confess, resting my cheek against his chest.

"You don't have to say anything, Blair."

Meeting his gaze, I whisper, "I'm going to miss you most of all."

The corner of his lips turns upward. "I'm going to miss you too, sweetheart."

"These last four months have been amazing," I add.

Lacey Black

He nods in agreement. "They've been pretty incredible. Like you," he says, running his hand along my cheek and sliding his fingers into my hair. "You're an incredible woman, Blair O'Connor. Don't ever forget that."

I give him a smile; one I don't really feel in my heart. "Thank you for everything."

"No need to thank me, beautiful. Just know you have a big group of people—hell, a whole town—behind you, supporting you, and cheering you on."

"And you?" I find myself asking, even though I don't feel like I have any right to ask that question.

"I'll always be there, Blair. Always."

A few more tears fall as he leans forward and presses his lips to mine.

One last time.

"Be happy, Blair."

"You too, Gabe."

He gives me a smile that doesn't quite reach his eyes before he finally releases me. There's this cloud of uncertainty hanging over us, and a ton of things left unsaid, but this is what we agreed upon. In the beginning, we decided to have fun while I was here, both knowing I was leaving at some point.

Yet, it still feels so unresolved and final at the same time.

I hate it.

I hate this.

But it's time for me to go.

With one foot in front of the other, I slowly walk toward my car. Gabe is there, opening my door and waiting while I climb inside. Aggie runs over once more and throws her arms around me for another big hug. "Bye, sissy!" she proclaims before returning to her mom's side and waving.

That one word. Sissy. I've never been called that before. Sure, she's talked about her sister, but I've never heard her refer to me as sissy. My heart squeezes so hard, I'm afraid I might be having some sort of medical emergency. I wave back, biting my lip to keep from crying out.

"Buckle up."

I look up and meet Gabe's gaze once more. With shaking hands, I do as instructed and place my finger on the start button, giving it a gentle push to start the car.

"Let me know when you get there," he adds, standing between the open door and where I sit. Then he bends down and leans in once more, gently kissing me goodbye. When he pulls back, he opens his mouth, but nothing comes out. He shakes his head, as if to push away whatever words he thought about saying, and gives me a smile. "Take care, Blair."

"You too," I whisper, the words barely audible.

Then, before I can say anything else, my door is closed and I'm alone, most of the people I care about in this world standing on the opposite side of the door. Gabe shoves his hands back in his pockets and steps back, giving me the space I need to leave.

Gripping the steering wheel with one hand, I put the car in Drive, and slowly pull away, throwing one final wave as I go. I have no clue how I manage to not cry as I carefully drive away from the park, from those I love. It doesn't hit me until I reach the city limits and pass his house.

What have I done?

I almost stop. I almost turn around and tell them I was wrong, that I can't go. That I've never felt so at home than I have these last few months with them.

But then I think about what was never said.

Gabe never asked me to stay. If he wanted me to, wouldn't he have at least given me the option? And what would I have done if he would have said those words?

You would have stayed.

But he didn't, which tells me our time together was exactly as it was supposed to be. Fun for a few months and then we both move on with our lives.

As reasonable and logical as that sounds, it doesn't help relieve the ache in my chest that only intensifies with each mile that passes. Something tells me no amount of time or distance will ever alleviate that hurt. I'll carry it with me for the rest of my life, like an old photograph in my wallet. Over time, it may fade, but it will always be there.

He'll always be there.

I'll forever love Gabe Rhodes and wonder what could have been.

CHAPTER *Twenty four*

GABE

Five.

That's how many nights she's been gone, and I'm downright miserable. I'm sure everyone around me knows it too. I've been a moody bastard all week. I haven't been this grumpy for this long since my marriage blew up and Amara left. Only this time, it's worse. The struggle to breathe through the pain in my chest is so much worse than it ever was when things fell apart with my ex-wife.

Because Blair was so much more.

"You okay?"

I glance up and find Frank standing in the doorway to my office. He's been back to work now for five days and easily fell into the same familiar routine we had before his heart attack. I'm definitely happy he's here, but I can't stop thinking about how great it was when Blair was working beside me every day either. The sad realization is I can't have them both.

"Yeah, great. Why?"

He gives me a knowing smile. "I've been talking to you for a couple of minutes, and you didn't even realize it."

"Oh. Sorry."

He waves off my comment. "Don't apologize. I know this week has been difficult for you."

"It's been great having you back," I quickly insist.

He leans against the doorjamb and just stares at me. "That's not what I was referring to."

Ahh, yes. Blair.

The elephant in the room.

"Have you talked to her?" he asks from his position by the door.

"We've texted a couple of times," I confirm.

"Texts?" He shakes his head and closes his eyes. "I'm sorry, Gabe. I wish I knew how to fix things with her. I'd do anything, which is why I've stayed away. That's what she always said she wanted. I was trying to respect her wishes, even though it killed me on the inside."

"I know," I reply, wanting to say more, but also not wanting to break her confidence with the things she's shared with me and I've learned over the last four months. I think her being here has gone a long way to heal old wounds, but not entirely. At least I saw her make some sort of peace with Patience, even if she only did it for Aggie.

"Big plans tonight?" he asks.

"No, just home. I thought about stripping out the old bathroom and getting that ready for new drywall and subflooring."

"Don't forget to flip your light on," Frank replies, adjusting the shoulder bag he's carrying.

"Why?"

He gives me a look. "It's Halloween, kid. Trick or treating starts in thirty minutes," he says, glancing down at his watch. "Which means it's time for me to get home. Aggie is getting ready, and I promised I'd be home to go with them."

"What's she going to be?" I ask, remembering Blair's adorable little sister as an octopus last year.

"She wouldn't tell me. Said it was a surprise. You need anything before I head out?"

"No, I'm good. I'll be right behind you," I tell him, powering down my computer and slipping it into my cabinet.

"All right, well flip on your light. Aggie will insist on stopping by."

"I'll have it on," I reply, mentally reminding myself to grab a bag of candy on my way home.

He nods and leaves, closing the big metal door behind him when he goes. Finally, I'm surrounded by silence, and it's not a welcome feeling. It's stifled me every night when I was home, and now it has followed me here. It's lonely and suffocating, and I don't like it.

I make sure everything is put away before leaving the building, setting the alarm as I go. Inside my truck, I still expect to turn and see her sitting in the passenger seat. Sadly, she's not there or anywhere I've expected to find her in my house. The walls feel just as sad and lonely as I do, especially late at night.

I'm saved from drowning in my own sorrow when my cell rings. I quickly start the truck so the Bluetooth picks up, and I see my sister's name on the screen. Not that I'm not happy to talk to Hallie, but I was really hoping I'd get to actually speak to Blair.

"Hello, sister," I greet.

"Brother. Are you home?"

"Heading there now," I tell her, backing from my parking spot and making my way to the street.

"Well, you're going to have company. I have to get out of this condo, or I'm going to go crazy. I'll stop and grab a pizza."

"Wanna grab candy too?" I ask, feeling only the tiniest bit of guilt for asking her to make a second stop, but I really don't want to venture into the store and have everyone ask me about Frank returning and Blair leaving. That doesn't sound like fun on a Friday night.

"Sure. You care what kind?"

"Whatever you think the kids would like. I don't expect to get a lot, but Frank mentioned Aggie would want to drop by," I tell her, grateful I can bypass the market and head home.

"Aww, I can't wait to see her," my sister says. "Oh, and do you have tequila?"

"Tequila?" I ask, smiling for what feels like the first time in nearly a week.

"Yeah. This feels like a tequila kinda night," she replies.

"Yes, I'm pretty sure there's some above the fridge."

"Perfect. I'll be there shortly. Oh, and cut up some cheese. I'm gonna need some extra cheesy goodness with my booze," she adds before signing off.

Shaking my head, I pull into my driveway and stop in front of the garage. I'll put my truck away later. Right now, I have to run in and see what kind of mess is all over the main living space, dig out some bricks of cheese from the fridge, and find the tequila. Something tells me she's not wrong. Tonight is probably going to call for a sleep aid much stronger than melatonin.

Thirty minutes later, I have the dirty dishes in the dishwasher and the floors swept. I even cleaned up my bathroom and made my bed so my sister isn't disgusted with the disheveled state of the two useable rooms upstairs. I'm just flipping on the front light after putting my truck in the garage when I hear my sister arrive.

"Pizza delivery!" she hollers as she enters.

"In here," I reply from the kitchen, watching as she kicks off her shoes and meets me at the island. "You don't have to take those off."

"Gutting the bathroom?" she asks, knowing me well.

"Started two nights ago." I leave out the part about not being able to sleep in my bed because I can still smell Blair there. The couch reminds me of that night last Christmas, so it's been my recliner to catch what little z's I've been able to grab.

She gives me a knowing look. Flipping open the pizza box and grabbing a slice, she asks, "Have you talked to her?"

"Just a few texts," I state, grabbing a paper plate and sliding it in front of her.

"She called me last night," she says with a mouthful. When she swallows, she meets my gaze and says, "I think she's miserable."

My heart rate jumps a few hundred beats per second, but I keep my voice and my features even. "Did she say that?"

"No, but I could just tell. She's working long hours again, even with that newer nurse practitioner there, who was all moved out of Blair's apartment, but apparently left it in a huge mess. Blair was not happy," she adds before taking another bite.

I reach for a slice, noticing right away the nasty pieces of fruit on top of the pizza. "You couldn't get half with just meat?"

"Hell no, big brother. If I have to suffer without my best friend again, you can suffer with fruit on your pizza," she sasses, shoving a huge bite in her mouth.

I don't bother to tell her I'm already suffering for the same reason she is, except her level of love for Blair and my level are totally different. I can't seem to breathe without her here.

Before we get too much into chatting about work, I hear a car pull into my driveway. "Got the candy?" I ask, wiping my mouth and taking a quick drink of water.

"I got baby Snickers and Twix because those are my favorites. Whatever's left after the kids leave, I'm sitting around and eating with my cheese and tequila."

I snort a laugh. "So, you're staying, I take it?"

"Yep. I brought pj's too. I figured we could hang out, get drunk, and hopefully, pass out. Maybe I'll actually get a full night's sleep for a change," she mutters as a knock sounds at the back door.

"We'll come back to that," I insist, referring to her comment. "Come in!"

The back door opens and in bursts a small version of Blair. A smile instantly crosses my lips as I take in Aggie, decked out in a small lab jacket, scrubs, and all the accessories to transform her into a doctor. "Hi, Gabe! Trick or treat!" Aggie bellows as she joins us in the kitchen, her parents hot on her heels.

"Trick or treat, Miss Aggie. Look at you."

"I'm a doctor, like Blair!" she proclaims, holding her jacket open and spinning so I get the full affect.

"Just like Blair?" Frank asks, chuckling at his daughter's enthusiasm.

"And Daddy too," she adds with a giggle.

Patience steps around to Frank's side and slips her arm around his back. "Aggie always loved that picture of Blair when she was little. Frank keeps it on his desk at home, and last month, Aggie decided she wanted to be Blair for Halloween."

"Happy Halloween, Hallie," Aggie says to my sister.

"You look just like your sister," Hallie states, smiling from ear to ear.

"That's because she's my sissy," Aggie announces with a toothy grin.

"How about I take a picture of you and send it to Blair."

"Yes!" Aggie proclaims, going into the living room with Hallie to pose for her picture.

"This was her surprise costume?"

Frank nods. "She made Patience promise not to tell me until tonight," he replies, beaming with love and pride for his youngest daughter.

"She's simply adorable," Patience adds, grinning widely. "She's been planning this since before Blair left. She made me take a dozen photos and send them to her already, and they have a plan to video chat as soon as we're done running around."

I glance at Frank, who just smiles. "As long as she's willing to have a relationship with Aggie and communicate through Patience, I'm a happy man," he says, patting his wife's hand. But I can see the pain laced in his eyes. It still really bothers him to not be able to patch up the relationship with his oldest child.

"Hallie says I can have extra candy!" Aggie announces as she and my sister return to where we stand in the kitchen.

"She did, huh?" Patience responds with a grin.

"But you can still only have two pieces before bed."

Aggie turns to me and says, "I'm going to have one piece with Blair."

My gut clenches, mostly because my brain instantly went to seeing her in person, because if Aggie sees her in person, that means I can too. But then reality sets in, and I know her sharing candy with her sister will be done over a video call. The realization is depressing.

"I'm sure you will both enjoy that," I reply to the little girl with eager anticipation in her green eyes.

Turning to her parents, Aggie asks, "Can we go to Kelly's house now?"

"We can," Frank replies.

"She always gots the good stuff too," the little girl adds with a happy nod, her pink frames slipping down her nose just a bit. Instantly I think about Blair and the caring way she'd gently push those glasses up her nose.

Fuck, will I ever stop thinking about Blair in every situation?

Frank and Patience carefully corral Aggie to the door so they can head to Kelly's house. Frank's nurse was telling me earlier how she always buys a full-sized candy bar for her coworkers' kids, so I'm sure that's what Aggie is referring to.

As soon as they're gone, I head back to the kitchen and watch as Hallie pours a few fingers of tequila into two glasses. "Looking to get good and soused tonight, huh?" I quip.

She shrugs. "Blair just replied to my texted pictures. She's on her way back to her apartment from work, and it just makes me sad all over again," she mutters, sipping her drink. "Oh my God, I forgot how much I hate tequila." Then, she takes another drink.

Taking my own glass and throwing back a hearty swig, I reply, "Then why are you drinking it?"

"Because it'll make me drunk and I could use drunk right now."

"Come on," I say, reaching for the bags of candy and the pizza box. "Let's flip off the light and take all this junk into the living room. I don't think anyone else is going to drive out here for trick or treating."

"That's the best suggestion I've heard all night," she agrees, grabbing the bottle of booze and following behind me.

I make a quick stop to flip off the light and make sure the door is locked before joining my sister on the couch. She instantly notices the pillow and blanket sitting on the chair.

Dammit, I meant to take that upstairs.

"What's this?"

I shrug and plop down on the couch, kicking my feet up on the coffee table. "Nothing."

"Bullshit. It looks like someone is sleeping down here. Unless you have a roommate, I'd guess that someone is you."

I take another drink, this one much smaller than the first one, and finally reply, "I don't like sleeping in my room."

"Because she's not there," my sister deduces accurately.

"Yeah."

After several moments she finally turns to face me and asks, "Why'd you let her go?"

I sigh, the alcohol in my gut settling like a lead balloon. I definitely could use more food before I consume the rest of my booze, but I don't really feel like eating right now either. "She wasn't mine to keep, Hal. It was always the plan for her to return to Illinois when she was done here."

"But you could have given her a reason to stay," she replies sadly.

The heart in my chest squeezes. I've felt such physical pain since she left, I wonder if the ache will ever subside. Perhaps I'll always feel it, the void. I'll always miss her in a way the hurt will never really go away. "Maybe, but she would have stayed for the wrong reasons, and I couldn't live with that."

Her eyebrows draw together. "What do you mean?"

"Just that. If she would have stayed because I asked her and then the relationship didn't work out, she'd resent me. She'd hate the fact she gave up her big city life at her big city clinic to move back to the town she hates, and for what? To be hurt in the end all over again?"

Hallie doesn't reply right away, so I take another sip of the liquor just to fill the time. When she does finally speak, it's not exactly what I was expecting. "Sounds like those are your issues, not hers."

"What?" Now it's my turn to look at her quizzically.

"You. You're scared. You're afraid she's going to leave you again, like Amara did."

"Blair is nothing like Amara," I counter, a touch of anger in my voice.

"I know that, but do you? I mean, you must not completely believe it if you're still guarding your heart, even after you agreed they're nothing alike. Stop letting your ex-bitch dictate your future." There's fire dancing in her eyes, and I'm not exactly sure if it's from ire or from the tequila. Possibly a combination of both.

My jaw practically unhinges at her statement, and when I go to argue, I find I can't speak the words. Am I afraid Blair will leave like Amara? I guess in a way, yes. If I were to ask her to stay and she did and was miserable here, I'd never forgive myself for causing her that kind of pain. She deserves so much more than to settle for a life she doesn't want but agreed to anyway.

She deserves the world.

When I'm finally able to reply, I mutter, "It was supposed to be fun, Hal. Fun while she was here and that's it."

"First off, gross. Second, things change, big brother. I saw the way both of you looked at each other. You love her, right?"

There's no hesitation. I nod, feeling my pulse thumping hard in my neck.

"Well, do something about it, because I'm certain she loves you too, but both of you are too stubborn to take that first step and admit it. Instead, you both revert back to your comfort zones of playing it safe and using excuses to validate your decisions. Well, your decision sucked, Gabe. You let her go without even giving her all the facts and the option to stay. You probably made her feel like you didn't want her to, that you were just doing exactly what you two crazies agreed upon, and that was having *fun* while she was here. You and I both know it turned into more, and I'm certain it's the same for her. Hell, I think it's been more since the very beginning."

My heart drops to my stomach. Did I make her feel like she wasn't important, was merely just a fling? A fun way to pass some time for the few months she was here? Sure, that's what it was supposed to be, but it quickly turned into much more than that. What started out as casual turned into a love bigger than I've ever felt. It's all-consuming and powerful. It's real and raw.

Jesus, I'm a fucking idiot.

"What do I do?" I whisper, trying to wrap my head around the fact I love her, didn't tell her, and then let her go.

Hallie sighs and throws her head back against the top couch cushion. "Hell if I know. My love life's a bigger mess than yours. I'm probably the last person you should want to give you advice."

I glance her way, resting my own head on the cushion. "I'm sorry your love life is a disaster. Why aren't you sleeping?" I ask, reverting back to her statement earlier before Frank, Patience, and Aggie stopped by.

She closes her eyes. "It doesn't matter."

"It does, Hal," I tell her, sliding over to sit closer to where she's sitting. Reaching for her hand, I give it a gentle squeeze. "It does matter, because you matter."

My sister offers me a small smile. It's still laced with a sadness I'm not used to seeing from her, but at least it's not total desolation. "Thank you," she replies, giving my hand a squeeze in return. "I'm okay, I promise. Working through a few things."

"You can talk to me if you need to," I insist, hating to see that look on her face.

"I know. Curtis is being a douchewagon cuntface and calling me at all hours of the night."

"And Logan?" I ask, even though she hasn't mentioned him at all. Something tells me there's something brewing between them, even if she's not willing to see it or wanting to fight it.

"What about him?" she counters with narrowed eyes.

"Nothing," I concede, throwing my hands up in surrender. "I just noticed you two seem to be butting heads lately. I figured he might be part of the reason you're so upset."

She sighs and covers her eyes with her arm. "It's not him."

"All right," I say, finally reaching for another slice of pizza. "If you need to talk, I'm here. If you need me to fix Curtis's face when you punch him, I'm here."

Hallie snickers a laugh and rolls to her side on the chaise part of the couch. "Deal." She leans forward and grabs her own slice of nasty fruit pizza and says, "Now, let's talk about how you're going to win back your girl."

CHAPTER *Twenty five*

Blair

Two weeks.

That's how long I've been back in Chicago, and I'm more miserable than ever before. The colors of fall surround me, yet I can't seem to find the joy I once found so easily when wandering my neighborhood streets. Everything makes me think about Gabe. The guy who opened the door for me when I stopped by my favorite deli the other night. There was something in his smile that tugged at my heart. Or how about the dad of one of my patients whose eyes were almost the identical color of blue. It was so startling, all I could do was stand there and stare until it became awkward and embarrassing.

Now, it's Sunday night and I have nothing to show for the weekend except sitting around and sulking. I worked all morning, despite not sleeping well last night, and when I finally did, my dreams were plagued with images of Gabe.

And really, it wasn't just him. Hallie was there, as well as Ellie, Logan, TD, Brody, and Ava. Aggie, Patience, and my dad too. Hell, even old man Foreman was present. Fortunately, without the infection under his foreskin.

Pushing thoughts of Pine Village and those I left behind out of my mind; I grab a bottle of water and some almonds from the cabinet and head for the living room. The letter my dad wrote is still sitting on the counter, unopened. I feel the weight of whatever's inside pushing down on me, yet I still can't bring myself to read it. The moment I sit down and look around, I see my stuff, but it doesn't feel right. It lacks the comfort and warmth of...well, home.

I recall the coziness of Gabe's big sectional sofa. Nights spent snuggled up on that couch, sometimes making love. Waking up in the middle of the night, our limbs entangled and feeling more content than I ever have.

I shake my head, doing anything I can to dislodge the reminiscences, but also knowing at the same time, it's no use. I'll carry him into my dreams later tonight too.

A knock sounds on my door, alerting me to a visitor. I glance at the clock and notice it's just after eight. Not exactly late, but not exactly the time friends drop by for a visit. Not that I have many friends here. The handful I've remained in contact with post-college all have spouses, kids, and busy lives, and the few colleagues I grab dinner or drinks with after work don't know where I live. Plus, none of them have a key for the front door, which means it's probably a neighbor or someone who lives in the building.

I make my way over to the door and look through the peephole. My heart starts to pound as I reach for the deadbolt and the knob lock, releasing them both. I pull open the door and instantly throw my arms around my mom. "What are you doing here?" I ask, completely shocked to see her standing at my doorstep.

Her soft chuckle is music to my ears. "Well, I thought I'd drop by for a visit."

I pull back and meet her gaze. "At eight at night? Coming from Merrillville?"

Her smile is small, and her knowing eyes are full of love. "I thought you could use a friend right now."

I feel the tears as I step back, allowing her to enter my apartment. She sets a small duffle bag down on the floor, letting me know she's planning to spend the night. So much emotion fills my entire body, it makes it hard to think, let alone breathe. "Thank you." I didn't realize how badly I needed my mom until she showed up at my door, but somehow, she knew.

"Come on," she says, leading me into my living room. "Let's chat." As soon as we're seated beside each other, she says, "Tell me about Gabe."

Even though I was hoping to not think about the man I left behind for just a little bit, I can't help but smile at her request. "He's the most caring doctor I've ever met, and Pine Village is lucky to have him."

She gives me that smile I'm accustomed to. "I'm sure he's a wonderful physician. Now tell me about the man you love."

Those pesky tears I tried to blink away fall. "He's...amazing. I've never met anyone like him, Mom," I whisper.

"So why did you leave?" she asks curiously. Her question is without judgment.

"Because," I start, but the words seem more difficult to find. "Because it was time for me to go. I was only supposed to be there four to six months."

She nods. "True, but that was before you fell in love."

I close my eyes, unable to refute. "I just...he didn't ask me to stay, Mom. If he wanted me to, he would have said something, right?"

She shrugs and squeezes my hand. "Maybe. Or perhaps he was just as conflicted as you and didn't want to ask because he thought you would go anyway."

My chest squeezes. "I would have stayed. If he would have asked, I would have stayed."

She gives me the softest, sweetest Mom smile. "I know. But I think everything happened this way for a reason."

I can't help but snort. "Yeah? And what reason is that? To make me miserable?"

"No, so you can learn how to forgive," she states so simply, so reasonably.

When I don't say anything for several long moments, she just grins and continues, "Your father, Blair. It's time to forgive your father. I made a lot of mistakes where you and he are concerned. I shouldn't have let you carry your anger as long as I have."

"But what he did to you—to us—was inexcusable."

She nods instantly. "You're right, it was, but at some point, I realized I had to let it go so I could be happy and free."

The tears fall harder now. "How? How did you let it go?"

"Well, my darling, I had help. I met someone. Actually, I had met him several years back, but we recently reconnected."

There's no way I can mask the shock written on my face. "Like...a man?"

She grins again, this one full of life and happiness. "Yes, Blair, like a man. His name is John, and the first time we met was about seven years ago. He asked me to dinner, which I accepted. At the time, you were in med school, and I was dealing with your father on a monthly basis, and—"

"Wait. What?" I ask, interrupting.

She sighs and meets my gaze. "Did you really think I was the one paying for your schooling?"

Her question confirms what deep down I already knew. There was no way my mom could pay for med school on her salary, and since it was covered each month, I never asked. I should have, but I didn't. Of course my father would pay for it, despite what happened. He was always so proud I'd chosen to follow in his footsteps, though I'm certain he would have paid for whatever field I would have gone into.

"No, I suppose it's not really a surprise. I never asked, and maybe I should have."

"I would have told you he was paying for it, Blair. I never hid it from you, I just never openly told you either. I apologize."

"Don't," I tell her and meaning it. "Go on."

"Anyway, I wasn't in the right place yet to date. I had tried a few other times, but I hadn't dealt with the hurt caused by the divorce. I wasn't happy, and that was on me, so I went to a therapist. She helped me realize I wasn't exactly happy in the marriage either. Oh, don't get me wrong, I loved your father, but we really hadn't been happy for a while before his affair. What he did was wrong, but so was me refusing to get over the betrayal and live my own life under my own terms. That's where you are, Blair. It's time to take control of your life and live it."

I close my eyes and think back over the last decade and a half of my life. I was able to hide behind my studies, focus completely on getting my degree. Then, I was so busy trying to make it in a large clinic, living in a suburb of a huge city, I never gave myself time to stop and process. I just continued to carry my anger like uncomfortable luggage.

"I'm not going to tell you what to do with your father. Only you can decide that. I am going to ask you to really think about what you want in your life, and who. I would be completely okay with you rebuilding a relationship with your dad, Blair. Don't ever feel like you're betraying me by speaking to him, because I'd much rather you be speaking to him than not. You both deserve that relationship. You both deserve to be happy. That's my fault for not encouraging it more, and for that, I'm so sorry."

I throw my arms around my mom and draw her close. "You have nothing to be sorry for. Honestly, even if you would have encouraged it, I still think I'd be where I am right now. I wasn't ready to forgive him, but I guess after spending those four months in Pine Village, I realized I missed him. A lot," I whisper, starting to cry.

She runs her hand across my head, gently tucking my hair behind my ear, just like she used to when I was young and needed comforting. "I think it's time you both heal, Blair. Despite his faults, your father is a good man and I know how much he loves you."

I nod and wipe away the falling tears. "He tried to talk to me, but I wasn't very receptive."

She gives me an understanding nod. "When you're ready to talk, he'll be ready to listen. I know it."

I take a deep, calming breath, feeling some of the weight on my chest lift. It's a fraction of the heaviness, but it's a start.

My mind starts to spin with ideas and plans, but I know I can't put them into motion while my mom is here. I don't get to see her very much, so I'll take this time and devote it to our visit. When she leaves tomorrow, then I can make the phone call I know in my heart I need to make.

Hell, a phone call I should have made way before now.

After, I'll truly be able to decide what I want to do. I'm pretty sure I already know my next step, but speaking to my dad will go a long way toward finally moving forward.

Honestly, I can't wait.

Turning to my mom, I can't help but smile. "So, tell me about John."

"Hello? Blair? Is everything okay?"

A small smile crosses my lips, even though the worry in his voice is evident. "Hi, Dad. Everything's fine."

My dad audibly sighs in relief. "Okay. Good. You scared me," he adds with an awkward chuckle.

"I'm sorry."

"Don't be. I'm just not used to getting many phone calls this late that don't have something to do with someone's health," he says, but I can't help but hear what he doesn't say. He didn't add the part about me never calling him at all, which I'm sure was why he went to the worst-case scenario immediately.

After a few long seconds of silence, he says, "How was your day?" as if trying to break the ice.

"I've been doing some thinking," I start, not answering his question.

"Okay," he replies, a hint of hesitancy in his tone.

"I, well, I just wanted to say..." I feel the tears starting to fall in earnest as I finally whisper the words I've been longing to speak to the man I've known my entire life, but shut out. "I read your letter. I love you, Dad, and...I forgive you."

I'm met with silence. At first, I wonder if we lost our connection, which would be my luck, but then I faintly hear a sniffle, and I realize it's not coming from me. My dad is crying. In my entire life, I've only seen or heard him cry once, and that was the day I left Pine Village. I don't know if it was the fact I was leaving or the hateful words I hurled at him like grenades, but the result was something I never forgot. "I love you too, Blair. I always have."

"I know," I state, meaning it. Deep down, I've always known, even if I refused to see it.

"Blair, you have no reason to apologize to me. I messed up terribly, and I'm aware of it. I've done things in the past I'm not proud of and hurting you and your mother are on the top of the list."

"I know," I repeat.

He exhales, as if taking his first deep breath since he picked up the phone. "Where do we go from here? I will follow your lead."

"I want to have dinner with you," I tell him, taking a seat on my bed.

"Sure. I would be happy to come to Chicago as soon as I can. Maybe next weekend? I'm sure Gabe will cover patient emergencies while I'm away," he says, almost absently.

"No, not in Chicago, Dad. I want to have dinner in Pine Village."

Again, there's a long pause. "Wow, okay. That'd be great. When do you think you'll be coming for a visit?" he asks. I can hear the excitement in his voice, even if he's trying his hardest to keep it at bay.

I take a deep breath and lay it on him. When I finish talking, he's silent once more, and this time, I'm certain it's because it's a good surprise.

"I don't know what to say," he confesses, clearly shocked. "Did you talk to your mother about this?"

"I did," I confirm. I don't need to tell him how we talked all morning about my idea, and she's the one who came up with big pieces of the plan. All he needs to know is she supports me and my decisions.

"Okay. Wow. I'm thrilled, Blair. Really."

"Me too," I reply honestly. "Oh, and when we have dinner, can Patience and Aggie come?"

"I—yes, of course. They'd love that, especially Aggie," he says with a chuckle. "You're all she talks about."

"I can't wait to see her."

After a few moments of silence, he says, "I really wasn't expecting this, but I'm so happy you called. I've been wanting to be able to tell you how sorry I am for so long; I was certain our relationship was beyond repair."

"Honestly, I thought it was," I tell him. "But Mom reminded me how short life is. If I don't take control over my own happiness, I'm not truly living."

"She's a very wise woman, and I'm not just saying that because I'm benefiting greatly from your decision," he replies with a laugh. "I really mean it. I want you and your mother to be happy, Blair. Both of you. Whatever that is or wherever it takes you."

Again, I feel the thickness of emotion lodging in my throat. "Thank you."

"No, thank you. For this phone call. For giving me the chance to be a part of your life again. You have no idea how great of a gift that is."

Smiling, I say, "I look forward to seeing you soon."

"Absolutely. Please let me know if there's anything I can do to help you. Oh, and I know I can speak for Patience when I say she'll be excited to join us for dinner."

"Good. It may be hard for me, but I want to try, Dad."

"As do we, sweetheart. Anything worth having isn't going to come easily, but we're both committed to rebuilding our family too. We'll take baby steps with you."

"Okay."

"See you soon, Blair. I love you."

Just hearing those three simple words causes my heart to leap into my throat. "I love you too," I croak out like a frog.

I hang up feeling much lighter than I have in years, and the exciting part is this is just the first step toward a better future. I have many more pieces to put together first, but when I'm done, the picture will be one I can be proud of.

I'm forging my own path, and it feels amazing.

Up next: Get my man!

CHAPTER
twenty six

GABE

This isn't exactly the message I want to give Frank the day before Thanksgiving, but it has to be done. I've put a lot of thought into it, into what I want for my life, and it all keeps circling back around to the same thing.

Blair.

I've talked to my parents. I've talked to my sister. Now, I just have to talk to Frank, and this conversation might be the toughest I've had yet.

"Knock, knock," I say, peeking around the doorjamb and finding Frank at his desk. It still startles me every time, even though I know he's there. I became used to seeing Blair sitting there, even after only a few months, and seeing her dad in the chair only serves as a reminder she's no longer here.

"Hey, Gabe. Come on in," he offers, setting aside whatever he's working on.

"I won't take too much of your time. I know you've got plans tonight with the family," I state, taking the empty seat across from his desk.

He gives me a smile, one that expresses his happiness. In fact, he's been a little different for the last week or two. He comes to work in a great mood and leaves the same way. Not that he's not usually in a good mood, but this seems different. Maybe it's because he's back to work without limited restrictions and able to keep doing what he loves. I hate the thought I might put a damper on that bliss with this chat.

"I've got time before I need to get home. What's up?"

"Well, I don't really know how to say this other than bluntly, so here goes. I'm leaving. At the beginning of the year, I'm relocating."

"Relocating? To where?" he asks.

"Chicago."

He masks his surprise well as he watches me. His head moves slightly to the left, as he says, "I thought you hated the city."

Swallowing hard, I reply, "It's not my first choice of places to live. I much prefer the slower pace of a rural community, but that doesn't matter. What matters is being with the woman I love."

If my comment surprises him, he doesn't let it show. "Okay. Sorry to see you go," he replies, standing up and extending his hand.

I have to admit, his immediate acceptance and the way he practically dismisses me catches me completely off guard. I suppose I pictured him arguing, maybe a little begging me to stay. You know, make me feel like I was a part of the team for nearly the last decade.

Then again, I did just indirectly tell him I'm in love with his daughter, assuming he caught that part, which I'm guessing he did. It wasn't that long ago he asked me if I loved Blair, and I wouldn't answer him. I thought if I was going to say it, she would be the first to hear, but now, since it's such a big part of my reasoning for leaving—my only reason, really—it felt imperative for him to know the facts.

Extending my hand, I give his a shake. "Thank you for the opportunity to work with you. I've learned a great deal and truly feel like I'm a better physician because I worked beside you every day."

He gives me a smile, one that makes his eyes beam. "You're an exceptional doctor and man, Gabe. You'll do well wherever you land, but just know there will always be a position here for you, son." Then he leans in, gently pulling on my hand and wrapping his arms around my torso in a hug.

The weight of my decision presses against my chest, but I know I'm making the right call. I can't stay here, not with Blair in another state. She might as well be in another country. If I want to be happy—truly happy in my life—then I know what I have to do.

The truth is, I want to be with her.

Here. There. Wherever.

I just want her, and it took her leaving—and maybe my sister knocking some sense into me—for me to see it. The love I feel for her is deeper than I ever expected, and the fact I haven't seen her in a month makes it a little hard for me to breathe. I need her. She's my oxygen. The sunshine that chases away the night sky. The reason I was put on this earth.

And she owns me completely.

"I plan to continue through the end of the year, unless you decide otherwise," I tell him when we pull away.

He waves off my comment. "Let's not worry about the details right now. I have dinner to get to, and I'm sure you have things planned with your family for Thanksgiving," he replies.

"I'm not going to my parents' until tomorrow," I remind him, even though we had this conversation last week. "Tonight, I'm just going to hang out at my house."

And continue to pack.

I've spent the last two weeks looking for a place in the same neighborhood as Blair. Thanks to my sister, she was able to help me find something about half a mile away, which will be a short ten-minute walk one way. I've been told the neighborhood is nice, safe, and has a park nearby where families take their kids to play. The apartment is on the second floor and should be available the first of the year, which is perfect. I was able to video chat with the manager to see the apartment, and I have the contract in my email ready to review and sign.

Maybe I'll take care of that tonight when I get home.

The next step is going to be listing my house. Since it's only half renovated, I know it might be a hard sell to some, but the market is doing fairly well, so I'm hoping a do-it-yourselfer will see the potential and snag it up. Then, I have to sell my truck. That was a hard pill to swallow, but it's necessary. My apartment only comes with one small parking space, and my truck won't fit. Plus, driving around and parking in a city like Chicago isn't exactly conducive for truck owners.

"Well, I'm going to head home to my family," Frank announces, pulling me back to our conversation. He walks over to his desk, slips his work into his bag, and locks up his computer. All I can do is watch as he practically ignores the fact that I told him I was quitting and goes about his day as if I didn't drop this bomb.

"All right. Have a good evening," I mutter, still trying to wrap my head around it.

"You too. Happy Thanksgiving," Frank adds, heading for the door. "Oh, if you want to stop by tomorrow evening, you're more than welcome. We're eating around five, or you can join us for drinks after dinner."

I nod in acceptance. Frank has always invited me over to join them for family dinners, and I've always made a point to drop by, even if it's just for a short visit. However, this time around, the invite feels off. He's so blasé about the whole fact I'm leaving, I'm not sure I can go over there and pretend everything is fine and dandy. As if I didn't make this huge decision that impacts the rest of my life.

But the decision is made.

If I want Blair—which I do—I have to be willing to make that happen, and if moving to another state to be close to her accomplishes that, I'm all in.

"Great! I'm sure we'll be seeing you soon," he states, slapping me on the back and giving me a friendly shoulder squeeze before walking right out the back door.

My legs are numb as I return to my own office and gather a few things for the long weekend. The office is closed on Friday, so I have four days at home to get things packed and sorted. Currently, we have no patients in the hospital, but even if that happens, I'll still have plenty of time to check up on them.

I pull into my driveway and put my truck inside the garage. I shouldn't need it tonight. I know most of my friends will gather in town at the bar for a drink, but I have no intentions of going. I haven't been in a joyful, friendly mood since Blair left a month ago.

Inside, I spot the boxes I've already packed up, along with the ones I'll either be donating or giving to my sister. As much as I hate to see my life in boxes again, I know I'm making the right decision. Should I tell her I'm coming before I actually sell my shit and move? Probably. But I'm afraid she'll tell me not to come because she knows how much I love Pine Village, and I refuse to give her that opportunity. I want to show her how much I care and want a future with her, and this is the best way to do that.

I run upstairs to change, throwing on a pair of black joggers and a long-sleeve T-shirt before returning to the kitchen. I grab a bottle of water and chug half the contents before making my way to the half bath downstairs. I have the new tile and walls done and am working on installing the new fixtures, vanity, and toilet. My goal is to get this room complete before I move, which only leaves the downstairs office, living room, and the extra bedrooms upstairs to complete.

Just as I get ready to level the vanity, my cell phone rings. I can't help the way my heartbeat jumps at the prospect of Blair calling, and even though I tell myself she wouldn't be home yet, since her clinic is open later than ours, it's still a letdown when I see any other name but hers.

This time, I see my sister's name and tap the screen.

"Hello?"

"Hey, big brother. I need a favor."

"What kind of favor?" I ask hesitantly.

"I have a friend who needs a ride. Her car broke down."

All I do is stand there, my brain trying to process her request. The last time she called me for a very similar ask was when Blair was stuck in the snow last December. Almost a year ago. Eleven months ago actually, and it changed my life forever.

"Hello? Are you there?"

Clearing my throat, I reply, "Yeah. Sorry."

"I hate to ask, but Markus isn't available for a little while and she's just down the road from you."

"Why don't you call TD? He can dispatch an officer to help," I reason.

Hallie sighs dramatically, reminding me of when she was younger. "*Because* he's busy too," she argues.

"Who is it?" I ask, realizing she hasn't told me who I'm going to rescue.

There's a beat of hesitation before she quickly says, "Ellie."

"Ellie? Is Brody with her?" I ask quickly, not that it would matter. I'll help regardless, which is why I'm already heading to slip on a pair of shoes.

"No, he's...not." Something in her tone is off, but I don't have time to try to figure out why now.

"All right, I'll run and get her. Where is she at?" I ask, putting my phone on speaker so I can lace my athletic shoes.

"Umm, just down the road, past the big curve to the south," she replies.

Again, memories flood my mind. That's where Blair's car became disabled. "Let her know I'm on my way," I state, scrambling to find my keys and coat.

The road isn't terribly busy, but as one of the only main arteries into town, it has enough traffic to become worrisome, especially when it's dark out. If her flashers aren't on or if she's not completely off the road before the curve, anything can happen if a driver isn't paying attention.

"Thanks, big brother. Let me know how it goes," she says, a hint of excitement in her voice.

"Will do. Bye," I reply, signing off and slipping my phone into the pocket of my sweats. I should probably run up and change into jeans, but I'm decent enough to pick up a friend and take her home.

I jump in my truck and back it out of the garage before pulling onto the road and heading in the direction of Ellie's car. I wonder what TD will say when he finds out she became stranded. He may not be ready to admit it, but he's been into Ellie for as long as I've been back in town. He's super protective of her and Brody, and I imagine he'll be upset when he finds out she needed help and he wasn't available.

Not seeing any other traffic, I'm able to go slow around the curve until I spot her car. Her hazards are on and she's well off the road, thankfully, so I throw my hazards on and start to pull off the road facing her, my front end to hers.

First thing I notice is the car. Ellie drives an older Nissan, and this is a Kia hybrid. I stop directly in front of the vehicle and just sit there, trying to figure out if my eyes are playing a cruel joke on me. It's supposed to be Ellie sitting here, but this woman isn't my friend. The woman looking back at me from the driver's seat is the most beautiful woman in the world.

The one I love.

I throw the truck in park, release my seat belt, and slowly climb from the cab. My eyes remain glued to the woman, as if she could disappear or change right before me. She gets out of her car and smiles, and suddenly, everything feels right in the world again.

Please don't let this be a dream.

"Are you okay?" I ask hesitantly, stopping at the front of my truck as she approaches.

"Yes."

All I can do is stare at her as I try to figure out what in the hell is going on. "Hallie said Ellie needed help."

She gives me a remorseful grin. "Yeah, sorry about that. I didn't want her to tell you who you were really coming to rescue."

"Why?" I ask, slipping my hands into my pockets to keep from reaching for her. I need to know what's going on before I do.

"Because I was afraid you wouldn't come if you knew it was me," she replies, rocking back on her heels and looking at me through guarded eyes.

Now, I move, reaching for her hand and gently pulling her against my body. She fits so fucking perfectly, it's as if she was made just for me. "I would go anywhere just because you were there," I whisper before lowering my lips toward hers. They hover there, her soft pants of warm air tickling my lips, as my gaze meets hers.

She gives me the softest, sweetest smile, and I know instantly I'm making the right decision. I *would* go anywhere, as long as she's there.

Blair goes up on her tiptoes and presses her lips to mine. The kiss is too short, but I'm not complaining. Soon, I'll be able to kiss her daily if I want to, and I'll take it.

"Can we go back to your house and talk? I have something I want to discuss with you," she says without stepping away from my embrace.

"Yes. I actually have something to talk to you about too."

She nods and finally steps back. "Well, the good news is my car is completely fine and not stuck in the snow, so I can follow you back to your place, if that works."

"That's perfect," I tell her.

Blair heads to her car and slides behind the wheel once more. She has it started and is ready to pull back onto the road before I finally turn and get back into my own vehicle. I wave her on, telling her to go ahead, and once she's on the road, I pull out, doing a three-point turn in the middle of the road so I'm pointed in the right direction. Following behind her, we take the curve and pull into my driveway.

There's something so right about seeing her car parked here.

I don't bother to put my truck away. Instead, I stop beside her car and climb out. The moment she's standing beside me, I take her hand and lead her to my house. Inside, we both kick off our shoes, take off our coats, and again, I don't release my hold on her. I'm terrified she'll disappear if I do. If I had it my way, I'd hold her forever and never let go.

Just as we step through the doorway of the mudroom, she stops and gasps, her eyes wide as she takes in the large kitchen and dining room area. "Oh my God, are you moving?"

"Yes," I respond. "That's what I wanted to tell you."

She turns to me with panic in her eyes. "You can't leave," she whispers. "Where are you going?"

I give her a gentle smile as I reply, "Chicago."

Clearly, that wasn't what she was expecting me to say. Her entire face shows her surprise as she just stares up at me. "I don't understand. You hate the city."

"Come in the living room so we can talk," I request. Keeping her hand tucked in mine, I guide her into the next room and sit beside her on the sectional.

As soon as we sit, she asks, "Why?"

"Because that's where you are," I tell her.

Blair's eyes fill with unshed tears. "I can't ask you to do that," she counters, shaking her head.

"You didn't ask. I made the decision, because being here without you isn't working out so well for me."

She smiles softly and places her palm against my cheek. "What if I told you being in Chicago without you hasn't worked out so well for me either?"

"No? That's exactly why I'm moving. I'm getting an apartment not too far from yours, and I've sent a letter of interest and résumés to a few clinics in the area. I think there's a good chance of one of them hiring me."

"Gabe," she starts, running her thumb across my bottom lip. "Don't go to Chicago."

"Why?" I ask, my heart thumping so hard in my chest, I'm certain she can hear it.

"Because as of today, I'm a resident of Pine Village, and I don't want to be here without you."

Her words don't really register, at least not right away. All I can do is watch her, waiting to find out if she's joking with me, but when she just looks at me expectantly, I realize she's serious. "Really?" I ask, so much hope in that one word.

She giggles and glides her palm across my several-days-old stubble. "Yes, really. I talked to my dad, and—"

"Wait. You talked to your dad?" I ask, hating that I interrupted her, but completely surprised by her statement.

Again, she grins. "Yes. We've talked several times over the last two weeks, actually. My mom helped me to realize how much I loved and missed him, and it was time to forgive what he did. I haven't completely gotten over it, but we're working on rebuilding our relationship. Together."

Now it's my turn to smile. "I'm proud of you, Blair. And at least now I know why he's been in such a good mood for the last couple of weeks, even when I've been a bear to work with."

"He told me you've been out of sorts and speculated it was because you were upset," she hedges, opening the door for me.

"Upset may not be the right word. Devastated, maybe? When you left, it tore me up in a way I can't even describe, but what hurt even more was the fact I was too stupid to tell you how I felt about you before you were gone."

She swallows hard as she asks, "How do you feel about me?"

"I'm in love with you, Blair. I think I've been in love with you since I saw you standing in the middle of that snowdrift in your fancy boots, and I don't want to spend another day living this life without you."

CHAPTER
Twenty seven

Blair

I'm in love with you.

Five words I never realized I longed to hear until just now, in this moment.

"I love you too," I whisper. My words cause the most breathtaking smile to cross his lips. A smile I want to see every day for the rest of my life.

Then his lips are on mine, kissing away all the pain and fear I've been carrying around since I returned to Chicago. All is finally right with the world.

He breaks the kiss much sooner than I want and meets my gaze. "You moved here? Really?"

I can't help but chuckle. "Yes. Hallie called her landlord, and he hadn't rented the condo yet. I was able to secure it immediately. And I was offered a job," I say, trying not to let my excitement show.

"Yeah?"

I nod coyly. "There's this great clinic in town with two amazing physicians. The owner really likes the idea of adding a pediatrician to the practice and is making plans to remodel some of the larger rooms to accommodate a third doctor."

Gabe shakes his head. "Jesus, I can't believe he's been planning all of this behind my back. I guess that explains why he wasn't at all concerned about me quitting earlier today. He knew I wasn't going anywhere."

I run my thumb across his bottom lip once more. "Well, we both are hoping you're not going anywhere."

"If you're here, then this is exactly where I'm going to be."

"Good," I say, feeling relief for the first time in weeks. "Now, what do you say you take me upstairs and show me how much you love me?"

I'm not sure I've ever seen Gabe move so fast. "Yes, ma'am," he replies, scooping me up in his arms and practically running for the second floor.

A bubble of laughter mixed with shock flies from my mouth as I tighten my arms around his neck. The moment he lays me down on top of his bed and covers me from head to toe with his body, I slide my fingers into his hair. "Gabe?"

"Hmm?" he coos, running his nose along my jaw and breathing me in.

My heart is trying to tap dance out of my chest as I confess, "I'm sorry I left. I shouldn't have."

He lifts his head and meets my gaze head-on. "I didn't give you a reason to stay, but that changes right now."

"You're reason enough."

Then his lips meet mine in a soft, yet demanding kiss. "I love you, Blair," he whispers without breaking our connection.

"I love you too."

We spend the next several hours showing one another exactly how much we mean to each other, and then again as the sun comes up the next morning.

Something tells me I'll never get enough of this man.

He's pretty irresistible.

"You ready for this?" Gabe asks, squeezing my hand as we face the door.

My heart is beating rapidly, a mixture of anticipation and excitement. "I think I've been waiting for this moment my entire life."

"Well, let's get inside then," he says, entering in his security code and opening the back entrance. Together, we walk into the clinic I now call home.

When I made the decision to move to Pine Village, I had a lot of loose ends to tie up in Chicago in a short amount of time. The pediatrics clinic I worked at was gracious enough to let me out of my contract, even though I could tell they weren't exactly happy about it. Especially since I had just returned from a four-month leave. However, once I explained why I was going—that I fell in love with an amazing man I couldn't live without and was working toward rebuilding a relationship with my father—they softened and agreed. They even wished me well and offered letters of recommendation. I didn't have the heart to tell them I didn't exactly need a letter where I was going.

It was always my destiny.

My apartment wasn't as accommodating. I was three months away from the end of my lease and opted to pay the penalty for an early out instead of trying to find someone to sublet. At the end of the day, it was just simpler and one less thing I had to worry about. I scheduled movers—the same ones I've used twice now—and packed up everything this time, bringing my entire life with me.

As soon as the door closes behind me, I can smell new paint. Dad told me he was going to do some remodeling in the larger rooms to turn them into smaller ones, but that project isn't scheduled to start until over the extended Christmas holiday.

Instead of going to Gabe's office, we turn to the left and step inside my dad's. What I see shocks me completely. My dad's office is, well, it's split in half. "What's this?" I murmur, meeting Dad's eager gaze as he stands beside the second desk.

"This is your office, Blair. The wall between us is temporary, so when the time comes, it can be removed, and you'll have the entire space to yourself," my dad informs me with a pleased grin on his face.

I take in the room. What once was one large room, there's a wall dividing it in half. I can see two desks, a series of new filing cabinets, and the two guest chairs are now positioned with one in front of each desk.

"I know there's no door between them, but you're welcome to close the one behind you if you need privacy. I promise to respect it," he adds, suddenly a little more nervous than he was when I first walked in.

"It's…perfect," I whisper, my voice hoarse with emotion and tears. "Thank you." I'm moving a moment later, throwing my arms around him and hugging him tightly.

"You're most welcome," he replies, clearing his throat. "I know it's not much right now, but I've been doing a lot of thinking over the last couple of weeks, and I'd like to retire next year. I'll be seventy years old, and even though I'd love to hang on and work beside you every day, I can't think of two better people to turn my clinic over to at the end of the year. That is, if you'll accept it."

I nod, choking on the tears streaming down my face. "I'd be honored to work beside you as long as you're here."

He reaches out and hugs me a second time, squeezing me a little harder than before. "Perfect. Now, what do you say we welcome the staff with the donuts Patience sent me with and get you settled in for your first day back."

I grin widely. "I'm ready."

"Me too, Blair. Me too." He takes a step back and adds, "Why don't you go ahead and get established at your desk. You should be all linked into the computer system and your schedule of patients is on your laptop."

Nodding, I walk over to the opposite side of the large room and take a seat at my desk. First thing I notice is the brand-new laptop waiting, along with letterhead and pens with the clinic logo on them. Then me eyes zero in on the double framed photos in front of me. The left side is a picture of Aggie and me from her school's reading night. We're both smiling widely, my sister's little glasses perched high on her nose as she has her arms thrown around me. The one on the left catches my attention right away. It's of Gabe and me, taken on Thanksgiving just four short days ago. We were at my dad's house—the first time I had been inside in more than a decade—and Patience insisted on a photo.

Now I know why.

Movement catches over the top of the frames, and I see Gabe sliding into the chair opposite me. "You like?"

"I love," I whisper, still so caught up in the overwhelming emotions of the moment.

"Good," he boasts.

"I take it you were in on this little secret?"

He just grins. "Maybe. I figured what was good for the goose was good for the gander."

I can't help but chuckle. "Touché, Dr. Rhodes."

Just then, the back door opens, and the staff starts to file in. "Good morning and welcome back!" someone hollers from the doorway.

"How about we go get a donut before they take the good ones," Gabe suggests.

"Let's do it."

He stands up, his eyes darkening just a shade. "That'll be later, Dr. O'Connor," he mutters quietly so no one can hear. At least I hope no one can hear.

My cheeks grow warm as I walk his way, meeting him at the doorway. "You're incorrigible."

He just laughs. "Yeah? Well, you're pretty irresistible."

And then he kisses me, right there in the doorway, with my father hopefully not watching just a few feet away.

If you would have asked me a year ago—hell, even six months ago—I never thought I'd be here, permanently working in the very clinic my father owns, but things change.

People grow.

Forgiveness heals old wounds.

Love happens.

And because of that, you get to experience some of the greatest thrills in life. Joys I would have missed out on had I not taken a leap of faith and followed my heart.

I may not know where I'll end up on this journey through life, but I do know I'll sit back and enjoy the ride.

Especially with Gabe by my side.

EPILOGUE
epilogue

GABE

My palms are sweating.

Why am I so nervous?

Perhaps it's because I've been thinking about this day nonstop for two weeks now, trying to figure out when the right time would be to ask. She has to know it's coming. Really. Blair is one of the most intuitive, smartest people I know, and surely, she could tell I was up to something.

I hear her car pull into my driveway.

Showtime.

I wipe my palms on my thighs again and head for the back door. Blair spent the entire day Christmas shopping with Patience and Hallie, so I enlisted the help of TD and Logan to get my surprise ready. We busted our asses from the moment she left this morning until about thirty minutes ago, when we got the text from my sister that they were headed back to town.

Opening the rear door, I step outside and make my way to her car. She's just climbing out of the driver's seat and smiles when she sees me approaching.

"I think we need to go car shopping for me pretty soon. I hear there's snow in the forecast next week, and I'm not sure my little Kia is fit for Wisconsin snow again this winter," she says with a chuckle.

When I reach her side, I press my lips against hers. "Consider it done. We can head to Hudson whenever you're ready."

She reaches around me and opens the back door. The seat is piled with packages of all sizes, and I can't help but laugh. "Yeah, I might have gone a little overboard for Aggie this year. I couldn't seem to stop finding the cutest stuff for her. Do you mind if I wrap them here? I figured since we're leaving to go over to my dad's in the morning for Christmas Eve, it would save me a trip of going home to do it."

She doesn't have to mention that a good chunk of her personal belongings are already here, since she sleeps in my bed most nights. In fact, that's part of tonight's surprise.

"I don't mind at all. I'll help you wrap," I insist, taking most of the bags and following her toward the house.

Blair opens the door for me and makes sure it's secured once she's inside. "I can't believe how cold it's getting. I'd be surprised if we don't have snow before next week," she says, kicking off her boots as I take the pile of purchases into the living room.

The moment I set everything on the couch, I reach for her hand. "Come with me. I have a surprise for you."

She grins and places her delicate little hand inside mine. "What have you been up to today?" she asks, walking beside me up the stairs.

"A few things," I reply, not giving anything away.

I bypass my bedroom and lead her to the end of the hall. "I had plans to turn these rooms into guest rooms at some point, but I was never in a hurry, since almost everyone I know already lives in town. But then your mom agreed to come for a visit, and I know you've planned to have her stay in your guest room at the condo, but I thought, what if..." I start, turning the knob and opening the door. "What if she stayed here? With us?"

I let Blair walk in ahead of me and take in the room for the first time. It still smells like fresh paint, and considering the second coat is probably still wet, I tell her, "Don't touch the walls yet. They're not dry."

"Oh my God," she whispers, slowly spinning in the middle of the room.

There's a queen-sized bed by the far wall with matching nightstands and a dresser. "The bedding is washed and ready. Hallie helped me pick it out, insisting it was a great fit for the room. We can get something else if you don't like it," I add, watching as she stares at the light purple and white bedding. The walls are painted white, except for the one directly behind the bed. It's a shade of yellow I probably wouldn't have picked myself, but I have to admit, now that I see the room put together, it's not so bad at all.

"You did this? For my mom?" she asks, turning shocked eyes to me. Donna agreed to come for a visit the day after Christmas, and Blair is thrilled. She's been talking nonstop about it since the plans were set in motion.

I shrug and shove my hands in my pockets nervously. "Well, I did it for you."

She moves, throwing her arms over my shoulders and launching herself into my chest. "I can't believe this. It's beautiful."

"I'm glad you like it. TD and Logan helped me finish laying the floors and patching the drywall. We got it painted, cleaned, and the furniture put together with barely any time to spare."

Meeting my gaze, her eyes fill with unshed tears. "My mom is going to love it. Thank you, Gabe." Then she goes up on her tiptoes and kisses my lips.

When we break away, I reply, "I have to admit, my work was partially for selfish reasons. Come on. Let's see the rest of your surprise."

She sniffles and swipes at a single tear. "There's more?"

Taking her hand once more, I lead her out of the guest room and toward my closed bedroom door. Stopping outside, I take a deep breath and turn the knob.

Inside, there isn't much change. At least not any you notice right away. I can see her looking around, trying to find whatever surprise I have for her. "This way," I say, walking to my closed closet.

The door isn't latched closed, so I give it a gentle push and wait.

"Holy shit," she mutters, making me laugh, as she steps inside.

"I did a little reorganizing, and thanks to Logan, he helped me build this island that fits shoes," I say, taking in our handiwork.

Half of the closet is now bare, with additional storage systems to accommodate sharing the space with someone. The island has cubbies on both sides to fit dozens of pairs of shoes, and there's a small bench on the end. Blair walks farther into the closet and looks around, noticing all the empty hangers with no clothes.

Wiping my palms on my jeans once more, I say, "I was hoping you'd fill that side with all your things."

She turns around and faces me. "Are you asking me to move in with you?"

I nod, my throat dry, as my heart beats wildly in my chest. "Yes. I know you just moved back into your condo last month, but you're here most nights anyway. I don't like sleeping without you, Blair. I want you in my bed, in my house, in my life. I want this to be *our* place. I want to build a home and a family with you. Here."

She doesn't say anything for a few long seconds, which only amplifies my erratic heartbeat. "Do I still get to take a bath whenever I want?"

A smile spreads across my lips. "You do that now anyway," I state, taking leisurely steps in her direction.

"True." She glances at my half of the closet before asking, "Can I still steal your clothes whenever I want?"

I openly laugh. "Again, you do that now anyway," I repeat, reaching her side and slipping my hands around her waist.

"Very true," she concedes, fighting a grin. "What if my clothes need more space?"

Locking my fingers behind her back, I draw her against my chest. "Then I will give you part of my half. Or I'll build you a huge closet across the hall in the unfinished room."

"I don't really have that much clothing," she says.

"No, but I'd do anything for you, including remodel the entire upstairs again to make you happy."

Blair shakes her head at my comment. "Not necessary. It's perfect the way it is," she says, leaning her head against my chest. "I suppose I should call my landlord again and let him know I'm moving."

I feel bad for the guy, considering he's been so helpful to Blair, and would gladly pay any fees he would charge with her vacating the condo so quickly after moving in. "Is that a yes?"

She looks up, her eyes full of happiness. "That's a yes."

My mouth is on hers a moment later, savoring the softness and tasting her sweetness. "How quickly can you move in?" I whisper, tracing her bottom lip with my tongue.

"How quickly do you want me?"

"Right now," I state, flexing my hips and rubbing my erection against her stomach. "I definitely want you right now."

She sighs, slipping her hand down to grab me through my jeans. "That's perfect, because this is the only place I want to be."

"I love you, Blair."

"And I love you, Gabe. Forever."

If you ask me, forever sounds pretty damn incredible.

The End

Don't miss a single reveal, release, or sale! Sign up for my newsletter.

http://www.laceyblackbooks.com/newsletter

BOOKS ALSO BY *lacey black*

Rivers Edge series

Trust Me, Rivers Edge book 1 (Maddox and Avery) – FREE at all retailers

~ *#1 Bestseller in Contemporary Romance*

Fight Me, Rivers Edge book 2 (Jake and Erin)

Expect Me, Rivers Edge book 3 (Travis and Josselyn)

Promise Me: A Novella, Rivers Edge book 3.5 (Jase and Holly)

Protect Me, Rivers Edge book 4 (Nate and Lia)

Boss Me, Rivers Edge book 5 (Will and Carmen)

Trust Us: A Rivers Edge Christmas Novella (Maddox and Avery)

~ *This novella was originally part of the Christmas Miracles Anthology*

BOX SET – contains all 5 novels, 2 novellas, and a BONUS short story

With Me, A Rivers Edge Christmas Novella (Brooklyn and Becker)

Bound Together series

Submerged, Bound Together book 1 (Blake and Carly)

Profited, Bound Together book 2 (Reid and Dani)

Entwined, Bound Together book 3 (Luke and Sidney)

Summer Sisters series
My Kinda Kisses, Summer Sisters book 1 (Jaime and Ryan)
My Kinda Night, Summer Sisters book 2 (Payton and Dean)
My Kinda Song, Summer Sisters book 3 (Abby and Levi)
My Kinda Mess, Summer Sisters book 4 (Lexi and Linkin)
My Kinda Player, Summer Sisters book 5 (AJ and Sawyer)
My Kinda Player, Summer Sisters book 6 (Meghan and Nick)
My Kinda Wedding, A Summer Sisters Novella book 7 (Meghan and Nick)

Rockland Falls series
Love and Pancakes, Rockland Falls book 1
Love and Lingerie, Rockland Falls book 2
Love and Landscape, Rockland Falls book 3
Love and Neckties, Rockland Falls book 4

Standalone
Music Notes, a sexy contemporary romance standalone
A Place To Call Home, a Memorial Day novella
Exes and Ho Ho Ho's, a sexy contemporary romance standalone novella
Pants on Fire, a sexy contemporary romance standalone
Double Dog Dare You, a new standalone
Grip
Bachelor Swap, A Bachelor Tower Series Novel
Perfect Kiss, Mason Creek Series book 9
Waiting For Love, The Love Vixen Series book 11

Burgers and Brew Crüe Series
Kickstart My Heart, book 1
Don't Go Away Mad, book 2
Same Ol' Situation, book 3
Wild Side, book 4
What's It Gonna Take, book 5

Home Sweet Home, book 6
Too Young to Fall in Love, book 7
Without You, book 8
Time for Change, book 9
You're All I Need, book 10

Pine Village Series
Pretty Remarkable, prequel short story
Pretty Incredible, book 1
Pretty Dependable, book 2
Pretty Drunk, book 3
Pretty Relentless, book 4
Pretty Wild, book 5
Pretty Desperate, book 6

Co-Written with *NYT Bestselling* Author, Kaylee Ryan
It's Not Over, Fair Lakes book 1
Just Getting Started, Fair Lakes book 2
Can't Get Enough, Fair Lakes book 3
Fair Lakes Box Set
Boy Trouble
Home To You, a second chance novella
Beneath the Fallen Stars, Never Too Far book 1
Beneath the Desert Sun, Never Too Far book 2
Tell Me A Story
Royal – Writing as Rebel Shaw
Crying Shame – Writing as Rebel Shaw
Watch and Learn – Writing as Rebel Shaw

ABOUT
lacey black

USA Today Bestselling Author Lacey Black is a Midwestern girl with a passion for reading, writing, and shopping. She carries her e-reader with her everywhere she goes so she never misses an opportunity to read a few pages. Always looking for a happily ever after, Lacey is passionate about contemporary romance novels and enjoys it further when you mix in a little suspense. She resides in a small town in Illinois with her husband, two children, a spoiled cat, and three rowdy chickens.

Website: www.laceyblackbooks.com
Newsletter: www.laceyblackbooks.com/newsletter
Email: laceyblackwrites@gmail.com
Facebook: https://www.facebook.com/authorlaceyblack
Twitter: https://twitter.com/AuthLaceyBlack
Instagram: https://www.instagram.com/laceyblackwrites/
Newsletter: http://www.laceyblackbooks.com/newsletter

www.ingramcontent.com/pod-product-compliance
Lightning Source LLC
Chambersburg PA
CBHW070635260626
47161CB00007B/2713